A KNIGHT FOR KALLEN

ALEXA ASTON

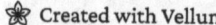 Created with Vellum

PROLOGUE
SOUTH OF ENGLAND—1293

Quentin's brow furrowed. His hair grew damp with sweat. He studied the cards in his hand and glanced casually at Renton. Damn, the ill-tempered nobleman seemed smug as he ran a hand through his dark, unruly hair. His host for this game sat across the table from Quentin as if he hadn't a care in the world.

He watched Renton gaze to his left. Quentin in turn viewed the old fool seated next to Renton. Soon the baron would quit the game. Only Quentin would be left to challenge his host.

God, but he wanted to win. Deserved to win. Why shouldn't he? At a score-and-one, he was the Earl of Nowland and bastard son of the king. His life should be richly blessed.

If only he could win this one hand.

The balding baron placed his cards face down. "Enough." He spat upon the rushes gathered on the floor and pushed away from the table.

Blond and buxom Lady Alita, always the perfect hostess and wife, moved from her husband Renton's elbow to the yielding nobleman. "My lord, would you care for some wine? I know a man's card play can work up a powerful thirst."

They stepped away, Alita's chattering striking a raw nerve with Quentin. She reminded him of his sister—the last person he wished to think of at this crucial moment.

His final opponent pushed the cards around in his hand. Quentin watched him, his heart pounding. Renton was notorious for displaying a casual but confident air. His cards could be worth less than a pile of dung, and no one would be the wiser. Quentin determined that his neighbor would not get the best of him.

Not this time.

Yet a quarter hour later the stakes were next to impossible. Quentin now found himself sweating profusely.

Tiny rivulets formed along his nape and coasted down his back. He had to win. He must.

"My final wager to add to this," Quentin heard himself say. His voice sounded tinny, coming from a long way off. Colors began to swim around the table, confusing him.

"What say you then, Nowland?" Renton growled. "You've no more coin at hand." He belched loudly and took another swig of his ale.

The man's vulgarity seemed the final straw. His heart full of hate, Quentin locked his jaw and narrowed his eyes, staring at his enemy. "The copse," he growled.

Renton's eyes gleamed. "The entire forest? Even the stream running through it?"

"Yes," Quentin said, his voice low and menacing. "The whole of it."

His host smiled. "You do realize that would include the hunting rights, Nowland? That it would become my land, an extension of Mangeron? That you could only set foot on it at my invitation?"

Quentin's gut tightened, but he smiled in return. "I understand perfectly, my lord." He paused a moment. "However, I don't intend to lose."

Renton laughed. "Then the copse, it is. I shall match you. My pair of steeds you've so admired, and your pick of brood mare to go with them."

He couldn't wait to possess those magnificent horses and all the foals that the mare would produce. "Agreed."

"Then show your cards, Nowland." Renton spread his across the tabletop slowly and then raised his eyes to meet Quentin's.

No! Quentin's blood screamed out. He wanted to take back the wager, scratch the entire night from his memory. He couldn't lose to Renton de Mangeron.

Yet he had.

He slowly laid down his own cards as if he were in a nightmare. Renton chuckled. The two men's eyes met.

Renton said softly, "*My* copse now." He reached out his arms and swept the stacks of gold coin on the table toward him. "And my gold."

Quentin smiled pleasantly, despite the fact his heart hammered unmercifully in his chest. He waved a hand nonchalantly. "It happens."

He looked around. Life went on in the great hall of Mangeron. Guests ate and drank as they listened to a minstrel. He returned his gaze to Renton.

"A fine match," he said, nodding his head. "I suppose I'm off for the garderobe and a willing wench, eh?" He laughed heartily, doing his best to disguise the pain that tightened about him, as real as any vise.

Renton's robust laugh caused Quentin to see red. "Mayhap I'll invite you to go hunting soon, Nowland. On my new land." He laughed again at his own wit as Quentin stepped away and crossed the room.

He was unbearably hot and needed fresh air. Quentin left the great hall, a headache already pounding mightily at his temples. They came infrequently but were painful when they occurred. He moved rapidly down the corridor, blind to everything except the fact that he'd lost. Again.

When would he get his gambling under control?

His blood and tastes ran royal, but his circumstances were not. Why must he always push himself beyond his means? He dreaded what would occur next. His tenants must be milked dry yet again. He could already hear their grumblings.

"By God's hooks," he swore, grinding his teeth. He'd suffered enough. It was time to make someone else pay.

Quentin had no idea where he went as he stormed down the stone-flagged corridor. He only wanted retribution.

And then he saw her. Renton's daughter. The raven-haired girl with her father's dark blue eyes was but ten-and-three, but she had the body of a woman. A very ripe woman.

Quentin decided it would be her. Here. Now.

He slowed his pace as he approached her. What was the chit's name? *Bevia.* Yes, that was it. Bevia.

"Bevia?"

She took notice of him and stopped in her tracks. "Oh, my lord. You startled me." She leaned down to pick up the doll she'd dropped.

Quentin bent and reached it first, handing it to

her. He gave her his most engaging grin. "I am most sorry for that, my dear."

He saw the effect his smile had on her. If he knew one thing, it was the way to a woman's heart. He had the height of Edward Longshanks, far beyond what most of the king's brood had been given, coupled with his mother's gray eyes and distinct, silvery blond hair. He used all this to his advantage whenever he could.

Bevia shyly returned his smile. "May I help you, my lord? Are you lost? I could—"

Quentin placed a hand gently on her shoulder. "As a matter of fact, I was on my way to your father's study, my sweet. He promised me the loan of a book. I first went to the garderobe and," he shrugged, "I seem to be turned around."

"I can take you there," she said eagerly.

Quentin gave her shoulder a squeeze. "Oh, would you? That would be most delightful, dear Bevia." He drew her hand through the crook of his arm. "I am quite looking forward to what I find there."

The girl led him down several halls, chattering much like her mother as they walked. Quentin murmured politely every now and then, and she didn't notice he wasn't listening to her.

But he was taking her in. Her breasts were full, her waist tiny. His heart quickened as he thought of punishing Renton through his daughter. 'Twould be most enjoyable.

Bevia stopped. "This is my father's solar. You must enter it to cross to his study. There's no other access, I'm afraid."

Oh, this was rich. Quentin would have Renton's daughter in the lord's own bed.

"Would you mind showing me, Bevia? I wouldn't

want to disturb anything. You know how particular your father is."

He saw her mouth purse with distaste. Renton was said to have a heavy hand. Quentin didn't know if it extended to his own family, but he felt sure it must by the expression on the chit's face.

"All right," she agreed reluctantly. She pushed open the door. A fire burned low in the grate, the only light of the room. They entered, and Quentin silently closed and locked the door behind them.

———

Flushed with drink and success, Renton pinched Alita's ample rump as they walked up the stairs. Most of the evening was now a blur after so many cups of wine and ale, but he remembered the most important event. He'd bested that pompous ass, Quentin of Nowland. The beautiful wooded area adjacent to his own property now belonged to his estate. Not his neighbor anymore. Renton would never foolishly gamble it away as the king's bastard had.

Renton threw an arm about his wife's shoulders. A quick romp with her and then sweet sleep awaited him. He paused as they reached the solar. The door was ajar. His guard went up. He never left it so. Neither did the servants nor Alita. It had taken training, but he was a particular man and liked things done his way.

Someone had been here. But who?

He motioned Alita aside and opened the door cautiously. The fire burned as mere embers now, the room mostly in shadow. Renton stepped in and examined his surroundings. No one was there. Still, he felt a presence and moved toward the bedchamber. In the doorway, he noticed the bed curtains, always opened upon his arising, had been closed.

Someone was in his bed.

And then he heard the singing. It was soft and haunting. A child's voice and a child's song. Relief filled him, followed by anger. What child stumbled into his bed? Now he'd want fresh sheets. He wouldn't lie where another had.

Renton moved toward the bed and lit a candle next to it before he drew the curtain aside. Chills ran through him.

His daughter sat propped upon the pillows, cradling her doll in her arms. Bevia rocked the toy and sang to it, her eyes glassy, her face pale. She was naked. Renton saw the blood between her legs and spilled on his sheets.

"Bevia?" he asked, touching her arm gently so as not to frighten her. "Bevia, who did this to you?"

His daughter gazed blankly at the wall and continued to sing eerily off-key.

———

Savina's back hurt from all the tiresome tasks assigned to her. She hated milking cows and loathed washing the undergarments of all the other nuns. Thank Sweetest Jesu her work was now complete. Though meticulous and conscientious as always, she'd finished quickly, and now she must avoid the abbess at all costs. That woman ruled with an iron fist. If God's love had ever been in that woman's heart, she'd killed it years ago. All Mother Superior now preached was work and more work. It may have made their convent rich in earthly stores, but Savina thought spiritual ones more important.

She brought her pail of milk into the kitchen and winked at the novices scrubbing pots. Their red, raw hands gave her heart a moment's ache. Savina said a quick prayer for them. All too often she had been in their shoes, as cleaning pots was a favorite punishment the abbess doled out.

Savina walked soundlessly on the stones, having perfected the art of keeping her presence unknown at an early age. The habit, still with her after all these years, came in useful upon occasion.

She heard voices in the main hallway and decided to see what news she might pick up. Mother Superior rarely let the nuns know what happened in the outside world. Savina may have chosen to live a sheltered life with God, but it didn't mean she wasn't curious as to what went on beyond the walls of the convent.

A man's voice!

She hurried her step when she realized it did not belong to any of the visiting priests. Savina moved close until she stood around the corner from the commotion.

"I tell you, I must see Julesa now. Your abbess, that is. Make haste, but summon her at once. Or better yet, simply take us to her. That will save precious time."

Savina heard the impatience in the man's voice. He also had a familiar tone. If she didn't know better, she would guess he was related to Mother.

The nuns conversing with him seemed hesitant to act. Savina peeked around the corner and decided she would take matters into her own hands. She marched out bold as a peacock.

"I am going to our abbess, my lord," she exclaimed. "I will take you to her."

The two nuns shot her a wild look of disapproval,

but Savina ignored them. Instead, she was most interested in the woman that stood next to the man. Actually, she realized it was a young girl as she drew near, and a beautiful one at that. One upon the cusp of childhood and becoming a maid, the girl possessed flawless skin and large, blue eyes. The eyes, though, were blank. Savina wondered for a moment if the girl were blind.

"Finally, someone who sees reason." The man waved the two nuns away and turned to stare at her. "Take me to your abbess now. The circumstances are none of your business, but time is of the essence."

"Of course, my lord," Savina said demurely, thinking the man a boor. She didn't need to know the exact nature of his visit, but he didn't have to sound so condescending. "Follow me."

Savina moved through the entry way and up a wide staircase. She tamped down the impulse to peek over her shoulder and assumed the nobleman would follow. She kept a brisk pace, as was her way, and hoped he and his charge could keep up.

As they approached the door to the abbess's study, Savina paused. Before she could speak, the man brushed her aside.

"I will handle matters from here," he said abruptly. Without knocking, he pushed open the door and swept into the room, dragging the girl behind him.

Savina knew Mother rarely spent time in the outer chamber. She felt it safe to enter and close the door. As she turned from doing so, she saw the man and the girl she assumed was his daughter vanish beyond the second door. Savina scampered to it. The door remained open a foot.

Plenty of room to hear... and not be seen.

"Renton! What on God's earth are you doing here? How did you get in? And who is—"

"I've no time for cordial conversation, Julesa. I have a problem. You will solve it."

Savina could almost feel Mother's appraising eyes as the room filled with the sound of silence. The abbess's intelligence was second to none. Savina knew she studied the situation, wondering how to turn it to her advantage.

"I assume you want to leave the girl here, Brother. She is your daughter?"

Savina grimaced at Mother's sharp tone. At least she learned the nobleman was kin to the abbess. He'd held the same air she did. It pleased her that she had guessed their connection.

"She is. Useless baggage to me now. Spoiled by that bastard Earl of Nowland. He did it for spite since I would never let him have her. I won't see my family ruined because of him."

"She appears... distant."

Savina heard a heavy sigh. "Bevia's always been a bit simple. By the Christ, she still plays with dolls at three-and-ten! I'd thought to make a good match of her, though. She's got Alita's looks. Men aren't interested in their wives having a brain."

Mother snorted. "Make this match. Why should anyone need know she was deflowered by a royal bastard?"

"Because she's with child."

A hush filled the air. Savina shivered, her heart going out to the blank beauty.

The nobleman let out a sigh. "The moment Alita realized it, I tried to arrange for a marriage to take place immediately instead of next year as planned. Unfortunately, the man I had chosen as Bevia's husband-to-be had a gravely ill mother. He refused to leave the woman's side and marry without her present at the ceremony. By the time the old fool passed on, Bevia's condition could not have been hidden from a randy groom on his wedding night."

"And so you bring her to me."

"What else can I do, Julesa? I refuse to let Quentin have Bevia or know of the child she will bear. Bevia is dead to me as of this moment. I have a coffer full of gold for your greedy hands, Sister. You're to keep her here permanently. No one's to know she's of my blood. Hopefully, the chit will regain some of her sanity after the child's birth."

"What does your wife say about this decision?"

"She will only be told Bevia is dead. Leaving her here is the best I can do."

Shock ran through Savina. She may not have seen her family for years, as all novices left their earthly relations behind when they committed their lives to God, but she knew her parents loved her to this day. And here this poor girl was, through no fault of her own, being written off as dead by her selfish, twisted father.

Savina vowed in that moment that she would care for this young girl, less than a dozen years younger than she herself.

"No one is to know of her existence, Julesa. The last word I will ask of this is to let me know if Bevia is delivered of a girl or a boy. I pray it will be a girl. The earl would have no use of a girl child if he ever discovered her existence. After that, no reminders. Ever."

Mother laughed harshly. "I understand everything you ask, Brother. And don't think I won't hesitate to call in a favor of my own when the time warrants. We both wield power in our own way. You may prove useful to me someday."

Savina realized this one conversation led her to understand Mother finally. She and this cruel brother seemed to be cut from the same cloth, one without heart, without soul. Savina didn't know how she would accomplish it, but she would become Bevia's protector.

Without thought to the consequences, Savina marched determinedly into Mother's study.

"Sister." Mother's low tones held little surprise. It was as if she knew all along Savina eavesdropped upon the private conversation.

Savina mustered as much innocence as she could project. "Yes, Mother?"

The abbess indicated Bevia. "You always seem to accomplish your tasks so quickly, Sister. I have a new one for you." Her eyes gleamed as she appraised Savina.

"I am most willing to do whatever you wish, Mother."

"This is Bevia. She will need your attention—night and day. You will be excused from all other chores with the exception of your prayers. You are to keep her with you at all times. You are not to make mention of anything you might have heard about her."

Savina winced at the hard look Mother gave her. "As you wish, Mother."

"Escort Lord Renton downstairs. Come back immediately to take care of your charge. Do you understand everything I've said?"

"Yes, Mother. I am to care for Bevia. I will not let her from my sight. I will protect her always, even with my life."

Mother nodded. "Good." She studied Savina a moment then said, "I've changed my mind. I will accompany Lord Renton to the gate. You may start caring for your charge from this moment forth."

The abbess rose. "Come," she motioned to her brother. "I know you are anxious to be off—and I must collect that coffer of gold which you mentioned. My best to Alita. And there's a boy now?"

"Yes," Lord Renton replied as he led his sister from the room. "My son Crispin. Much younger than Bevia. He will be heir to Mangeron one day."

They left the room, and Savina turned to Bevia. She slowly approached the girl and took her hand.

"We are going to spend lots of time together, Bevia." She stroked Bevia's hand, hoping it would soothe her. The glassy eyes remained unfocused.

Savina silently sent a prayer to the Virgin, asking for Her divine guidance. God worked in mysterious ways. He had finally used Savina's eavesdropping to give her a mission in life.

And Savina would guard Bevia from all evil.

Especially Mother Superior.

1

NORTH OF ENGLAND—1311

Savina paced nervously, anticipating the arrival of her invited guest. Had she done the right thing? Would he accept Kallen as part of his own family?

More importantly, would Kallen accept him?

She sat behind the massive desk that had belonged to Mother. Once a large woman who'd dominated a room, the abbess had dwindled away, little by little, consumed by an illness that ate away at her body over two long years.

Savina ran a trembling hand along the smooth wood. This would never do. She must remain calm. She must be in control of the situation. Reaching for a carafe, she poured herself a cup of wine. As she leaned back into the chair and sipped at it, her mind wandered.

Where had the years gone?

It seemed only yesterday she charged into this very room, ready to take Bevia under her wing. She'd made Bevia and the child she birthed her own, growing to love them both with a fierceness that only grew stronger over time.

Now Bevia lay dead of fever, years in the ground, joined recently by the convent's abbess.

And as the new abbess, elected by her fellow nuns to lead the convent, Savina now chose to take it upon herself to play God, hoping in the next few minutes to change Kallen's future. Hoping to save her from an empty life in this sterile convent, a place that had never suited Kallen, even as a young child.

The knock startled her from her reverie. Savina composed herself, placing a placid look on her face and dropping her hands to her lap.

"Come."

A red-cheeked novice with eyes of sky blue opened the door and smiled shyly. "Mother? Your visitor has arrived."

Savina returned the smile, grateful she could show her love for her fellow sisters with such a simple gesture. "Show him in, please."

The door swung open, and her heart almost stopped in her chest when the raven-haired stranger stepped through it. Oh, he was so like Bevia. His dark blue eyes held kindness. Savina knew instantly she had done the right thing. This man's posture and demeanor spoke nothing of the arrogant lord she remembered as Bevia's father.

"Thank you, Sister. You may return to your duties."

"Yes, Mother." The novice closed the door behind her.

Savina indicated the chair in front of her desk. "Please, Lord de Mangeron, have a seat. I know your journey has been long and may have tired you. Would you care for a cup of wine?"

The nobleman cocked an eyebrow at her. "You roused more than my curiosity with your cryptic note, Abbess." He seated himself. "Yes, wine would be appreciated. And to be told why you summoned me would be even more appreciated."

She laughed and poured out the wine. As she handed it to him, she said, "I was sorry to hear of your father's passing."

A shadow crossed the man's face. "I thank you. Not many have offered such kind words. How did you know of him, Abbess?"

Savina shook her head. "My lord, I have a tale to share with you that is most troubling. I hope when I've concluded, you will be the man I have prayed you would be."

She rubbed her temples, preparing herself. "I met your father once many years ago. You would have been a young boy then. He brought your sister—"

"Bevia?" The lord sat up, wine sloshing from his cup. "You knew Bevia?" he asked eagerly, his face now boyish.

Savina nodded. "I knew Bevia from the time she was three-and-ten until she died of a fever eight years ago. She was my friend."

"Impossible!" the man proclaimed. "Bevia died in a riding accident nigh on a score ago. She'd gone to court with my father. Her loss devastated my family."

She gazed steadily at the man before her. "No, my lord. Your father revealed he would tell you and your mother that Bevia died, but she did not. She lived here at the nunnery until her death. With her child."

"Her... *child*?" He stood, waving his hand wildly in front of him. "What reason would you have to lure me here with such lies?"

"Lord de Mangeron." Savina's tone rang firm yet soft. She'd discovered long ago shouts and anger did little good. As she expected, he quieted, confusion marking his features.

"Please sit, my lord," she commanded gently.

He did so, bewilderment spreading across his countenance.

"Lord Renton brought Bevia here many years ago. His sister Julesa was then our abbess. He gave her a coffer of gold and demanded she keep Bevia and her unborn child here forever."

"My sister was... with child?"

"Yes." Savina sighed, uncomfortable sharing with him this part of the tale. "The Earl of Nowland had violated her. Your father did not want this man to have her or the child, and Bevia's betrothed would not have wanted her when he learned of her condition. This is why your father pretended to the world that his daughter died. He said he did not want ruin brought upon the family."

"God's wounds!" Lord de Mangeron's face crumpled. Tears slid down his cheeks. "I was but eight when Bevia died. She played with me, sang to me. I thought she was an earthly angel gone to live with the heavenly ones."

He brushed the tears aside. "I so loved her, Abbess. There were no other children after me. Bevia was all I had." Crispin slammed his fist upon the desk. "Yet I can barely remember her face after all these years have passed."

Savina grinned. "Oh, but you will. You'll see her in Kallen. Her daughter."

"My niece?" Crispin sat back down, dumbfounded.

"Yes. She has her mother's fair skin and luminous smile. Only her hair is different. A silvery blond instead of Bevia's raven locks."

Crispin's mouth grew hard. "The earl's is such an unusual color. By the Christ, I will kill the bastard!"

Savina came around from behind the desk and placed a hand on his shoulder. "No, my lord. I see that you are a good man. You will put your hatred aside and instead lavish love on your niece, who's had no family for many years."

He studied her a moment. "Kallen, you said?"

"Yes." Savina smiled. "Bright, willful Kallen. She is intelligent, my lord. A great beauty, as Bevia was. Sometimes I wonder how one so sheltered in a nunnery can seem so worldly."

"I must see her at once." The nobleman stood. "We must return to Mangeron. She must meet her grandmother and my wife, Deva. She is with child. The babe will be Kallen's cousin."

Crispin began to pace rapidly in the confined space. "My mother's spirits have been flagging as of late, Abbess. Losing my father was a hard blow since she loved him dearly. Bringing Bevia's child home to Mangeron will make all the difference."

He came to stand in front of the window. "My men are just beyond your walls. I shall send word to them that we are to return at once."

Crispin turned to face her. "My gratitude at this news cannot be expressed adequately, I'm afraid. I do thank you for caring for Bevia and Kallen. I promise I will do everything in my power to see that Kallen is restored to our family in every way. Now let us go to her."

"I fear not, my lord."

The nobleman appeared stunned. "But why? I am sure she is eager as I to make our acquaintance."

"Kallen has no knowledge of your existence," she said bluntly.

"You never told her of us? Why?"

Savina raised her hands to her temples and massaged them again. "I have only been abbess for two weeks, my lord. Your Aunt Julesa, the former abbess, forbade any mention to Kallen of her family. She was to remain here always, never to be known by you."

"What cruelty was this?"

"'Twas your father's express wish that it remain so, and his sister abided by his words. He said Bevia and her child were dead to him and his. When Julesa died, I made an instant decision to send word to you. I knew your father had recently passed on. As the new abbess, I thought it best to inform you of Kallen's existence.

"But you see," she continued, "I could not risk telling Kallen of you. What if you had not come today? What if you did not wish to acknowledge this bastard child of your sister's? Having knowledge of you, and then learning of your rejection, would have been more than Kallen could bear."

"I see," Crispin said. "Then I place myself in your hands, Abbess. Kallen has been in them for years. My trust is in you. I will handle the situation as you see fit."

Savina nodded, relieved that Kallen would not be ripped away from her. "It will take me a bit of time to pray for the wisdom will take to tell Kallen the truth. Once she has adjusted to the idea, I will send for you. You can then escort her to her new home."

Crispin frowned. "How long will this take?"

"I would give her a few weeks to become accustomed to the idea, my lord. She has known nothing but this convent for eight-and-ten years."

"But my wife's babe will come in five or six weeks'

time. I cannot leave again so close to the birth. No, Abbess, Kallen must come with me now."

Savina fought the panic rising within her. "Then mayhap you could give me a week with her. Even two. Enough time to prepare her adequately."

Crispin pondered her words for a moment. "I shall leave immediately for Mangeron. will take me a week to reach it. I will then send my emissary to return and bring Kallen home to her true family."

His face displayed a deep agony. "Deva has already miscarried one child. I dare not be away from her. The man I send, though, is my wife's brother. Sir Griffith is like my own kin. He will guard Kallen well. Is this satisfactory?"

"Yes," Savina agreed. "'Tis best you stay with your wife at such a time. I will break this news to Kallen. I promise she will be ready when Sir Griffith comes to return her safely to her new home."

Crispin stood and took her hands in his. He kissed them with tenderness. "Abbess, you have made me so happy this day. I am now an uncle, and soon to be a father. God's blessings are rich indeed."

She squeezed his hands in return. "I shall pray that your wife delivers a child in good health, my lord. God's grace be with you."

"And also with you." The nobleman turned and left the room, his step light.

Savina wrapped her arms tightly about her. The easy part was over. She had faced a strange nobleman with a sordid tale of the evils his father and an earl had taken part in many years ago.

Now came the hard part. Telling Kallen.

2

Griffith awoke with a start. He sat up quickly, cold sweat laced through his hair. He ran his hands through the wet mass, tugging on the ends, trying to force himself to leave behind the dreams.

They came infrequently now, never more than once or twice a month, but with a fury that always took him by surprise.

"She's dead," he whispered. His words hung in the still of the room, but his heart and mind raced far beyond those four walls. He closed his eyes tightly, willing the visions to flee.

Yet the dream lingered in the early morn. The familiar sick feeling washed over him. He swallowed hard, pushing back the bile that rose each time.

Carina could not come back to him except in these nightmares. The soft, pliant woman who'd worshipped him with her warm brown eyes and given her body to him night after night lay rotting in a grave, their stillborn son clasped to her bosom. Griffith hadn't wanted them parted. His father thought it foolish and wanted a separate casket carved for his grandson, but his mother understood and overruled her husband. Griffith got his wish, and now his son lay with his mother for all eternity.

He pushed aside the blanket and swung his legs to the floor. His head fell into his hands.

When would the ache end?

Two years had passed, yet after one of these nightmares, Griffith still experienced the hurt afresh. He saw Carina's long, dark hair, matted with sweat, the faraway look in her eyes. And the blood. Christ's wounds, there had been so much blood.

Griffith's mother forced him to hold the dead babe. The child was the last thing on his mind as his wife lay dying, her very essence draining from her. He didn't regret the time spent with the babe, though. He needed to see the boy, innocent that he was. If he hadn't held him, he might still blame the child for Carina's death.

Now, he only blamed himself.

Carina was a petite thing, shy, never questioning him. He loved to spend hours simply gazing at her beauty. His father warned him that one with hips so narrow would never make a good breeder, but Griffith wouldn't listen. He wanted a son, and Carina wanted whatever her husband did. Having the child cost her life.

It cost Griffith the only happiness he'd ever known.

He stood and moved to the bowl of water, splashing it over his face. The nightmare began to fade. But the consequences of his actions never would. Griffith vowed never to love again, never to get a woman with child. The Sommersby line would die out with him.

He dressed and went down for morning mass. The ritual meant nothing to him. He never set foot inside a chapel while at home. Deva, though, would question him if he did not make an appearance, so whenever he visited at Mangeron, Griffith went to mass as she expected.

He slid into the pew next to her, crossing himself and kneeling to pray, or at least go through the motions of prayer. He didn't believe in prayer anymore. A God that would let Carina die was no God to him. His impassioned prayers to spare his wife's life had been ignored. If a woman of pureness and light such as Carina could be sacrificed, Griffith wanted no part of that God's world.

His mind wandered throughout the mass, flitting aimlessly from one topic to the next, never staying in one place for long. He found it better that way.

"Are you hungry, Brother?"

Griffith's wanderings fled, to find Deva's hand resting lightly on his arm. He rewarded her with a smile.

"Of course. When am I not ravenous?" he said lightly.

"Then come. Let us break our fast."

Deva led the way out from the chapel, her steps slow as her hands rested atop her huge belly. They crossed the bailey in the early morn's gray light.

"'Tis rain later today, I think," he noted. "Is not Crispin due home soon?"

She frowned. "I hope so. Tomorrow will be two weeks he has been gone."

"What business took him to this convent so far away? You have remained vague on that point, Sister."

Deva shrugged. She lifted her skirts as they climbed the stairs to the castle's entrance. "I am not hiding anything from you, Griffith."

He heard the odd note in her voice. "Then 'tis something Crispin keeps hidden from you?" He brought an arm about her shoulders in comfort.

"Nay, my husband is not one to conceal anything from me. We are closer each day we are together." She frowned. "I fear even he knew not what business awaited him there."

Griffith gave her a squeeze. "I am sure your lord husband will soon return and share all with you."

They entered the great hall. Griffith seated Deva and positioned himself next to her on the dais. Servants quickly brought bread and cheese.

"A little of the weak ale this morn, my lady?"

Deva nodded, and the servant poured her a full cup. She raised it to her lips and sipped it slowly.

"Ah, ever so much better," she proclaimed when she'd drained the cup's contents. "I think I may be able to partake of a few bites of bread now."

"Still queasy?" Griffith asked. He knew Deva's stomach had been fickle throughout the entire time she had been with child.

"A little. Only in the early hours before I eat something. This time." A shadow crossed her face.

He took her hand in his. "All will be well this time, Sister. You will give birth to a strapping lad."

She smiled. "I hope so, though Crispin cares not whether 'tis a boy or girl. He only wants the child to be healthy."

Griffith's own stomach twisted. He'd lost his beloved wife. He refused to lose his only sister as well.

A servant approached. "Your husband approaches, my lady."

Deva rose. "Thank the heavens he has returned," she exclaimed. Before they could exit the great hall, Crispin burst through its doors, his arms held wide.

"Saints be praised, but you are the picture of health, Wife." He embraced Deva and then spied Griffith. "And the Devil Himself here with you." Crispin shook Griffith's hand. "Thank you for coming."

"Your message sounded urgent, Crispin. I came as quickly as I could."

Crispin placed a protective arm about his wife. "I needed you here to look after Deva. I trust no one but you, my friend." He grinned. "Foolish, I know, but then again, you do have a few redeeming qualities."

Griffith smiled. "Such as? Quick, flattery for a guest should be required, Crispin, especially one who dropped everything to attend your wife while you were gone."

His friend laughed. "You need no flattery from me. You've heard it your whole life, Griff. Were you not always the best bowman? The best hunter? The most skilled at dancing and the lute? Were you not always the smartest and fastest among those who fostered with Quentin? The one who could but crook his finger and have half the village girls in a swoon? Nay, Griff, you will gain no accolades from me. I lavish all compliments upon my sweet Deva alone."

Crispin nuzzled his wife's neck, and soft giggles erupted.

A pang of jealousy tore at Griffith's heart. Crispin and Deva's very closeness, their love, blanketed the room. He took a deep breath.

"As you two seem to have much to catch up on, I shall go make myself useful elsewhere."

His brother-in-law raised his head and turned his attention to Griffith. "Actually, you could be very useful to me, Griff. I have need of your knightly services."

Griffith cocked his head. "Can you afford me,

Crispin? Or 'tis a favor you seek, with no compensation?"

Deva laughed. "Come, let us go to the solar. We can speak in comfort." Her eyes gleamed at her husband. "I am most curious about your trip, my lord, but even more so about this favor you require. I would have you tell all and tell it well."

Crispin bowed to her. "My lady wife, I can refuse you nothing." He glanced to Griffith. "Come, then. Let us adjourn to more private quarters. But instead of the solar, we shall go to my mother's room."

Deva shook her head. "She is no doubt still abed, Crispin. She rarely ventures forth this early. I would not have her disturbed."

Crispin raised his brows. "I think, my lady, for this news, she will jump from her bed and lead us all in a merry dance."

Griffith followed the couple up the stairs, intrigued by Crispin's words. What news would have the withdrawn noblewoman spring from her bed? He knew her health to be moderately good although she did pass a great part of the day in her bedchamber. Griffith had not spent any noticeable amount of time with the older woman since his sister had married into the de Mangeron family. He wondered what news Crispin would share that might make his mother come alive again.

They arrived at her door, and Crispin knocked gently. He entered before he received a response. Lady de Mangeron sat with a mountain of pillows stacked behind her. A tray across her lap held a small pewter cup and a slice of bread smeared with butter. Her skin, while still fairly smooth, was a pale, ashen color, barely distinguishable from her graying hair.

She turned stormy eyes upon them. "I don't recall inviting any of you in, Crispin."

Her icy tone rolled off her affable son. "Mother, you will thank me for this intrusion in but a moment's time, I assure you."

Haughty brows arched in protest, but Lady de Mangeron kept silent.

"I have news, Mother. News that will first take you aback, but I'm sure you will embrace it, much as I did."

The old woman perked up, Griffith thought. She shifted on the bed. "Go on. 'Tis not as if I can do anything else but listen. Certainly not ready myself for the day with an audience present."

Crispin laughed. "You old charmer. All right." He knelt next to the bed and took his mother's hand in his. "I have news about Bevia."

Lady de Mangeron's eyes widened. Her mouth twisted. "Nay, Crispin, I cannot talk about—"

"No, Mother, you will not talk. You will listen."

Griffith hid his smile. Crispin, normally the most placid of men, and certainly nothing like his ogre of a father, silenced his mother with but a few words. Griffith's surprise at his friend's confidence made him take a step closer. Whatever Crispin was about to reveal would be more than interesting.

And why would it concern Bevia, now dead longer than Griffith could even remember. They had been but young boys, fostering with the Earl of Nowland when news of Bevia's death reached them. What could Crispin have discovered after so long a time, especially at a convent?

A chill ran through him, a premonition. His gut told him that his friend's words would change his life.

"Bevia did not die at three-and-ten, Mother. She suffered no riding accident in London."

"No accident?" his mother echoed. "No accident? I do not understand."

"No accident," Crispin confirmed. "When Father took her away, you knew she was with child, did you not?"

Lady de Mangeron's face flushed with color. Her head dropped. Griffith saw the tears begin to fall, staining the lace coverlet on her lap. Silence fell heavily upon the room.

Finally, she raised her head, her eyes watery and bright. "Yes, Crispin, I knew. The Earl of Nowland took advantage of your sister, and we discovered she was with child. Your father took her to London to try to make a quick match." She shuddered. "'Twas there she died."

Crispin clutched her hands. "No, Mother. He took her to a convent where Aunt Julesa was abbess. She remained there and gave birth to a child. A daughter."

"I have... a granddaughter?" Lady de Mangeron's words were but a whisper.

Crispin nodded. "Yes, you do. Bevia died eight years ago. Her daughter has been alone there ever since."

Deva gasped. "She's there now, Crispin? Did you see her? Did you not bring her home with you?"

"Nay, Deva, she remains there with the good sisters. But I would like her to come and live with us, here at Mangeron."

"Of course she must live here," Deva insisted. "She is your niece, Crispin. And she's been without family for so many years. How lonely she must be."

"Mother?" Crispin looked at Lady de Mangeron, her mouth trembling. "Shall we bring Kallen home?"

"Kallen. My granddaughter's name is Kallen." The old noblewoman began to sob. "Yes, my son. Bring her to us. We shall correct the terrible mistake your father made so long ago. Oh, Bevia. My poor, sweet Bevia."

Deva turned to Crispin. "I shall stay with your lady mother. I know now what you require of Griffith." She sat upon the bed to comfort her mother-in-law.

Crispin motioned Griffith. They stepped into the hallway, and Crispin led them into the solar.

"I cannot leave Deva again, my friend," Crispin told him. "'Twas enough to travel away from her these past two weeks. I worried constantly about her and the coming babe. I must stay with her."

He looked hopefully at Griffith. "Kallen knew not of her family for all these years. My father paid to have Bevia and Kallen remain there forever, hidden from the world. When Aunt Julesa died recently, the new abbess summoned me. 'Tis why I went to the nunnery."

"Why did you not bring your niece home with you? Why the need for a second trip, Crispin?"

"I wanted to, but the new abbess is strong-willed. I gather she has been Bevia's and Kallen's protector all these years. She wanted time to break the news to Kallen gently. In case I refused to have her, the girl would never have known of her family."

Griffith nodded. "You wish me to go and fetch this found relative back to Mangeron?"

"Yes, my friend. I have never asked anything from you before."

"Even though you could have?"

Crispin nodded. "Even so. Will you do this for me, Griff? Bring this niece of mine back into our fold?"

"Will that cancel my debt to you?"

Crispin smiled. "I will then be in your debt, Griff. As I have been ever since you introduced the heavenly Deva to me."

Griffith nodded. "I shall do as you ask. When do you wish me to leave?"

"On the morrow. 'Tis sure I am Kallen will be eager to return to her family and Mangeron."

3

"You think to pawn me off upon strangers?" Kallen bellowed. "I'll not go, Savina. I'd rather sell myself on the streets of London than do what you ask."

Savina laughed. "You always have had a bit of drama in you, Kallen." The nun clucked her tongue. "I would have thought with my new title as abbess of this convent that you might show me a touch of respect."

"Respect? You encouraged me to question any and everything from the time I toddled about, unsteady on chubby feet. You, my eternal friend, nurtured what you called my mischievous spirit. I might never have become the troublemaker I'm known to be without your words of advice, Savina. And you think I should show you respect simply because of an office you now hold? Why, you have become Evil Incarnate. 'Tis the spirit of Mother Superior that now inhabits you. I declare she has invaded your very soul, else you'd never think to throw me out into the cold."

Savina bit her lip.

Kallen knew she always did that to keep from

laughing. Anger bubbled up again, but she held her tongue.

In truth, she was frightened. Savina's wild tale of a wicked earl somehow ruining her mother, and the part Bevia's own father played in leaving her here at the convent without his family knowing, was too fantastic. And now she was to go to this family of strangers when she'd known nothing but the walls of this place?

The thought scared her—and yet it intrigued her.

Kallen had long ago grown weary of the confining routines of the nunnery, how the nuns shunned her for being different, how she had no calling to serve as a Bride of Christ. She often longed to see what lay beyond this boredom, but she'd no money to finance such an adventure.

She loathed the thought of being a servant, for she hated to clean. Mother Superior saw to that. She instructed the nuns to give Kallen the most deplorable cleaning tasks found both inside and outside the convent. Kallen never had a chance to learn to sew, nor had she been allowed to cook, as others residing within the nunnery's walls did on a regular basis. She didn't think she could beg on the streets, for she had far too much pride.

Now, though, was her chance to escape. She had family, the very thing she'd longed for. Why did she rebel at the chance to see them?

"I know you to be as curious as I once was, Kallen. I have been as a mother to you, and you have been the daughter of my heart. I now speak to you, however, as a friend. You must go with this trusted knight. He will take you to your uncle and his wife."

"You'll finally be rid of me!" Kallen accused. "Oh, I

always suspected you knew of my origins. Who my father was. You hid the truth from me, Savina."

Her friend grew serious. "'Twas Mother Superior who kept the truth from you. I only followed her orders."

"The abbess would not have recognized the truth if it had bitten her, Savina. You know it to be so."

The nun grinned. "You are correct, Kallen. But she is no longer here. Nothing binds you to this place. You should be eager to leave. To start a new life. You've often said you felt like an outcast among the pious nuns. Here is your chance at freedom. Take it. Go to Lord and Lady de Mangeron. Or are you afraid?"

Savina knew her too well. Kallen lifted her chin high. "I'm not afraid. I am just going to miss you, 'tis all. I don't know if you'll be able to manage without me underfoot."

The new abbess threw her arms about Kallen. "Oh, my precious love, my dearest child. Do you not know I will be beside myself without you in my life? Pushing you from my nest is by far the hardest task God has ever given me to do." Savina gripped Kallen's shoulders. "'Tis right, though. You must fly on your own now, my sweet dove.

"Besides, I have a nunnery to run. After years of darkness, I find my work is cut out for me. I intend to bring God's love and light back into the lives of these good sisters. Christ Himself knows 'tis far too long since they've seen it, much less been given a kind word."

Kallen rested her forehead against Savina's and basked in the warmth of her friend's love, the friend who had been more like a mother to Kallen than her own. Then she pulled away.

"When am I to embark upon my adventure?"

"I expect you'll be gone in two days' time."

Griffith decided to go himself, instead of sending a messenger to the gates of the convent. The delicate nature of his mission led him to believe that action the most appropriate. He halted Satan as the nunnery came into his sights and turned the horse in order to face the band of men that had accompanied him.

Crispin had sent nothing but the finest knights on this journey. They numbered ten. All were not only skilled warriors but loyal to the de Mangerons. A man of his time, Renton had ruled his home and his men through fear. In Crispin's short tenure as earl, things at Mangeron had changed for the better. These men accompanied Griffith because they wanted to, because it was what their liege lord asked of them. They'd been told very little, other than they were to escort an important member of the de Mangeron family safely home.

Griffith decided that his friend could share what he wanted of Kallen's past with his people. He would simply accomplish his task and return home, his debt to Crispin finally paid. This trip was nothing but a pleasant interlude in his otherwise dull life. He would see the girl back to Mangeron without incident and then return to...

To what?

It didn't matter. Nothing did anymore, except Deva's happiness. He would move heaven and earth for his beloved sister. If returning this Kallen to the castle made Crispin happy, then Deva would bask in her husband's glow. That was reason enough for Griffith.

"I must visit with the abbess for a spell," he informed those gathered near. "She has kept a safe watch over Lady Kallen for Lord de Mangeron. I may be gone a few hours, but I shall return to you no later than nightfall. Make a temporary camp, for we will stay only the one night. 'Tis likely Lady Kallen will wish us to make haste and travel as far as possible on the morrow."

Griffith gave specific orders to a few men and then spurred his horse toward the gates of the convent. He was allowed within, a slight nun of no more than a score taking his ebony horse and promising to water and feed it well. Griffith thought it wise to keep Satan's name to himself. No sense in frightening off the good sister, much less denying Satan a little bit of spoiling after their week-long journey. Although the horse could be a handful at times, Satan seemed relatively well-behaved for the moment.

Another nun accompanied him through the massive oak doors into the nunnery itself, where the hall's floor gleamed from long hours of polishing. He followed her up a wide staircase and down several turns along a dim corridor before they stopped before a door.

It opened almost immediately, and Griffith found himself in the company of a slender woman with small laugh lines about her eyes. Her severe black habit was tied with a leather belt. Her wimple and veil hid her hair. Tiny in stature, he perceived her to be capable and loving at the same time, a fine balance he assumed all abbesses must maintain.

"I heard a man's footsteps and knew it had to be you. I am Sister Savina, abbess of this humble convent." She bowed her head graciously.

"Sir Griffith Sommersby, Abbess. I am sent by

Lord Crispin de Mangeron to escort Lady Kallen back to Mangeron."

"Oh!" The nun looked taken aback. "I suppose I've never quite thought of her that way. She's always been plain Kallen to me since the day she emerged kicking and screaming from Bevia's womb." The nun pondered things a moment. "I rather like it. Lady Kallen. It suits her."

Griffith admired this nun's plainspoken manner. She had none of the devious double-talk most churchmen espoused.

"Did you have a hand in raising Lady Kallen, Abbess?"

The older woman laughed aloud, her eyes merry. "Oh, more than a hand, my lord. I've been the only mother Kallen has known. And quite a handful she is. Why—"

A sudden blur burst from the other side of the door and flew across the room, stopping in front of him.

"Savina, you're telling tales again, aren't you? Now that you're the new abbess, I would have expected better from you. Besides, I thought you wanted this nice nobleman to take me off your hands. Do you not think telling him wicked accounts about me might cause him to regret his mission and leave without accomplishing it? You are impossible, you know."

The girl turned to face Griffith and inclined her head a brief moment before raising it and locking her gray eyes to his. "I am Kallen, my lord. Not nearly as bad as Savina warns. Probably not very good, either, but I will leave you to be the judge of that after we've spent some time in each other's company. I hear that it will be a week's journey or more to this... place we venture."

Griffith could only stare. He hadn't really pictured Kallen de Mangeron in his mind. It hadn't been of importance to him.

Before him was more woman than girl, though. The most ethereal beauty he had ever seen. There was a look of Crispin about her, around her eyes and mouth. Griffith suddenly wished he could remember what Bevia had looked like.

Even so, this woman was striking. Tall, curvaceous, and with the most flawless complexion he'd ever seen. Her gray eyes, sparkling with mischief now, complimented the silken, straight, silvery blond hair. Griffith had never seen a woman with such natural beauty. Those at court would envy Lady Kallen's original looks.

Then it hit him. Her hair was the color of Quentin's, the man who'd raped her mother. Hair this unusual would be the talk upon every servant's lips, and the oldest of the family's servants would certainly put together what had happened—Bevia's removal from Mangeron and her sudden "death." A child now returned home after so many years.

Would the de Mangerons truly be accepting of Kallen? Crispin had not seen her on his trip to the convent. How would he and his mother react? Could they welcome Kallen into their castle and wipe away the sins from the past?

Griffith suddenly felt very protective of Kallen de Mangeron.

4

The Earl of Nowland greedily sucked on the plum the whore held to his lips. Its juice spilled downward, falling upon her naked breast. He bent his head and licked it before returning to the fruit itself. The woman's sultry laugh echoed in the small bedchamber of the inn.

A room he couldn't afford. A whore he couldn't afford.

Damn the king!

His half-brother had reneged again on the quarterly allowance. The fool thought to tease him, mayhap make him beg as he'd done in the past. If Quentin didn't get that money out of Edward soon, he'd be forced to order his bailiff to squeeze more from his tenants. The thought that they might sense his desperation made his blood run cold.

Not like clamping down on his equals. Quentin had spent a lifetime playing a chess game with the nobility. Some viewed him with fear; others with indifference. Being a royal bastard had its advantages, but lately his leverage slipped.

If only his mother had not expired three years prior. She had been key to most of his success. Her sixth sense and visions gave him an insight into his friends and enemies that most men would kill for. Quentin had the ability in limited quantities but no control over it. He saw it as more curse than anything productive.

Only the women in his family seemed to possess the gift in full force. He'd heard tales that his grandmother and aunt had been quite powerful, and his sister had shown even more talent. Unfortunately, the power drove her to madness and death by her own hand.

His mother, though, proved quite useful to him over the years. Quentin had no qualms about keeping her a prisoner the last twenty years of her life. It helped him become a rich man, but it brought him many enemies.

Now times grew desperate. His fortune dwindled rapidly. The second Edward, his half-brother who now sat on the throne, was a true royal bastard in every sense of the word, playing games with him.

If only he had a child, a daughter, who could aid him in seizing the crown...

Fury built within him, and Quentin took it out on the whore, slamming into her again and again, ignoring her cries of pain. Rage consumed him. He was angry with his wretched wife, who'd only delivered stillborn sons before she died. He was furious at his fate, wishing he could control England's destiny from the throne, where he belonged.

Spent, he rolled off the sobbing woman and fumbled with his clothes. Once dressed, he smoothed his hair and tossed a coin onto the bed. The whore glared at him. He shrugged and left the room.

Barley greeted him in the hall. "My lord, 'tis news ye should be hearing," the servant told him, yellowed teeth exposed in a wide smile. "I've someone in the stables who wishes to speak to ye. Will ye come and talk with him?"

Quentin sighed inwardly. Barley, though loyal, irritated him to no end. He hoped it was pleasant news.

They crossed the tavern's taproom and stepped out in the cold afternoon, the gray, overcast sky reflecting his current mood.

"Over here, my lord." Barley motioned toward the stable, and they stepped into the wooden building. Dimly lit, the servant quickly snagged a lantern and scurried to the back. Quentin followed with an easy gait, never wanting others to see him in a rush.

"This here 'tis Maitland from Mangeron. He works in the stables there and is sweet on the younger Lady de Mangeron's personal maid."

Quentin began to pay attention. He'd placed spies all over the land except on his neighbor's property. The one castle he most wanted inside information from proved time and again the hardest to penetrate. During Renton's time, Quentin had a few in place, but ever since Crispin took over as lord, fidelity reigned among the servants.

He quelled any outward curiosity as he studied the lad before him. The boy was no more than ten-and-six, if that.

"So you've a sweetheart in the castle, boy. What of it? Why would this concern an earl of the realm?"

The stable lad shifted uncomfortably from foot to foot. "Aye, I do. And I've heard tell that you seek to learn all about the de Mangerons. Will you pay then?"

Quentin laughed affably. "I already know quite a bit about my neighbors, Maitland. But, yes, I'd pay if you had information that did me some good."

The boy grinned nervously. "'Tis something you would wish to know. You do pay? 'Tis a trinket that my Celia wants. I intend for her to have it." He shuffled again, staring at the ground.

Quentin concentrated on the boy's silhouette for a moment and caught a quick glimpse of color around him. Damn, but the ability teased him constantly. His mouth went dry in anticipation.

"Speak up," Barley prodded. "The earl ain't got all day for the likes of ye. Tell 'im what ye told me, and be quick about it."

The boy raised his head and swallowed. Quentin placed a bland expression on his face, hoping to soothe the boy with a passive air. No sense scaring him off in case what he knew was of value.

"Celia... that's my girl. She works for the young mistress."

Quentin smiled. "Yes. I'm sure she's lovely."

Maitland grinned. "She is indeed, my lord. Pretty as a budding flower come springtime." He paused. "Celia told me that the de Mangerons have a relative coming to stay. A Lady Kallen."

Quentin's brows knitted together. He could think of no close relatives they had by such a name. *Who was this Kallen?*

Aloud, he asked, "And what relation is she, lad?"

The stable boy's face scrunched up. "That's the mysterious part. No one's quite saying. No one knows for certain. But Celia," he added, "heard my lord and his lady talking about it. Master called Lady Kallen his niece and said she'd make a great companion to the mistress and the babe. Said his mother was delighted that Lady Kallen was finally coming home."

Quentin's thoughts crystallized in an instant.

Crispin only had one sibling from which a niece could spring.

Bevia...

His mind reeled at the implication. Bevia died years ago. Or so he'd heard from the court gossips. Had she in fact lived and produced a daughter?

Quentin knew with certainty that Lady Kallen was Bevia's offspring. Bevia's... *and his*. That was the only possible explanation. He had a living child.

A girl.

Quentin realized with a surety that transcended time that this Kallen was more like him than Bevia. That she would possess the sixth sense the women in his family held. That she could see him to his ultimate destiny.

King.

He would finally be able to take the throne.

She would be young. Quentin quickly figured she must be around eight-and-ten, mayhap nine-and-ten. Young enough that he could still mold her. Obviously, she'd been brought up in isolation. That meant a convent.

He nearly exploded with glee. A serene, convent-bred girl. She would have the power. She would see the auras.

Kallen de Mangeron's fate was tied to his.

Quentin turned his attention to the servant in front of him. He offered the boy a reassuring smile. "Yes, that is quite interesting. Do you know where she comes from? Will Lord de Mangeron see to her return to her home?"

The boy shook his head. "Celia said Master is mad for his wife. He won't leave her so close to the birth of their child. He's sent Sir Griffith to escort her back to Mangeron. He left over a week ago with a guard of ten men. Celia heard he'll return in another week with Lady Kallen in hand."

Immediately, Quentin realized where Kallen had been kept all this time. Renton's sister became abbess years ago at a convent far to the north. He was certain that was where Renton had hidden Bevia a score ago. He would assemble a group of men. They would meet Griffith Sommersby's little party before they arrived at Mangeron.

And they would kill every man in it.

5

Kallen stepped out into the cool day. Mass now ended, her fast broken, her few personal articles gathered together, she was ready to embark upon her journey to Mangeron, which was far to the south. Savina arranged with Sir Griffith the day before for them to depart early this morning.

She gazed about her, the sight so familiar, a place she dreaded and longed to break free from. Yet suddenly it called to her like a siren's song, begged her not to leave the protected land nestled behind stone walls.

What would the outside world hold for her? What would her family be like? Would they truly welcome her as Savina had promised?

Kallen shivered, wondering if going to strangers was the right choice. Her home had always been the convent. Bevia had been as a sister to her, and they grew up playing together, side-by-side with their dolls.

Eventually, she outgrew their child's play, and she became mother and Bevia her child, especially during those long months when Bevia slipped away, illness eating at her. Savina became her only family after that. Savina, her lifeline, her rock. How could she leave her truest and dearest companion behind?

Kallen watched as the gate opened and a group of riders entered the convent's land. Her insides fluttered uncontrollably. Leaving couldn't be right, not if she felt as sick to her stomach as this. Suddenly, it didn't matter anymore that she was different, that the nuns had been unkind, that they poked fun of and were cruel to her over the years. Those were just echoes of Mother Superior's feelings.

Surely it would be different with Savina as abbess now. The nuns might not ever grow to love her, but they would tolerate her, for the new Mother's sake.

She turned to Savina, the only one who'd come to see her off, and fought her spreading panic. Before she could speak, though, a sense of calm enveloped her, the sheer beauty of color surrounding Savina reassuring her.

Savina's aura was pure silver. Her goodness and selflessness, her virtuous grace was evident in the color that bathed her. As Savina watched her, Kallen saw shoots of blue, like wisps of smoke, rise from the silver. Kallen felt her friend's peace, the contemplative air, and the bits of sadness at Kallen's leaving.

The older woman smiled. "'Tis your day, Kallen. The one you always longed for." She cupped Kallen's cheek, her hand light and smooth, and she stroked Kallen's face with her thumb. "I will miss you, my child. You will be in my prayers, every morn and every eve."

"Savina, mayhap I—"

Savina cut her off. "I know you don't trust others much, my girl. But you have a sweet spirit about you.

These de Mangerons will grow to love you, despite your curiosity and mischievous ways."

She couldn't help but smile. Savina knew her too well. Yet still Kallen's uncertainty lingered.

"I don't know if I can do this," she confessed. "I already am cautious about every word I speak. I fear I might slip. They might learn that I... *see things*."

Savina spoke softly. "Remember, Kallen, your sight is a gift from God. God will one day use you and your gift for good."

Kallen bowed her head and closed her eyes. She wondered how her new family would feel about her if she told them what she could do. If they would think her sight a gift from God.

Savina lifted Kallen's chin, and she opened her eyes to view her confidant one last time. The nun's eyes misted with tears, and Kallen felt hers do the same.

"Go now, and may the Almighty be with you always." Savina kissed Kallen's cheek and held her tightly for a moment before she drew away.

The abbess turned to the escort party, which had stopped a short distance away. Kallen watched as Sir Griffith came toward them. The nobleman was tall, his warm brown eyes the color of his hair, his build strong and powerful. Kallen knew this man would protect her well until she reached her new family.

"Take good care of her, Sir Griffith. She is a gift from God."

The nobleman bowed to Savina. "Lady Kallen will be in good hands, Abbess. I shall send word to you when we arrive safely at Mangeron."

Savina wiped away a tear. "Then if you'll excuse me, my lord. I must return to my duties." She glanced at Kallen. "The Lord be with you."

"And also with you," Kallen replied.

She watched Savina hurry briskly back into the convent. A feeling of immense loneliness washed over her. She would never let these men see it, though.

Being with so many men at one time worried her. Father Michael came around occasionally, but this company of men and their thundering horses already intimidated her. Kallen squared her shoulders. She decided to tamp down her fears and speak boldly. They would not see a coward in her.

She turned and smiled with a confidence she didn't feel. "I am ready, Sir Griffith," she told her escort.

He offered her an arm and accompanied her to the men gathered on horseback. "I have brought a gentle mount for you, my lady. Have you done much riding?"

Kallen laughed. "Much? I'd say none at all."

Griffith groaned inwardly. He should have expected as much. Totally convent-bred, he guessed Kallen had probably never left the grounds of the nunnery, much less experienced what a woman of her class and breeding would have under ordinary circumstances.

"This might make things a bit difficult," he said aloud.

Kallen giggled. "Are you already dreading the journey, my lord? Do you see me holding on for dear life as I bounce upon the back of a runaway mare? Mayhap you should plan on a fortnight and no less before we reach Mangeron."

That's exactly what he pictured. "No, my lady, I'm sure we'll make excellent time."

"Have you accounted for the number of times I'll

be tossed from my saddle? And then will be the time lost picking twigs and leaves from my hair. After each fall, of course. You will want me to look presentable, I'm sure, to any passersby."

She sighed. "At least the bruises will not show overmuch. I shall try my best not to land face down any time I am thrown, but I cannot promise no broken bones shall occur."

The men snickered good-naturedly, and Griffith himself couldn't help but smile at the picture she painted.

"Then do you have a suggestion, Lady Kallen? Or would walking better suit you? Of course, Lord de Mangeron did not give me enough coin to buy the number of pairs of shoes you would wear out if we allow you to go afoot the entire distance."

He watched Kallen cock her head suddenly and stare at Satan. She frowned a minute and then nodded. "This horse will let me ride him. He promises to be on his best behavior. I think I could handle him."

Griffith shook his head as several of the men let out loud guffaws. He shot a warning look at them before he turned back to Kallen. "My lady, I fear Satan can be quite ill-tempered at times. If you hesitate to ride a gentle mare, I'm afraid riding Satan is quite out of the question."

Kallen cocked her head once again as she gazed at Satan, almost as if she were listening to him. An eerie feeling passed quickly through Griffith as he watched her.

She brightened. "No, I think we understand each other. Please ride with us, my lord, since I am inexperienced in the saddle. I'm sure you can make suitable corrections in my riding. By the time we reach Mangeron, I'll be quite skilled."

Kallen stepped over and began to stroke Satan's velvet nose. The horse nickered in a way Griffith never heard before. If he didn't known better, he'd think his horse had just fallen in love.

"Very well then. I shall mount up, and we shall ride together." He climbed into his saddle and leaned down. Grasping Kallen by the waist, he lifted her up in front of him.

Calling out to the men, he said, "We may not travel as far today as I expected, since Lady Kallen is unused to riding. We shall take several breaks along the course of the day."

The group responded amiably, and Griffith spurred Satan on and out the gates of the nunnery.

"Don't be frightened," he told Kallen. "Satan can be testy, but he's a good steed."

"Oh, I know he is, despite the fact he was mistreated."

———

Griffith stiffened behind her. She'd done it now. Kallen wished she could leap from the horse and kick herself. She'd promised herself she wouldn't err. She'd begged God to keep her tongue from flapping in the wind. She wanted to be accepted for herself and certainly didn't want her new family frightened of her. Or her so-called gifts.

"How did you know Satan was mistreated?" Griffith asked warily.

Oh, there was that tone. The first time she said something that made another exercise caution around her. Quick, think of something. What?

Then she heard the whisper of how she could smooth things over.

Thank you, Satan, she said, not aloud, only in her mind.

But she knew Satan heard her. Animals always did. Just as she heard them.

"Why, I saw the scar along his side when you mounted. On an all-black horse, 'tis rather obvious. And I couldn't help but notice the marks between his eyes. Now, my lord, do not think I accuse you of these things. I'm sure they happened long before you rescued Satan."

He tensed again. Maybe she shouldn't have used the word *rescue*. That might have given it away.

Quickly, she added, "I perceive him to be in fine condition now. I'll wager you are much kinder to him than the previous master that abused him. I can guess you must brush him every day and indulge him in all sorts of treats." In fact, Kallen knew this to be the case, for Satan had just told her so.

She always had been in tune with animals. She even saw auras about them and could sympathize with the word pictures they sent her about their past lives. Satan's former master had been very brutal and unkind, to man and beast alike. Griffith stumbled across him beating Satan one day and thrashed the man thoroughly before buying the horse from him. Satan was eternally grateful Griffith interrupted that day and tried his hardest to be of good service to his master.

He did sometimes throw little tantrums, mostly as a test to see if Griffith really loved him. Griffith did, for he never struck the horse, only gave him a quick tongue lashing when Satan proved to be slightly ornery. Satan loved Griffith very much and would do anything for his master.

Griffith relaxed behind her somewhat. "I do spoil

the brute, I suppose. I found him in an intolerable situation and was glad I could remove him from it. He's ever loyal and steadfast. I cannot imagine a horse as fine as my Satan."

"I can see why," Kallen remarked. "He's very beautiful. Although he is a bit uncomfortable to ride." She shifted around, wishing she could throw her leg over as Griffith had. This must be how ladies sat upon a horse, she guessed. Kallen already wished minutes into it that the long ride to Mangeron was behind them.

"I wish 'twere over, as well, my lady."

Not again. Kallen sighed. She had a bad habit of voicing her private thoughts aloud. Now that she would be in mixed company, she must be more aware of her loose lips. It was one thing to speak aloud when alone at the convent; it would be entirely different to utter her opinions aloud among strangers.

"Have you pets, my lord?" she asked abruptly, hoping to change the subject.

Griffith answered, "None. Did you leave any behind?"

"Not really," she replied. "I've kept mice and rabbits over the years. I longed for a dog or cat, but Mother Superior would never grant my request. You don't suppose there are any of those at Mangeron, do you?"

"Why, in abundance. Crispin loves dogs. For now, they are his children, and he spoils every one of them rotten. His wife, my sister Deva, is with child, though. I fear the dogs won't have run of the castle for long. As for cats, there are many out in the stables. I'm sure if you wish to befriend one and have it brought into Mangeron proper, Crispin will allow it. He wants you to be happy."

Kallen mulled over that thought before she spoke. "Why does he wish me to be happy?"

Surprise shone on her escort's face. "You are a niece to him, my lady. Your mother Bevia was his older sister. She cared for Crispin and played with him when they were children. He missed her a great deal once she was gone."

Kallen stared into the nobleman's eyes. "But why would he care about me? He doesn't know me. He has never seen me."

"You are family, Lady Kallen. Crispin would do anything for you. He regrets not knowing you existed and is eager to reunite you with your family. Deva, too, longs for a sister. We have none, only each other. Deva always wished I were a sister and not a pesky older brother. Lady Alita, your grandmother, has been in poor health of late, but the simple news of your return to Mangeron has her sprung from her sickbed and dancing upon air."

She eyed him warily. "Surely, you jest?"

"Well, mayhap about the dancing part, but the lady is getting up and moving about some. They all are ready to welcome you with open arms."

Kallen frowned. "But what if they don't like me? What if I don't like them? I can be difficult, you know. Very stubborn and sometimes argumentative. At least that's what Mother always said. Savina simply implied 'twas my inquisitiveness that led to my problems with Mother Superior."

"Then I shall hope to make a lasting good impression upon you, Lady Kallen, for I would not want so stubborn a person as an enemy."

A flock of birds flew overhead, jumbling Kallen's thoughts. She could read the minds of most animals, but a bevy of birds often threw her off-balance, all of them flying by at once. She'd learned to filter out their mass thoughts and only hear a gentle buzz when they passed. She hadn't seen them coming, though, and so had been unprepared.

"What were you saying, Sir Griffith? I swear those birds made me lose track of our conversation."

He laughed, an easy laugh that made her tingle in a funny way.

"You are most delightful, my lady. You speak bluntly and do not have the manner of most noble-women in society."

Kallen grimaced. "I was afraid of that. I grew up so isolated, I won't be sure if I am breaking society's rules with my frankness, for I have never mixed in it. Mayhap you can give me a signal when I fall astray. Scratch your head or blink your eyes rapidly. Or you could tug on your earlobe or snap your fingers. No, snapping might draw attention. Hmm. Now that could be a good thing, because attention would fall from me to you, but if you snapped often enough, there might be those that would figure out our game. Why don't you—"

"Why don't I let you be? You are charming as is. The de Mangerons will fall in love with you and do your bidding after having only known you a day." His dark blue eyes twinkled at her as he added, "Or mayhap it will take two."

Kallen smiled. She liked this Sir Griffith.

Even if his aura confused her to no end.

6

They stopped after three hours. Griffith knew Kallen would already be sore even after so short a time. If he'd realized the circumstances, he might have thought to bring a litter. That would have tripled their time on the road, though, and he knew Crispin wanted Kallen safely at Mangeron as soon as possible. Definitely in time for the birth.

Besides, he'd enjoyed riding with her. She had a refreshing energy and enthusiasm about her. She reminded him of a young colt before being broken, full of verve and vigor, content to run wild through the meadow with no destination in mind.

He also appreciated her frankness. She didn't realize she broke most of the rules society placed upon a young lady, for the set of convent rules she'd lived by for the past eighteen years must have been far different.

Griffith had never met a person with more questions. Where were they actually going? How far was that? Why did it take a week to get there? What was the castle like? Who lived in it? How many tenants did the de Mangerons support? What kind of crops did they raise? Did they tend any animals? What were meal times like? How often did they say prayers?

The morning certainly passed quickly as he answered all of Kallen's questions.

Most of all, he'd enjoyed her scent. *Roses.* He hadn't been pleasured by the scent of a woman since Carina died. Riding in such close proximity, though, he couldn't help but inhale the subtle aroma rising from her skin and hair. She was a breathtaking beauty and totally unaware of her flawless skin and light gray eyes and what that combination—along with her lush figure—could do to a man.

And that troubled him.

He had no worries among the men that accompanied him. All knew Kallen to be nobility linked in some way to the de Mangeron family. He had no fears they would take advantage of her in some way. Far from it. Instead, they would protect her with their lives, if necessary.

It was others he worried about. Sooner or later, news of Kallen's great beauty would leak, and courtiers would come calling in droves. Even though Crispin shared with Griffith before he left on his mission to fetch Kallen that he planned a betrothal for her, he had guessed men would come crawling from the woodwork itself, seeking to attach themselves not only to a powerful family, but also to bed a celebrated beauty.

He didn't want Kallen to become callous or amused by the entire process. He certainly did not want any of those noblemen to take advantage of her extreme innocence with their guile and courtly manners.

By the Christ, he still felt protective of her. It was a strange feeling, one he'd thought dead and buried.

Carina had brought this out in him long ago. No woman had since. He was a man, not a saint. There had been other women since his wife's death. Yet none stirred this sense of being a champion that Kallen de Mangeron did in him. It surprised him.

And scared him.

It frightened him that he longed to run warm fingers through her cool, silvery blond hair. To stroke her cheek and see a smile begin to curve her lips. To bend and kiss her ripe mouth, taste her, touch her.

It could not be. She was his charge for a week. Nothing more. He assumed he would see her on occasion when he visited Deva and Crispin at Mangeron. Eventually, Kallen would marry and be gone from there. He wouldn't give her a second thought.

But she was here now—and giving him much to think about.

Griffith determined to set such foolish notions aside.

———

Kallen watched Sir Griffith as he checked on the men, issuing instructions, checking supplies, discussing the weather. He was unique in her experience because meeting a large variety of people did not occur in a convent setting. A priest appeared every now and then to offer mass, while on occasion a traveler might take refuge in the convent overnight.

But no one's aura had been that of Griffith Sommersby. She frowned slightly and then tried to relax and concentrate. She could always see more if she remained calm. Kallen picked up on more when he stood in front of something with a neutral background. As he went and treated his coal black horse to an apple, the colors exploded, taking her aback.

Blue and red always were brightest of all the colors she saw. They were easily recognizable in others. Most people had one dominant color that surrounded their person, especially around their head. These became the easiest to read. Others had not only the aura about their head but a main aura banded about their body. With some, the hoops of light were thick, usually with varying shades of one color, perhaps two.

Kallen knew various colors could indicate a range of personality traits, but if she were around a person long enough, she could begin to guess at what their aura told of them. Blue could mean someone was spiritual and sensitive, contemplative and empathetic, generous and honest, sad or wistful, or several other characteristics. By getting to know someone, Kallen usually could predict what traits that person possessed and many times how he or she might react in certain situations, simply due to their overall aura.

Over the years, she found that auras reflected health, character, mental activity, and the emotional state of others. Especially in the case of her mother, Bevia's aura showed disease long before the onset of her symptoms.

Griffith Sommersby possessed the most complicated auras she'd witnessed. Kallen found that a person's aura rarely changed, only doing so over a long period of time. Sir Griffith's changed not only from yesterday, when she'd first laid eyes upon him, but while he engaged others in conversation. She realized each individual had many facets to his personality, but her aura reading had taught her most people's personalities were dominated by a handful of traits.

Sir Griffith was a contrast from yesterday to today, and sometimes even minute to minute. He'd had flashes of red and blue, brown and green, turquoise and yellow, even purple and gold. The colors swirled about him, first one prevailing and then another, in such a multitude of shades that it caused Kallen to grow dizzy.

How was she to know what her protector was like? She wondered if all the people at Mangeron were as complicated as this man.

The colors surrounding him, thanks to her experience, revealed to her a few things. He was patient and easy-going, but he possessed an air of sadness about him. Those were his definite blues. The turquoise showed him to be organized and of a practical nature. Kallen saw evidence of this in how he directed the party of men. His purple bands indicated his leadership and bold spirit. Beyond those, she was utterly confused. No individual had ever affected her so.

She was aware, too, of more than this unusual confusion. Sir Griffith himself did something to her insides. At first she'd thought it was due to leaving Savina and her old life behind. Yet the sick feeling changed into a quickening inside her, an excitement, a nervousness.

It was due to his touch. That's all she could guess. Kallen had never experienced a man's touch before. The closest she came was when Father Michael gave her the host at communion on his rare trips to the nunnery. As he placed the wafer upon her tongue, she always felt the heat from his hand near her lips. But he'd never physically touched her.

Griffith Sommersby had done nothing *but* touch her since they left Savina behind. Oh, Kallen knew there was nothing untoward in these contacts. He must have his arms about her to guide Satan's reins. He helped anchor her against him as they rode, which lessened her bobbing up and down.

Yet his touch was fire itself, the heat rising from his very male body in a scent unknown to her but far from unpleasant. He smelled of his horse, his leather riding gloves, and something else that was all male. That was what brought the tingling inside her. From her lips to her toes, her body tingled and throbbed like never before.

That was why she'd asked question after question, trying to take her mind to other subjects and places. She was naturally curious, and she would have asked all these questions in the week to come, but Kallen feared she'd exhausted every idea in her mind in the space of three hours. The words that flowed fast and furious finally dried up.

That is when Sir Griffith had them stop.

How would she get back up on that horse with him and pretend nothing had happened? She ached with something so new and fragile, something she had no way to understand and feared she didn't want to begin to try to do so. She wished Savina had explained to her how complicated the outside world could be.

"Lady Kallen?"

She turned and smiled pleasantly as he approached her. Suddenly, she caught a glimpse over his shoulder of another man, one she hadn't spotted in the group before. She always casually studied a crowd, picking up on its differing colors, but this man had remained hidden to her. Until now.

Whoever he was, he wasn't to be trusted. Of that, Kallen was certain.

Deep red surrounded his entire body, the band

fairly glowing with immense anger. A solid band of black totally encircled his head. Kallen sensed a great evil within him. This man was strong and intelligent. And very dangerous.

"Are you ready to mount again and continue upon our journey?"

Kallen's mouth went dry, and she nervously licked her lips before biting down upon them. She couldn't guard her words, for she had none to give him.

He laughed. "Surely, the ride hasn't been that painful? We are but a few hours into our travels, my lady."

She turned and gazed into his eyes, eyes that were the deepest of blues. That tingling started again, and this time he hadn't even touched her!

"No, my lord. I am ready to proceed. I just have a few more questions, 'tis all."

The nobleman placed her upon Satan's back and swung up behind her. She adjusted her skirts but tried to remain perched just away from his body.

"Please, my lady, lean into me some. We shall ride again even longer than before. I would think I could cushion you somewhat rather than see you jostled about."

"Of course," she murmured, easing back into his hard, muscled chest. His arms came about her as he took the reins and nudged Satan. As they rode, the man she'd spotted passed them. He nodded to Sir Griffith before riding at a quick pace and was soon out of sight.

"Where goes that man, my lord?"

"That man is Sir Rodger, my second-in-command. He rides ahead to check the roads. Nothing for you to worry about, my lady."

"He's not to be trusted." There, she'd said it. Kallen knew she had to get it out, else it would eat at her over the next hours and days.

She turned and studied Sir Griffith as he frowned. "I'd say your fancies run wild today, Lady. Rodger fostered with me and your uncle Crispin. We have fought together in battle. I find no better way to judge a man than one who has swung his sword at your side."

Kallen reflected on his words. She hesitated before she said, "Yes, I can see he is fit and would be brave in battle. I wish I could explain to you why I feel as I do. I simply tell you he should not have your trust. I fear he is a dangerous man."

His arms tightened about her. "Do not be evasive with me. If you witnessed something to support such accusations, I will hear it now."

She saw orange shoots spring forth from him and knew he was very emotional now. It was the first time this particular color sprang from him. Kallen already knew him to be a very controlled man, so the sudden orange came to her as a surprise.

"Nothing specific, my lord. 'Tis nothing I can justify."

"A gut feeling, then?" he asked.

Kallen nodded. No further words could explain to him why she felt this way about the man unless she revealed her secret—and she refused to do that.

Her escort kept his eyes steady on the road as she watched him. "We all have those from time to time. Sometimes, they can be wrong, even unreasonable. I thank you for your warning, but I have known Rodger for nigh on a score. I will trust my own instincts in this case."

Kallen heard the dismissive tone in his voice and kept silent.

———

Griffith swore he would break the silence that weighed so heavily between them. But league after league, he could think of nothing to say. His anger grew stronger the farther they traveled.

How dare Kallen, a stranger, accuse Rodger of being untrustworthy and dangerous. The little innocent had no experience with what danger truly was. If only she could meet the earl, her father. Then she would know pure evil and deepest treachery.

Why would she fix upon Rodger as a danger? Griffith could not begin to guess what brought Rodger to her attention, much less why she seemed so strong in her conviction.

He took a deep breath and tried to sweep it from his mind, as he did anything that troubled him overmuch. He neither worried nor let anything disturb him in his present situation. Let life come as it would; he bore no interest in it. As for his brief infatuation with the woman seated before him, it was over. He'd been blindsided by her immense beauty when they'd met, but Griffith Sommersby would be smitten with no woman. His days of writing romantic poetry and dreaming of a life with a woman he loved were gone forever, banished from his existence.

Griffith realized he pushed their traveling party farther than he'd first wished, a petty reaction to his anger at Kallen. He thought previously to stop once again and then another time to make camp for the night. Instead, they'd ridden on without pause until now.

Dusk would soon arrive. He motioned to those around him. "We'll make camp in the grove to our left. There's a stream just beyond it."

The group rode to the copse and dismounted, the men fully aware of their individual tasks. Some gathered wood to begin a fire, while others brought back water. Two set off and soon returned with their kill, quickly skinning it and tossing bits of meat into a pot already boiling with water.

He realized Kallen watched all of the men perform silently, efficient in their tasks. He'd given her no task to complete on their journey, as befit her station. He did know that she needed to move about to get over her soreness.

Griffith went to her. "My lady, after such a long day in the saddle, 'tis best for you to move about for some minutes. Your joints will ache with soreness enough when you arise on the morrow. Walk now and you will help them some."

His tone was even and orderly, and even he realized it lacked the earlier warmth from before.

"I wish to have some time alone to attend to my needs." She looked about her, and Griffith understood that nature called out to her.

"Come with me." He escorted her to a private place a short distance from where they set up their camp.

"I shall wait for you here. Take your time."

Griffith waited some minutes until Kallen returned. As she moved toward him, her beauty, a breath of freshness, struck him again after a long, tiring day.

"I regret my harsh words from earlier," he apologized. "I would have us be friends. After all, we are almost family."

Kallen nodded. "I would like that."

She smiled at him sweetly, and Griffith felt a stir-ring within him. He couldn't escape the feeling of wanting to touch her in a most intimate way. How could he remain friendly with her with such thoughts bouncing about his head?

As if to pick a fight and put distance between them, he said, "I hope you have now pushed aside your foolish notions about Sir Rodger."

His conscience ached as he saw the hurt sweep across her face.

"I wish you could trust me more, my lord. I cannot explain to you why I feel thus, but I implore you to be ever watchful as far as this man is concerned."

He nodded stiffly and offered her his arm. They returned to the campfire, and he seated Kallen against a tree. He searched around and saw Rodger, a gleam in his eyes as he stared across the way at Kallen.

A wave of emotion flew through Griffith. Jeal-ousy? Anger? He did not bother to try and classify it as he headed toward Rodger.

"Found yourself a new sweetmeat?" Rodger asked idly as Griffith approached him.

He tamped down the urge to strike the man. "Nay, Rodger, do not be vulgar. The lady is concerned, being around so many men. She has spent every night under Mother Superior's watchful eyes at the nun-nery. I merely tried to calm her fears. I assured her we are her protectors."

Rodger nodded. "That we are, Griffith."

Still, he suddenly viewed Rodger with new eyes. They had never been close friends, but rather good acquaintances after being thrown together often during the years. He wondered if Kallen saw something he was blind to after so long a time.

Griffith went about setting up guards for the night. He'd take the first watch himself.

And watch Rodger like a hawk.

7

Kallen wondered how she could have been so wrong. She watched Sir Rodger as the day progressed, and his aura shone totally different than what she'd been privy to the day before. Did all of these Mangeron men change like the wind?

No. The others in the escort party had not. She began to learn names today and instead of questioning Sir Griffith incessantly, she'd paid closer attention to those surrounding her. For the most part, they rang true to her previous experiences. A single shade or perhaps two wound about each man, the hues varying, but none changing as radically as Sir Griffith's did.

As for Sir Rodger, his aura all day seemed in keeping with his position and responsibility. It showed him to be good with the men and solicitous toward her, very unlike the bands of red and black she'd witnessed yesterday. Mayhap she had been overtired and misread the shades entirely.

She must be more wary now that she was out and about in the world. She might experience these difficulties more frequently. Kallen wished at times that the auras would be gone, and then she wouldn't have to worry as much.

Still, they provided her some comfort. All except Sir Griffith's, that is. His aura was ever-changing, despite his steady outward appearance. The man proved a constant challenge to read. Savina had long said that still waters ran deep. Kallen believed this phrase applied to Griffith Sommersby like no other being.

"We shall stop for the night," he announced. The escort party slowed their steeds and dismounted, shaking out their limbs.

Sir Rodger came over to her. "My lady, be sure and stretch your back. Sometimes people forget to do so and regret it later."

"I shall. Thank you for such good advice. Do you have any more for me?" Kallen hoped to draw him out and discover more about this man.

He laughed. "Nay, unless 'tis about horses. They are my life. It will serve you well to learn to ride once you reach Mangeron. Lord de Mangeron has fine stables. You'll like it there, though I fear life will be quite different than that of your peaceful convent."

Kallen frowned and the knight laughed again. "You will find happiness there. Mangeron 'tis a safe place, with good people."

Sir Rodger turned and studied the motions of the men a moment. Then he said, "I neglect my duties." He bowed to her and walked away.

Kallen moved about after their brief conversation, speaking to several of the men. One called out, "Will you tell more stories 'round the campfire tonight, my lady?"

"If it pleases you, I shall."

She heard many of the men murmur their approval. She had always possessed an active imagination, according to Savina. She enjoyed telling her tales to these men the previous evening.

Sir Griffith approached her. "Are you adjusting to life on the road?"

Kallen shrugged. "As best as I can, I suppose. I haven't much to do except ride and watch the men. Everything's so orderly and disciplined, I fear I contribute little to the proceedings."

"And the men? Are you comfortable around them now?"

Kallen knew he spoke of her aversion to Sir Rodger, but she answered in a general way.

"Yes, I do like the men a great deal. They're plainspoken and mean what they say."

He frowned. "Why wouldn't they say what they meant?"

She shook her head, trying to hide a smile. "Spoken like a man who lives mostly among men. Oh, my lord, if you only knew of the hidden whims women possess."

"Even nuns?"

Kallen laughed. "*Especially* nuns."

He nodded. "I gather your life among so many women might be more like life at court than I'd first thought."

She shuddered. "I hope not. The nuns, for all their piety, could be quite disapproving and vindictive. For all their supposed Christian charity, there were times aplenty when Satan took hold of their tongues and let them play havoc. Begging pardon to your own Satan, of course."

"Of course." He smiled, and her heart thumped rapidly. "Yet I must defend my own sweet sister while we speak evil of women as a whole. Deva is not a typical woman, such as you describe. She is full of grace and light."

"And she is with child. You said she will soon be delivered?"

Sir Griffith cracked his knuckles loudly. Kallen noticed the gesture that he seemed unaware of and wondered about it.

"Yes, we are all most happy this time."

"This time?" she asked, puzzled by his choice of words.

He hesitated a moment and cracked another few joints. "Yes. Deva lost a babe before. It devastated her and Crispin. 'Tis why your uncle wished to remain at Mangeron with her while I was sent to fetch you."

"He loves her," Kallen mused. "'Tis a love match then?"

Raking a hand through his dark hair, he nodded. "Yes. They both told me on separate occasions 'twas love at first sight for each. Crispin indulges Deva in her every whim. Deva waits on her husband with adoration shining in her eyes. They are good for each other."

Kallen sighed happily. "I like that. I know I shall like them."

She decided to ask this nobleman about himself. His auras confused her—the deep sadness lingered about him today—yet his inner layers showed great spirit and a carefree nature lighter than air buried far within him.

"Why are you so sad, my lord?"

The knight flinched as if she'd slapped him. "'Tis neither happy nor sad am I," he snapped. "Nor 'tis any of your concern. I simply do the task at hand."

He stormed off without another word. Kallen realized what seemed an innocent question to her held far more significance for him. She wondered what could have wounded him so, for him to act in such an abrupt, rude manner. It upset her that seeing auras once again had her in trouble, and she questioned Savina's wisdom in thinking this talent was a gift from God. She wished fervently her troublesome second sight would vanish once and for all. It might help her exercise more control over her tongue.

Sir Rodger hurried over. "Shall I try to smooth things over, my lady? I'm sure Sir Griffith did not mean to bark at you so. I will speak to him if you so desire."

She saw the men glancing from her to their leader and back again. She looked into Sir Rodger's warm, brown eyes, full of concern, and relaxed. Mayhap she had been wrong about him, after all. She hadn't really lived much before these last two days. Besides, his manner seemed gentle enough, and his aura stayed consistent as they spoke.

"I am fine, sir. I'm sure Sir Griffith is simply tired. Please, leave him be. Tend to your duties, and I thank you for your kindness."

―――――

Griffith didn't know the last time he'd been such an ass to a woman. Usually, a glib comment rolled from his lips with ease. So why did Kallen de Mangeron seem to get under his skin? Her question startled him, as she gave no warning in advance. He figured it only natural that she would ask of his own background since she'd proven so curious about those with whom she would soon live.

Yet he assumed she would eventually ask where he currently lived, whom he'd fostered with as a boy, what battles he'd seen as a soldier. She might ask what his relationship was like with her uncle or if Crispin intended to spoil his new niece or nephew.

Instead, she'd shocked him with her penetrating stare. Those steady gray eyes seem to see all, know all, as she asked him why he appeared sad. Of course he was sad, damn it all to Hell and back! He'd lost his beloved wife and a son, so tiny, so perfectly formed, every finger and toe precious to him. He'd lost his will to live, his zest for life. Even his poetry fled his soul. Only a shallow husk existed now where Griffith Sommersby once dwelled.

He'd stumbled alone through the world ever since, appearing calm and capable to everyone, yet withering inside. He went through the motions, did what others expected, but life held no real pleasure for him.

Until this woman-child from a convent came along. Kallen pulled Griffith toward her in a way no words could explain. His physical attraction grew by the hour, so drawn was he to her beauty.

But it was her spirit that beckoned him even more. Her eagerness as she drank in the world. Her curiosity and questioning nature. Her excitement in being caught up in a new world and new experiences. It intrigued him, and he wanted to know her. He found himself captivated in a way completely foreign to him.

Griffith thought he'd never find another like Carina, one that would cause such a spark in him. He stayed loyal to his wife's memory to this day. But Kallen was nothing like Carina. They were different as day from night.

He ran his hands through his hair in frustration,

knowing nothing would ever change his love for his wife.

Yet Kallen continued to attract his attention.

He forced himself to push all thoughts of Kallen de Mangeron aside and returned to the camp. The men's eyes dropped to the ground as he approached. No one referred to his strange outburst.

"Stew'll soon be ready, my lord," he was told. "Venison and a bit of vegetables. Still a bit more of the bread the good sisters sent, as well."

"Very good," he replied.

He kept his distance from Kallen as they ate, but as he sat directly opposite her, she was never far from his vision or his mind. He smiled to himself as the men begged for more of her stories and watched the pretty flush that came to her cheeks.

Kallen began with a tale of pixies, ones who strayed far from their course and caused more mischief than they should. As she spoke, Griffith lost the meaning of her words and simply stared at her animation. She used her hands a great deal, and her facial expressions caused her to resemble the different characters in the tale she wove.

She was breathtaking to watch.

Her voice grew to a mere whisper, and the story ended. The Mangeron men sat spellbound for a moment then began to babble at once, arguing as to the story's close, fascinated by its unusual ending. Griffith watched Kallen sit back, satisfied, glowing more brightly than the fire before them.

A sudden boom filled the air, and the men quickly took up their arms, encircling Kallen as they peered out into the black night.

8

T*hunder!*
"Thank God," Griffith murmured.

For a moment, he'd thought a band of attackers plagued them. He mentally ripped himself from the pleasant daydreams looking at Lady Kallen brought even as he lowered the sword he'd raised.

"My, but you are a most impressive lot!" Kallen proclaimed. She turned in a circle, her eyes gazing up. "One thunderclap and you all hold swords high to ward it off. Now that is an event I should like to witness. 'Twould make a grand story, the merry men of Mangeron fighting off thunderbolts from the sky. Those merciless Vikings would have nothing on you, I dare say."

Sheepishly, the guard of men lowered their weapons and chuckled as the first pelts of rain began to sting their faces.

Though he prayed no more, Griffith offered up silent thanks that Kallen was so unworldly. She knew little of dangers on the road and how a band of men could have their way with her and still offer her up for ransom, all in a day's work.

He also silently cursed himself for letting down

his guard. Usually, he was in tune with the elements of nature and his surroundings. He would force himself to pay strict attention for the rest of their sojourn.

The rain soon doused their fire, pouring down through tree limbs that offered little protection.

"Wish we were back at Lord Percival's, where 'twas dry and full of good cheer," Rodger said, and several of the men nodded their heads in agreement.

"Who is Lord Percival?" Kallen asked.

"A nobleman another day's ride from our position," Rodger answered. "We celebrated St. Crispin's Day at his castle on our journey to the convent."

Griffith continued. "Your uncle Crispin is named for the saint of the same name. The twenty-fifth of each October is his feast day, full of good food and merriment."

Kallen frowned. "I've never celebrated in such a manner. The nuns only recognized three holy days, that of Easter, Christmas, and All Saint's Day, on the first of November. But Savina told me I would adore feasts. She used to tell me of St. Swithin's Day and St. Catherine's Day, but never did she mention St. Crispin's Day."

"My lord?" called Rodger. "Surely Lady Kallen would enjoy All Hallow's Eve tomorrow. We should be near Lord Percival's by then."

Griffith considered it. He had accepted the hospitality of Lord Percival on their way toward the nunnery, joining in with Percival's tenants in making merry. Dare he overstep his bounds and call again as they returned to Mangeron?

Then he beheld Kallen's eager face, glowing in anticipation despite the droplets of rain cascading down it, and he decided they would stop.

"'Tis only right to allow Lady Kallen to witness All Hallow's Eve in the proper atmosphere," he declared.

The men cheered and their spirits lifted, despite the constant downpour.

"I can't wait to meet this wonderful Lord Percival and celebrate such a day," Kallen told him as he helped her bed down for the night. Griffith arranged several blankets on the ground and placed several more atop her.

"You won't stay totally dry, but I hope you are warm. As soon as the rain ceases, we will rebuild the fire," he told her.

Her brow creased. "I know I shall have trouble falling asleep, trying to picture it all in my mind."

"Nevertheless, sleep is what you need. Close your eyes, my lady. I must go stand watch."

She sat up. "Do all the men take turns at watch?"

Griffith nodded. "Yes. Why do you ask?"

Kallen shrugged. "No reason. Only I suppose I should also take my turn. They must be terribly tired after missing out on their rest."

Her solemn expression was the only thing that kept Griffith from laughing at her words.

Keeping his own face grave, he said, "I thank you for your kind offer, my lady, but I do not think you are as skilled in weaponry as my men. Who knows when a wild animal might crash through the camp and need to be slaughtered?"

Her eyes grew large, and a fearful expression filled them. "No, I do not think I would be of much help in such a situation." She thought a moment. "Still, if you are lonesome for company and would like to pass the time in conversation, simply wake me, my lord. I would be happy to share this duty with you."

"Thank you," he said softly. "I shall let you know

if I have need of your services. But for now, go to sleep."

Griffith moved away from where she lay, touched by her kind offer and generous spirit. The words tugged gently at his heart.

He was glad now he'd agreed they would stop at Lord Percival's castle. He would enjoy watching Lady Kallen experience her first All Hallow's Eve.

The next morning broke cold and damp, but at least the rain had cleared. Griffith stretched and stood, happy to see the fire roaring once again. His stomach gurgled noisily as he went to warm himself before they broke camp.

Rodger handed him a mug of ale and a hard crust of bread. Griffith tugged on it with his teeth and chewed patiently.

"Mayhap we can replenish a few of our stores at Lord Percival's," Rodger commented. "Fresh bread would be most welcome."

He nodded as his eyes searched the camp, making sure all was well as the men prepared to leave.

But where was Kallen?

"She's gone down to the stream," Rodger said, reading his thoughts. "Wanted to wash her face and comb her hair."

"I shall check on her. See that we are ready to disembark when I return."

Griffith made his way to the clear stream he'd drunk from the night before. As he came through the trees, he saw Kallen as she knelt before it, dipping her hands into the water and bringing it to her face.

He stood there a moment, drinking her in. Her clothes were a bit rumpled, but the wrinkles would shake out as they rode. Her hair was a tangled mess, though. Griffith watched as she tried running a comb through the snarls.

"Good day, my lady."

"Sir Griffith! You came quiet as the fog."

"A good soldier learns to tread softly around his enemies."

Kallen cocked her head and studied him. "And would I be your enemy?" she asked in jest.

"Nay, my lady, but those knots in your hair might be your own worst enemy."

She ran a hand through her locks self-consciously. "'Tis snarled indeed," she agreed. "In the past Savina helped me make myself presentable."

Kallen attempted to move the comb through her hair once again, but it stuck midway through the stroke. She eyed Griffith. "Would you please help me, my lord? 'Tis easy to comb when dry, but I fear the rain has caused it to become hopelessly entangled."

"Then allow me. We'll have you ready and on the road in no time."

Kallen came to her feet and offered her back to him. Griffith patiently worked the comb through the silken tresses, mentally swearing at himself.

Why had he offered to help her in such a womanly endeavor?

The feel of her soft locks against his callused hands brought a chill down his spine. As he worked through the tangles, he was very aware of Kallen's nearness. The faint scent of roses still clung to her skin and hair, despite the hard rains of last night. Her nape called out to his lips, and he fought the temptation to brush them against it. He steeled himself from the strong emotions she stirred within him and concentrated until he completed his task and the silken hair hung freely down her back to her waist.

Griffith placed the comb into her hands. "There now. You are much more presentable. Lord Percival won't know what struck him when he meets you." He kept his tone light despite the quick beating of his heart.

Kallen turned. "Are you sure we will not impose upon him? Surely, his wife would have a say in what guests reside under her roof."

Griffith wondered again at her odd notions. Crispin might consult Deva about something so trivial, but most men would never seek a woman's permission in such matters. Kallen had much to learn about the outside world.

"Lord Percival will be delighted by our company. He and Crispin know each other well. It will be perfectly all right. We will be most welcome."

Her gray eyes locked upon his. "Then if you say so, I shall accept it as truth."

"Come. Let us ride to his castle."

As they returned to the others, Kallen said, "Speaking of riding, I would like to try and ride that mare you brought along for me."

Griffith faced her in surprise. "Why now? In truth, it is not a wise decision, my lady. You have no experience in controlling a horse. I would not see you injured before you reach Mangeron."

She sighed. "No, really, 'tis all right, my lord. I've spoken to Carrie about it, so put your mind at ease."

Griffith laughed aloud. "You've spoken to Carrie? And she told you she would not throw you or frighten you in any way?"

Kallen's eyes shone with a bit of mischief. "Let us say that we have come to an understanding. Please. This is something I would like to try and do. If I am unsuccessful, I will admit defeat and ride with you again."

He shrugged. "If you really find it necessary, my lady."

"Oh, I do." Her eyes gleamed.

"Then your wish shall be granted."

It was only after Griffith gave Kallen some quick instructions and they'd ridden several miles did he remember something.

He had never told her the mare's name.

Yet she'd known it somehow.

9

Kallen enjoyed riding. It was everything Carrie promised when she'd fed the mare bits of an apple last night. She'd been afraid the horse would choke on its size, but Sir Rodger graciously offered to slice the fruit into small pieces.

Carrie had been delighted with her treat and eagerly passed word pictures to Kallen, showing her what it would be like to ride atop her. Of course, the horse knew of Kallen's inexperience and promised to trot gently at all times. She especially agree to watch for any holes along the path. Carrie revealed she had no fondness for the road. She explained she would much rather run across the pasture at Mangeron, the wind causing her tail to shoot straight behind her. Her sire resided in Mangeron's stables, and Carrie shared with pride the knowledge that he oftentimes carried the master around the estate.

As they rode, Kallen took pleasure in her running conversation with Carrie and found herself relaxed as the miles of countryside passed by.

"You have taken to your horse as one born to the saddle, my lady," Sir Griffith complimented. "Anyone who saw you would never suspect 'tis your first day atop one."

She smiled. "I give all the credit to Carrie. She's of a sweet temperament."

He returned her smile. "Unlike my Satan?" He stroked the horse's neck as they rode. "Although I must say, my boy has been oddly well-behaved since we left the convent."

"He might have been in need of a journey, my lord. He is probably the type of horse who feels bored if his life is too easy."

The earl nodded. "Mayhap you are right. He has always risen to the challenge during battle. Much as many men I know."

Kallen hesitated before asking him a question. She didn't want a repeat performance from yesterday. "And you, my lord? Are you one for war, or do you prefer staying closer to home?"

A shadow crossed his face. The blue band surrounding him deepened in shade. "Once I was for the steady life, close to home. However, when the king calls, a knight must obey. I actually relish the challenges of war."

A piece of the puzzle fell into place for her. The tragedy Griffith had suffered must have been one of family, possibly the death of someone very close to him. That was why the home fires no longer burned brightly for him.

Kallen changed the subject. "Are we far from Lord and Lady Percival's estate? Is their castle as grand as that of Mangeron? How does my uncle know them?" She wrinkled her nose. "And however will they have enough to feed the dozen of us, unannounced as we are?"

Sir Griffith laughed. Kallen saw as he relaxed, the

dark blue band receded.

"I have taken care of that and sent a rider ahead with a message that we soon arrive. As to feeding us? Well, my lady, you will be surprised how much food their banquet table will hold for a celebration."

He raised a hand to shade his eyes. "I see my messenger returns. If you'll excuse me."

He lightly tapped Satan's sides and darted ahead. Then he turned and peered over his shoulder at her, his white teeth gleaming in the sunlight. "And, no, nothing compares to Mangeron," he called out.

Kallen felt herself grow warm at that smile. She did have the oddest feelings when Sir Griffith was near. She watched as he spoke with the arriving rider, nodding a few times before returning to her side.

"All is well," Griffith informed her. "Lord Percival cannot wait to be the first to entertain a relative of Crispin de Mangeron. It will be quite a coup for him."

She felt herself blush. "Surely, he realizes I am no one important?"

"Nay, my lady, you are a de Mangeron. They fairly strut their importance to the world. If my sister had not married into the family, they could have made her an honorary de Mangeron, for she, too, can put on airs with the best of them."

Kallen was unsure what he meant. He'd spoken fondly of both Crispin and Deva.

Sir Griffith must have seen her confusion. "I tease you, Lady Kallen. Have you never been teased?"

He smiled again, and her stomach turned upside down. She put her hand to it, trying to calm it.

"Are you all right?" he asked quickly. "Is the road too rough? Shall we slow our pace?"

She sensed the heat creep up her neck and spill

onto her cheeks. "Nay, my lord. I suppose this teasing is simply too new for me to understand."

The knight nodded. "I gather the nuns had no great sense of humor?"

"The only laughter I heard came from Savina and my mother, upon rare occasion. Mother Superior told me 'twas a sin to laugh, that it showed my slovenliness and sinfulness. Savina, though, told me laughter was God's gift to his angels, and they shared it with the humans on earth."

"Your Savina sounds wiser to me by the minute. I hope that her new position as abbess will change the lives in that convent for the better."

"You have no great love of nuns. Or the Church, for that matter, I gather."

His face showed amazement at her perception. Kallen bit her lip to silence herself, yet she couldn't help but believe she'd revealed what she had to show off to him a bit. Despite his own respect for authority, bands within his aura told her that respect did not extend to the Church.

That saddened Kallen. Despite the poor side of Christianity Mother Superior and most of the nuns had shown toward her, Kallen had always been steadfast in her belief in God and His kindness. Savina encouraged her in these beliefs, promising Kallen that she was special in God's eyes.

She looked at him with sadness in her heart. "I hope one day you will come to love Our Lord. He is far more compassionate and giving than anyone on His earth."

Griffith opened his mouth to speak and closed it. He'd almost growled at her, bad temper and all again, ready to tell her never to dictate to him, that he knew there was no God nor goodness in men, particularly those of the Church.

Yet how did Lady Kallen grasp his stance regarding the Church, especially since he kept such blasphemy to himself? Or how had she known the mare's name without being told? He couldn't remember an instance when it had been mentioned. What was it about her?

She hid something. Griffith was sure of that. He wondered if a night such as All Hallow's Eve would reveal exactly what.

———

"Welcome to my home, Lady Kallen," boomed the voice. "'Tis I, Lord Percival, here to greet you and your party of men."

Kallen only stared in amazement at the nobleman, whose aura was a warm brown, indicating his steady, reliable nature. Her experience with men was exceedingly small, yet she imagined even this man's great stature would surprise most who met him.

"And I share in his welcome, my lady."

Kallen forced her eyes from the giant of a man and met those of her hostess. Thank the Dear Lord the gray-haired woman before her was of a normal height. The blue and green bands surrounding her blended into aquamarine. Kallen thought the noblewoman one who would attract people that needed help and guidance.

"Lady Percival." She bowed her head. "I am most happy to visit with you and your husband."

Lady Percival slipped an arm through hers. "See to her things, Bowman." She gestured at a servant as she looked Kallen up and down. "What you need is a hot bath and a change of clothes, my dear. Traveling—especially great distances—can be so miserable. Let's see to your comfort and leave these men to their business."

As they strolled through the castle, Kallen marveled at its size and beauty.

"Your home is lovely, my lady," she remarked. "I have not witnessed such grandeur before. Your staircase is the largest I've seen."

Kallen cast her eyes toward the walls. "And all these tapestries. They are magnificent. I cannot imagine how long it took to weave them. This is truly the most beautiful home in all of England."

"Ah, that's because you have not seen Mangeron yet." Lady Percival's green eyes gleamed. "'Tis the grandest of homes. I've only seen it twice before, but that castle is a sight that truly stays with me."

"I cannot imagine anything more beautiful than your home," Kallen said truthfully.

"I thank you for your kind words. Now let us get you into a hot tub and wash that beautiful hair of yours. 'Tis such an unusual color." Lady Percival cocked her head to one side. "I'm trying to remember where I have seen it before."

She led Kallen into a large room where servants filled a tub with steaming water.

"Pour in the lavender now," their mistress instructed. She fussed over the servants until everything met with her expectations and then dismissed them.

"I shall help you myself," the noblewoman shared. "We shall have ourselves a nice chat."

Kallen soon found herself scrubbed from head to toe with the scented water. Their chat consisted of Lady Percival telling Kallen all about herself and her husband, their tenants, and some of the evening's activities. Kallen merely nodded or murmured a word of encouragement every now and then. Lady Percival was fully capable of conversing for the both of them.

"There now." The noblewoman finished running a comb through the last of Kallen's tangled strands. "I think a nap is in order once we've let your hair dry by the fire. The festivities will last late into the night. We want you to be awake to enjoy them all.

"Sir Griffith, too," her hostess added with a smile. "A most charming man. When he wants to be."

Kallen's attention, which had wandered during the lady's running monologue, returned.

"I thought hearing his name would bring you back around."

Kallen blushed and combed her fingers through her hair. She retreated to stand in front of the fire.

"Don't worry, my dear. I think most women are taken with Sir Griffith's fine looks. He's a bit of a loner, though. Has been ever since Carina passed on."

"Who is Carina?" Kallen asked the question, but in her heart she already knew the answer.

"Why, you wouldn't know, I'll venture. All locked away in that convent, no news of your family or the outside world. Yes, I know you're being returned to your family at Mangeron. That's why you don't know much about anything, I suppose."

Kallen bit her tongue hard, making sure she wouldn't speak rashly.

Lady Percival studied her a moment and then said, "Carina Sommersby was the earl's young wife. Quite an acknowledged beauty. She died in childbirth, I'd say a good two years or so ago."

"And the babe?" Kallen's voice was a whisper.

"A boy, I recall. Dead, too, just as his mother was

soon after delivering him. Sir Griffith has never been the same since his wife's death."

Kallen absorbed this information. It made sense —his deep bands of melancholia, the sudden anger that came and went if the conversation turned too personal. She also knew loss. Bevia had died when Kallen was only ten, but she had been most of Kallen's world. Her heart went out to Sir Griffith, losing both his wife and his infant son.

"I'd best be seeing to your escort party now, my dear. Try and rest for tonight's festivities. We are so honored to have you present for our celebration. 'Tis sure I am that you'll remember us to Lord and Lady de Mangeron once you arrive at your new home."

Lady Percival left the room, and Kallen went to lie down. She closed the curtains about her, but sleep did not come.

10

Kallen opened her eyes and found herself in the dark but for the tail end of a fire glowing in the grate. It took her a moment to adjust to her surroundings, and then she remembered they had stopped at Lord Percival's estate on their way to Mangeron.

She pushed aside the bed curtain and stepped down from the bed. Before she could fumble about in the dark to find a candle, the door opened. Lady Percival's silhouette appeared in the doorway.

"Have a good nap, my dear?"

She smiled. "Yes, quite pleasant, thank you."

Kallen thought it best to keep to herself how Lady Percival's revealing words of Griffith's past actually haunted her efforts to fall asleep. Only her extreme fatigue finally brought the much-needed slumber for far too short a time.

Her hostess moved across the room and stirred the dying embers in the fireplace. She lit a candle and gestured for Kallen to come closer.

"Here, I've brought one of my daughter's gowns she left behind on her last visit. It should fit you perfectly."

"But won't she mind?"

Lady Percival laughed. "She'll never see that size again. She's bred twins once and is with child again. I doubt she's even missed it. You are welcome to it. I'd like to see the gown worn and get some use from it. 'Tis too pretty to waste."

Kallen reached out to stroke the luxurious velvet. The kirtle was a dark midnight blue trimmed in silver around the cuffs. A matching surcoat went over it.

"Why, I would feel like royalty in something so rich," she proclaimed.

"Then try it on. You shall be queen at least for this day. Or night, I should say."

Kallen slipped into both pieces and stepped back, looking to the noblewoman. "Does it seem—"

"'Tis lovely you are, my dear girl. All our men shall fall madly in love with you. You should brush your hair again and you may borrow one of my circlets or veils."

They adjourned to the solar, where Lady Percival handed Kallen a circlet. Kallen had never worn one before and stared at it.

"What, those nuns had no pretty circlets? Here, let me adjust it for you." Lady Percival anchored it atop Kallen's head. "You are beautiful."

Kallen felt like a queen. Her old, plain clothes set aside, she was now garbed as one of the nobility. She hoped Lady Percival spoke the truth and would let her keep the beautiful clothes. She would wear this to Mangeron and make her uncle and his people proud of her.

"Come, we don't want to miss out on the feast," the older woman urged.

Kallen followed her hostess downstairs to the great hall. A large candelabrum stood in the center of the hall, lit with a hundred or more gleaming candles. The fire also burned brightly. The room held more people than Kallen had seen gathered at one time. Their boisterous talk almost made her flee the room.

A hand touched her elbow and held onto her. Kallen turned and saw Sir Griffith standing next to her, wearing a tunic of dark hunter green. Her heart skipped a beat at how impossibly handsome he looked.

———

Griffith smiled down at Lady Kallen, who seemed transformed in a surcoat of deepest midnight, her hair hanging loosely about her shoulders, the silken tresses calling to him to stroke them as before. Griffith shrugged off such poetic thoughts. Poetry had no part of his soul anymore—but Kallen de Mangeron's beauty did take his breath away.

"Would you care to be escorted to the table, my lady?" he asked. "The feast is about to commence."

She nodded, and for once Griffith thought the cat had her tongue. Usually, she was talkative. And yet this quieter Kallen appealed to him as much as the other did.

As Griffith led her to the head table, he noticed the appreciative glances of many men studying her as they passed. Lady Kallen seemed oblivious to their stares. He gritted his teeth. He would take special care tonight not to let her stray far from his side.

He seated her and slipped into the spot next to her. A servant appeared and poured them cups of spiced wine. Lady Kallen took a sip and wrinkled her nose.

"'Tis very strong," she remarked before she coughed gently. "You may have mine if you wish."

"Do not worry, my lady. Plenty of food will match the drink. I shan't let it go to your head."

Immediately, servants with trays came by each trestle table, setting a chilled soup and salad in front of the celebrants. Lady Kallen began with the soup, exclaiming how delicious it was, and attacked it with gusto.

"We rarely ate salad at the convent," she told him, "much less with such sweet eggs. What are these?"

He grinned. "Those are hard-boiled eggs stuffed with a honey and mustard blend. A wonderful treat and one of my favorites."

"I've never tasted anything so divine."

"If you have a taste for sweet things, then try these." Griffith pointed to the bowl of nuts.

She picked up one and studied it speculatively. "Could this be an almond?"

He nodded. "One that has been dipped in sugar and baked. "Try it." He popped one into his own mouth and sighed. "Food for the gods."

Lady Kallen followed suit and smiled as she crunched the sugared almond. "'Tis wonderful indeed," she exclaimed.

"You mentioned the nuns did not celebrate many feast days."

A shadow of sadness crossed her face. "No, the former abbess was very strict. We always offered prayers for the saints, but our meager fare rarely changed. We ate a lot of boiled cabbage and beans and bread, sometimes accompanied by meat. Cheese upon rare occasions. Mother never, ever allowed sweets. The abbess frowned upon them as being sinful."

Griffith's heart ached for this young woman. He thought of the countless times he'd partaken in sweetened foods, something he took for granted. "No wonder you enjoyed the almonds. I can't wait for you to see what the last course will be."

Lady Kallen considered all the food before them and turned back to Griffith. "You mean more food will come?"

He laughed. "'Tis a feast, my lady, several courses in all. This is but the first. Feasts start with light dishes that are easy to digest. Then heavier items will be served, followed by many sweets. You may stuff yourself as a fatted goose. 'Tis the way to show our hosts your appreciation."

She caught Lord Percival's eye and smiled. Their host returned the smile and raised his cup to her.

As she looked back at him, Griffith offered her a piece of cheese that he sliced with his knife. "You'll find the servants will bring a different kind of cheese between courses to clear our palates."

"I can't imagine more food. This is already so plentiful and filling."

"Then let me take your mind off it if you wish. Do you know any of the history behind All Hallow's Eve?"

"Nay, my lord. The first I've heard mention of the term was when your men spoke the name."

Griffith shaved another piece of cheese from the small round and handed it to her. "The Church does not like to remember that this festival originated with Samhain. The ancient Celts recognized this day as the start of their New Year. Sometimes they referred to it as the Feast of the Living Dead. The Druids believed that souls never died. Instead, they would be recreated in a new baby or in an animal, depending upon the type of life a person led."

Lady Kallen shivered. "I would hate to come back as a rat, filthy and forever despised."

"I doubt you would. You seem much too nice. Mayhap a cuddly kitten or a sweet ewe? That I would believe."

She blushed. "You tease me again, my lord."

A servant interrupted their conversation, bringing the main course.

"Beef, pork, mutton, pickled carrots, and pears." Griffith pointed each item out to her. "And the best is yet to come."

"Tell me more about Samhain."

He chewed thoughtfully for a moment. "Well, the Druids thought sins could be expiated through gifts or sacrifices to Samhain. 'Twas fairly grisly. They burned horses and black cats and even imprisoned men in cages of wicker and thatch, feeding them into a large bonfire.

"The bonfire was to guide good spirits on their journey and banish the evil ones. Eventually, the Church turned the day into one of their own favor. All Hallow's Eve is to recognize the blessed dead, those made holy—or hallowed—by their obedience to God. Christians are to welcome the dead souls visiting from Purgatory. Many will visit where their family is buried and clean the weeds from the burial plots. To-morrow, some may even picnic next to their dead."

"I am amazed by this," Kallen shared. "Mother Superior and Savina never mentioned this day."

"'Tis probably its roots in Celtic lore, no doubt, that caused their silence. It has turned more into a day to celebrate, though some still fear the dead that might return. I've been to Scotland where they drink a special brew on this night to ward off those spirits that slip past the bonfire. The Scots and even the Welsh try to keep evil witches away on this night by hanging horseshoes over their doors."

Griffith took a deep swig of the wine. "All that talk makes me thirsty."

"I enjoyed hearing about it, my lord."

Suddenly, her gaze strayed from his. He turned to see what distracted her.

"I see the *solteties* are arriving," Griffith said.

"The what?"

"The *solteties*. The special sweets created for a feast such as this. Some are made of a sugar paste in the shape of flowers, hearts, or cherubs. I guarantee you, my lady, you will learn a fondness for *solteties*."

A servant appeared at their table and placed a variety of *solteties* in front of them. Griffith thanked her and pointed one out to his companion.

"Try this one. 'Tis a sweet little cherub."

Lady Kallen examined it with distrust. "'Tis more art than food. Mayhap I shouldn't." She turned away from the sweets.

"Nay, you shall like it more than anything we've partaken of this night. Please try one."

Her face betrayed that she still had doubts, so Griffith picked up the sweet and brought it to her mouth.

"Open, my lady. Have no fears."

She opened her mouth slightly, and he brought the cherub to her lips. She bit off the tiniest of pieces. A low moan escaped her lips.

Griffith eased the rest of the sweet in, his fingers grazing against her perfect mouth for a quick moment.

The contact made him go weak with sudden desire. His mouth grew dry. His heart began to race as he watched Lady Kallen savor the delicacy with eyes closed. She let out a heavy sigh.

Her eyes opened, a bright light shining in them. "That was heaven on earth."

Griffith stammered, "You have... there's a bit of..."

She frowned at him in confusion.

Swiftly, Griffith brushed the corner of her mouth with his thumb, removing a bit of sugar glaze. The touch brought a quick thrill to him again. Lady Kallen appeared puzzled, as if she couldn't quite figure out the answer to some problem.

They stared at each other a long moment before Lord Percival boomed, "And for the head table, here's Cook's greatest masterpiece."

Griffith dragged his gaze from Lady Kallen's and saw a large platter covered with impressive details.

"Why, 'tis a fish!" she blurted out.

Percival chuckled. "'Tis shaped like a fish, Lady Kallen, but a hundredfold more tasty than one." He motioned for the dish to be cut. Soon servings were placed at each trencher.

Lady Kallen eyed her piece of the fish suspiciously. Griffith hid a smile.

"Go ahead," he encouraged. "Take a bite."

She hesitated and then plunged in. One bite told the story. "'Tis a spiced cake! I heard the men talking about this earlier."

He took a bite and chewed, taking a calming breath before he answered her. "Yes. Some cooks have practiced for years to create exotic *solteties*. They will take a common shape and disguise the dessert within. Many take the shape of humans and represent a particular saint, famous warriors, even the king himself."

Lady Kallen eagerly consumed the delicacy. "You were right, my lord. I fear I will grow quite fond of sweets."

She grinned mischievously and leaned toward him, as if to share a confidence. "If 'twere my castle and my feast? I would start the celebration with the *solteties*."

Griffith let his smile shine. "Then you would be a very popular hostess, my lady."

"'Tis time to bring in the apples," Lady Percival declared, her voice ringing through the great hall.

A quick curse slipped from his lips. "*Not the damn apples.*"

11

Kallen wondered why apples would put Sir Griffith in such a foul mood. Ever since Lady Percival announced their arrival, her companion sat sullen and silent. All their earlier conversation about Samhain came to an abrupt end.

She turned her attention to the baskets of large apples, a deep, rich red in color. It seemed as if several dozen arrived now with various servants. She wondered if this last course of apples would end tonight's feast. Mayhap Sir Griffith did not favor apples. He might have been disappointed that no more *solteties* would appear.

"We will commence with the peeling," Lady Percival bellowed, her voice carrying over the giggles that broke out across the room.

"Each unmarried female is to receive one. Please distribute them quickly," the noblewoman ordered.

A servant came by and handed Kallen an apple, winking as he did so. The gesture surprised her.

"Gentlemen, please hand over your eating knives to any nearby ladies. Ladies, you may begin peeling when you are ready. And don't forget, you must peel in one long strand and recite the rhyme for true love to avail itself."

Kallen turned to Sir Griffith. His scowl frightened her as much as the angry red band now surrounding his body.

"What—"

"Hello, my dear." Lady Percival appeared before them with a broad smile. "Are you ready to peel your apple?"

Kallen shook her head. "I am not familiar with this custom, my lady. If I—"

"Oh, nonsense. I shall help you." Their hostess turned to Sir Griffith. "Your paring knife, my lord?"

The knight handed his knife to Kallen, his jaw set as if in stone.

"Now, my dear, begin to peel your apple's skin and recite after me. And mind that you do so in one long strand."

Kallen's fingers shook. She took a deep breath to steady herself.

"I pare this apple round and round again, my sweetheart's name to flourish on the plain."

Carefully, she began peeling the fruit, repeating after Lady Percival.

"I fling the unbroken paring o'er my head, my sweetheart's letter on the ground to read."

Kallen absently repeated the words but concentrated more on removing the peel, especially because she had no experience in doing so. Fortunately, the knife did not slip and the task actually seemed easy. Soon, she'd sliced until she had one long swirl.

"Excellent, Lady Kallen," Lord Percival told her as he came to stand next to his wife. "You peeled accurately and with remarkable speed. What other hidden talents have you kept from us?"

She felt her face flame. "'Tis not hard to peel an apple, my lord."

"Toss the peel over your left shoulder," he said.

She did as instructed and turned to see where it landed. The peel had fallen directly upon Sir Griffith's left boot.

"Don't move, my lord," Lady Percival commanded. "We must read what the peel says." She bent to the ground and studied the shape.

Kallen knelt beside her hostess. "Exactly what are we looking for, Lady Percival?"

Her hostess frowned. "The peel should form a letter, dear. That letter should tell who your sweetheart is."

Kallen glanced down at the long strand of skin. "'Tis no letter that I recognize, my lady, and that makes perfect sense. I have no sweetheart nor plan to acquire one any time soon."

The older woman sniffed. "'Twould have been easy to read had it not landed upon Sir Griffith's foot." She took the hand Lord Percival extended and stood. "We cannot determine your true love this way, Lady Kallen."

Kallen's blush ran up her neck and spilled onto her cheeks, causing her to grow warm. "Nay, my lady. I tell you that I have no sweetheart. This peel could not tell me anything, for there is nothing to reveal."

The noblewoman studied her carefully. "*You* may not know, but the apples *always* do." She smoothed her hands along her surcoat. "We cannot try this test again tonight. 'Twould be bad luck, you know."

Lady Percival thought for a moment and then smiled. "We shall use a snail for you instead. That will solve matters."

Kallen thought she'd misheard the noblewoman.

The great hall was filled with shouts of laughter and raised voices, as ladies everywhere were announcing to their friends the identity of their revealed sweetheart.

"Come, my dear." Lady Percival took her hand and dragged Kallen toward the fire. She saw large wooden bowls of hazelnuts close by. Several women were counting out nuts and placing them in front of the fire's grate.

"Ah, 'tis the hazelnuts. Let us watch a moment," Lady Percival said.

Kallen spied a girl about her age who set down three different hazelnuts. She solemnly chanted, "If you love me, pop and fly; if you hate me, burn and die."

After a brief space of time, the second nut jumped from its place. The girl smiled broadly and crooked her finger at the crowd of bystanders.

"James, 'tis you who leaped." She ran to the man and threw her arms about him, and he kissed her soundly as those gathered nearby cheered.

Lady Percival whispered, "'Tis a way of divining your future husband, dear. All three nuts were named, and it seems that James is where the future leads."

She patted Kallen's shoulder. "I shan't have you do that. The snail is much more telling. I hate to put out this fire, though. We shall just use a small corner instead."

At the snap of her fingers, a servant appeared, a snail cradled in his palm.

"Just set it on the edge here, Bowman. No wood is here, and the ash has turned thick."

Kallen watched in fascination as the snail began to slither along the gray ashes.

The noblewoman nodded, a satisfied gleam in her eye. "Do you see, Lady Kallen? 'Tis a *G* the creature's produced."

Kallen thought it a rather poor *S*, but she didn't want to upset her hostess. "Yes, 'tis definitely a *G*, my lady," she agreed, thinking it could also have been a *C*, *O* or even *Q*.

"Just as I thought. Considerate little creature." She took Kallen's hand, and they returned to where Sir Griffith and Lord Percival stood.

"Find what you wished to discover, Wife?" Lord Percival put an arm about his spouse's shoulders.

"Yes. 'Twas definitely a *G*."

"Hmm." Lord Percival seemed pleased. "Having used the snail will save you from the apple bobbing," he continued. "That can be a messy business. Sometimes I think 'tis the only reason for the bonfire, to allow the bobbers to dry out. Poor souls."

Kallen glanced around and saw that large wooden tubs had been brought out and placed about the room. Both men and women were plunging their faces into the water over and over. Suddenly, a cheer was raised as a man lifted an apple from the water, having captured it with his teeth. He removed it from his mouth and carefully examined it, calling out, "*Tabitha!*"

"Tabitha! Tabitha!" those around him repeated.

A blushing redhead took a step forth, her hands behind her back. The man handed her the apple and then lifted her from her feet and swung her around.

"I can see you are confused, Lady Kallen. 'Tis all the ancient customs we follow," Lord Percival explained. "If an apple peel does not take on a shape of a letter, then people may bob for apples. They are marked with the name of a possible lover."

"I do think they'll suit, do you not think so, my lord?" Lady Percival asked her husband.

"'Tis tradition. Of course, they'll suit." He looked at Kallen.

"We did not put your name upon any apples, my lady. You are but a stranger to those present, passing through. We thought it best not to try and link you with a lover through such a tradition."

Mortified at the thought, Kallen mumbled, "I see."

Lady Percival linked her arm through Kallen's. "'Tis quite all right, dear. We divined the *G* by the snail. And just to assure you that is correct, I shall give you an apple to place beneath your pillow tonight. You should dream of your love. But you must awaken before dawn and sit outside and eat this same apple. If you do not feel cold, you will attain your desired sweetheart."

Kallen's confusion mounted. She only knew a handful of men, and none of their names began with the letter *G*. She decided this old custom was quaint but full of nonsense. If Lady Percival insisted on presenting her with an apple, she would take it. She had no intentions of sleeping with it, though, much less wandering about a strange bailey in the dark while she ate it. 'Twas a sin to break her fast before attending mass, especially on such a special day as All Saint's Day on the morrow. She would not adhere to this tradition, no matter how kind the Percivals had been.

————

Griffith stepped across the room, approaching Kallen and Lady Percival. He saw the color spotting her cheeks. She obviously needed to be rescued. "This nonsense will continue for a while, my lady. Would you care for a bit of fresh air?"

Kallen nodded, and he could see her relief as her shoulders relaxed. "'Twould do me good, my lord. Thank you." She turned to her hosts. "If you would excuse us?"

"But of course." Lord Percival smiled benignly at Kallen. "We shall follow you shortly. The bonfire will be lit once the bobbing ceases."

"Come."

Griffith took her elbow and led her from the boisterous noise in the great hall. He found the door, and they moved out into the moonlit night.

"The wood for the bonfire has already been laid," he told her. "'Tis just outside the castle walls. Mayhap you saw it when we rode in earlier."

They strolled slowly through the inner and then outer baileys, the crowd noises dissipating with the distance.

"All Hallow's Eve has some very strange customs," Lady Kallen remarked.

"Some use it as an excuse to couple with another," Griffith told her. "A pair might have had eyes on one another for a long time. This feast day and its customs simply give them an excuse to join up."

"I wonder if true love exists between a man and woman," she whispered, her tone serious. "I know God loves us, both sinner and saint alike, and I have felt the love of a friend, that of Savina. It seems silly, though, to think just because you bob for an apple bearing a certain name that this person will fall in love with you."

Griffith clenched his fists. "I would think that sometimes true love grows between a man and a woman. Most marriages of the nobility are arranged, but in time, I have known couples who come to love one another deeply."

As I loved Carina.

The words echoed in Griffith's head. He had loved every hair upon her head, the dimple in her smooth cheek, her slender legs and shapely ankles.

Yet he realized he'd thought of his wife little upon this journey back to Mangeron. His thoughts were taken up with being sure all were safe, taking the right routes, stopping at appointed times.

And in thinking of Kallen de Mangeron.

She was the first woman to make him forget Carina—if only for a little while. And despite the guilt he felt, he reasoned that it was good every now and then to escape from his burden. He'd spent two years in misery, the separation from his wife much like a physical pain. Nothing interested him. No one brought laughter into his life. He lived in a void, absent from all feeling.

Yet he'd come to see the world through Kallen's eyes during the past few days. Each discovery became something new, each mile and day brought new experiences, and he had shared them along with her.

Was it time to release Carina from his heart?

Nay, he could never forget his sweet wife. But did he have room in his heart to keep her memory alive and still go on living? He'd been as dead himself since she'd been placed into the ground with their son. Had such grief been so wrong? Had he retreated from the world, using Carina's death as his excuse?

Did he even want to awaken from his nightmare? Was it easier to live in misery, or did he have courage enough to try and enjoy life once again?

Griffith smiled gently at Lady Kallen. "Your uncle

and my sister are radiant examples of what love can bring between two such as they."

"I was sure of it," she declared. She turned her head and studied him a moment. "Your sour mood of earlier has left, I see."

He looked at her blankly.

She sighed. "From the moment Lady Percival commanded the apples to be brought out, you sulked. You seem to be in much better spirits now, my lord."

Griffith nodded. He and Carina had shared their first kiss on All Hallow's Eve. He had bobbed for the apple with her name on in, knowing which one it was, determined to claim it before any other man did.

Yet now his mood was light, as if a heavy burden lifted from his soul.

"I dare say I am in high spirits, my lady." He turned and listened a moment. "'Tis noise coming from the castle. It must be time to head toward the bonfire."

Her eyes sparkled with anticipation. "I cannot wait to see this bonfire. It will be the first I have ever laid my eyes upon."

"Then I shall escort you through the gates and to a place of your choosing."

He slipped his arm through hers and led her toward the opened gates and out to the huge stack of wood. As they strolled, he pointed out various constellations to her.

"'Tis Cassiopeia there, and over here the ram."

"The stars all have names?" she marveled. "I shall never view the night sky in the same way," she mused.

Griffith gazed down at her. *And I shall never look the same way at you.*

12

Kallen sensed the change in Sir Griffith. In the dark, with only moonlight to mark their way, colors shone brightly. The constant shades of blues that dogged her escort began to blend into one band, and even that band became faint. Instead of indicating how sad and wistful Sir Griffith was, how he lived in the past, the new blue showed more that he was honest and patient, even contemplative. Kallen knew the nobleman had come to some life decision about his deceased wife, but she had no idea what sparked this change.

Now his bands grew more vibrant than before in their color. As she saw earlier, he was a rainbow of colors, unlike anyone she had ever encountered. The yellow revealed his intellect and good mood, while the purple showed his athleticism and confidence. A different band that had not appeared earlier, one of bright green, showed a healing or new growth within him. He possessed more balance now than when they'd first met.

Kallen also became aware of the quickening of her heartbeat, the lopsided turn of her stomach, how every breath came shallow and quick. What did these things have to do with this nobleman? They were connected, as she did not experience these symptoms when away from him.

She beheld the structure they approached and blurted out, "I can't imagine how many trees were felled for such a stack of wood. 'Tis almost wasteful, I would think."

He laughed heartily, a sound she found comforting. "You must keep that notion to yourself, my lady. Lord Percival's workers would take it as insult. Every All Hallow's Eve bonfire must burn brightly. 'Tis how this land has always done things, back to ancient times."

"Then I shall be a perfect guest and smile at its great height, I suppose."

"Where would you like to stand? Here?"

Kallen glanced around as others in the crowd began to approach. "Yes, I can see all from this spot, and hopefully the blaze won't singe me."

After a few more minutes, Lord Percival's tenants surrounded the stack of wood. The nobleman made his way to the front and gave a long-winded speech that Kallen found she could not possibly listen to. Instead, she became fascinated by the many couples that paired off. Was it the apples and such nonsense that led men and women to act so cozily? Or was Sir Griffith correct in thinking many of these already knew whom they wish to couple with, the feast day and its customs being their excuse?

Her gaze skimmed the group present. Many men had their arms about a woman, while others stole kisses as the clouds drifted across the sky, hiding the moon's light momentarily. Although she thought seeing such actions would cause her embarrassment, she found quite the opposite was true.

She longed to be receiving such amorous attentions.

And she wanted very badly that they come from Sir Griffith.

The thought shocked her. She had never, ever contemplated such wicked doings. Mother Superior often railed against the sins of the flesh. No, Kallen admitted silently, her daydreams had been about what life was like outside the convent, what it would be if she could wear bright, pretty clothes, about wishing she could discover she had a family somewhere.

Never about kisses and caresses.

Until now.

Suddenly, Kallen sensed a new awareness within her. Sir Griffith stood next to her, slightly behind her, giving off a heat that radiated sweet warmth. She was aware of him as a man—his scent, his height, his strength.

Instinct told her this spelled trouble.

She lifted a hand in front of her and stared at it, wishing for once she could read her own aura.

"Are you growing hot from the blaze, my lady?"

His voice startled her from her reverie. "Why do you ask?"

The earl shrugged. "I thought mayhap the flames grew too warm for your comfort."

Kallen looked up and realized the bonfire was already lit, the flames reaching their fingers into the night sky. The crowd, illuminated by the strong light, watched in amazement.

"'Tis an awesome sight," she said weakly, not believing she'd missed its lighting.

"Quite impressive indeed." He placed a hand

upon the small of her back. "Are you certain you don't want to retreat a bit?"

Retreat? The only thing that warmed her was the heat of his palm as it penetrated her surcoat and kirtle.

"Nay, I like the warmth," she said softly, willing him to leave his hand there.

And he did. Kallen leaned slightly into it, feeling his strength, savoring his masculine scent.

"Are you weary, my lady?" he asked softly.

"A bit."

"Then we should make our way back to the castle."

"Nay, wait a few more minutes, my lord."

His hand floated up to her shoulder, and Kallen leaned more into him. Within his grasp she felt totally protected, a strange and new feeling.

One she liked very much.

Griffith realized Kallen was more tired than she imagined. They had traveled several days now, which she was unused to, and she'd ridden alone for the first time today, an action that always brought about soreness. The late hour and the rich foods she'd consumed also added to her fatigue. He should escort her back to the castle now.

But he chose not to. The feel of her against him was too pleasurable. She smelled of lavender, one of his favorite scents.

"Are you chilled, my lady?"

She hesitated a moment. "Just a little," she admitted.

Griffith pulled her close, placing her in front of

him, wrapping both arms about her. "Here, share my warmth as you enjoy the burning fire." He held her gently as she leaned against his chest. Without thinking, he brushed his lips upon her silken hair, his eyes closed. He couldn't remember the last time he'd been so content.

They stood like that some minutes before the burning wood began to shift. As parts of the fire fell, the people gathered jumped back amidst squeals and shouts.

"We should return to the castle," he murmured close to her ear, wishing to nibble on her lobe with his teeth. Just the thought sent a quick shiver through him.

"Come." He turned away from the bonfire and dropped his left arm from her front, but he kept the right one about her shoulders. She voiced no objection as they continued through the crisp night, the smell of burning wood wafting through the air.

They spoke no words until they reached inside the keep.

"May I escort you to your room?"

Lady Kallen nodded. They climbed the stairs slowly and walked down the stone corridor, their footsteps echoing in the heavy silence. A few lighted sconces guided their way.

"This is my bedchamber."

Her voice sounded far away to him. The night took on a surreal air, and he wanted nothing more than to remain by her side.

"I wish this night would never end," she said wistfully, echoing his own thoughts.

Griffith had not been impulsive in years, but suddenly he felt young and foolish. He spied an alcove directly across from her chamber door and without thought to the consequences pulled her into it.

"My lord—" she began, but he cut off her words with a kiss as he backed her against the wall. His hands ran down her arms as he entwined his fingers with hers.

The kiss started slow and sweet as he softly brushed his lips against hers, back and forth. He heard her sigh and became more daring, running his tongue along the seam of her mouth. Her lips parted in surprise, and he gently thrust his tongue inside, tasting the sweet nectar within.

Oh, she was heavenly. He raised her hands and brought them to his shoulders. She instinctively locked them around his neck. He wrapped his arms about her and drew her close. He wanted to feel her body next to his, feel her heart beating rapidly against his chest.

And he did. He deepened the kiss now, wanting more from her, giving of himself to her, his fingers running through her silky strands. Her body began to tremble, her own fingers playing with the hair at his nape, soft moans escaping from her.

Griffith tore his mouth from hers and moved to spread kisses along her jaw, down to her neck, and even lower. The sweet curve of her breasts had taunted him all night, and he ran a tongue along each, delighting in her shivers and moans.

He wanted nothing more than to peel her surcoat away to reveal her perfection, but if he did, he was afraid he wouldn't be able to control himself. He reclaimed her mouth with his and cupped her face between his hands. He pressed one more fervent kiss upon her lips and then released her.

Lady Kallen opened her eyes and stared up at him.

In the dim light he could see her swollen lips, her breasts heaving as she tried to catch her breath. She leaned against the wall for support, her silvery blond hair mussed and tangled.

She was the most beautiful sight he could imagine. Griffith wanted to offer some explanation for his actions, knowing these were her first kisses, but the words froze in his throat.

Instead, he took a step toward her and captured her waist in his hands. He bent and took possession of her mouth once again, his hunger for her surprising him. The surprise faded as her mouth became his world, all thoughts simply on Kallen and pleasing her. He took. She gave. He possessed. She allowed him full rein.

They clung to each other like ones starved for affection. Griffith had allowed no one to come near him emotionally since Carina's death. He realized beyond Savina, no one had ever cared for Kallen. He wanted to be the one to comfort her, protect her, bolster her self-confidence in her new and strange world.

Slowly, he broke the kiss and gazed down at her.

She smiled up at him. "'Tis much nicer than bobbing for apples."

13

Kallen relaxed as Sir Griffith grinned at her words. They sounded ridiculous to her ears, but they came from the heart all the same. She took a step, but her knees gave way.

He caught her and held her close, his chin resting atop her head. He began to speak, but Kallen didn't hear his words. The euphoria running through her made it impossible to concentrate on what the nobleman said. It was as if God had picked her up and gently tossed her among the clouds, allowing her to float weightlessly above the earth. Her pulse still raced; her body continued to tingle.

She never wanted these sensations to end.

"Kallen."

His calling her name her brought her back down to earth.

"Hmm?"

"Kallen. Are you listening to me?"

She smiled lazily and sighed. "I am now."

He brushed back the hair from her face. His hands rested on her shoulders. "You must return to your room."

"No," she said quietly. "I want to stay with you."

He gave her shoulders a squeeze. "No, sweet Kallen. 'Tis late. You must sleep now. We will set out early on the road tomorrow. We have lost time due to our stop at Percival's. We must make that up. Crispin is eager for your return."

Kallen studied the aura that glowed about him. The red wasn't the deep red of anger but rather an orangish-red. She'd never been exposed to this color dominating anyone before, but she guessed it had to do with passion. She still felt the heat emanating from him, and her body responded. It spoke to her as a woman, not the girl who had ventured from the convent.

Kallen placed a hand upon his muscled chest. His quick intake of breath let her know he was as affected by her as she was by him. He wrapped a hand about hers and held it there, even as his gaze held hers.

"I cannot explain to you why I kissed you, my lady. I apologize for—"

"No. Please. Do not ruin such a beautiful moment with apologies. I have been drawn toward you ever since you came to the convent. I knew not what it was at first, but now I do. I have feelings for you, Griffith Sommersby. I know not why nor where they will lead, but I enjoyed your kisses very, very much."

He touched a hand to her cheek, his thumb tracing her lips. Kallen's heart began to race in anticipation.

"And I am drawn to you, Kallen de Mangeron." He bent and kissed her forehead gently. "My duty is to return you safely to Mangeron. Let me fulfill my charge to my friend, your uncle. Once there, I shall ask his permission to court you. We shall see then what our future holds."

She frowned. "So, no more kisses until Uncle Crispin grants permission?"

He gazed at her sadly. "No, my sweet Kallen. I should return you to him as untouched as when I found you."

Disappointment washed through her. She'd never been more alive than in these last few minutes. Mangeron seemed an eternity away.

"Would you... could you... give me one more kiss for good measure? Something to remember in the days to come?"

Griffith beamed at her. "My lady, your wish is my command."

He took her in his arms and lowered his mouth to hers. Once more, she was lost in the magic of his kiss. It hurt her physically when he broke it and took her hand, leading her back to the bedchamber's door.

Kallen touched her fingers to her own lips and then to Griffith's before she opened the door and entered the room. She closed it and leaned against it. The woman who exited this room hours before was not the same person who returned. She wrapped her arms around herself, wondering how she had existed without Griffith's kisses. Kallen brought her fingers to her mouth and kissed the tips, knowing Griffith's mouth had been there only moments before.

A single candle glowed next to the bed. Beside it sat an apple, plump and red. She remembered Lady Percival's words from earlier and how she'd scoffed at them. So much had changed in the space of a few hours.

Kallen crossed the room and picked up the apple. She slid it under the pillow and undressed. As she climbed into bed and drew the curtains about her, she asked God to send her sweet dreams of Griffith Sommersby.

"It was a *G*!" she cried aloud. "For Griffith."

She smiled and brought the bedcovers over her. Her hand rested under her pillow, clutching the apple.

———

Kallen awoke slowly. She stretched lazily, contentment washing over her. She had dreamed of her true love, just as Lady Percival promised. She removed the apple from its hiding place and wondered if she should follow custom and go outside to eat it. She would appear foolish if caught, but she decided to chance it.

Quickly, she dressed and combed her hair, slipping the apple into her pocket. If anyone saw her, it would not be so obvious what she was up to.

As she left her chamber, all was quiet. She descended the stairs and tiptoed past the great hall, where many still slumbered after the night's feasting. She stepped out into a day that was still night. Fog hovered about her and she hurried across the bailey toward the stables. As she walked, she removed the apple from her pocket and bit into it.

The fruit was ripe and sweet. She chewed thoughtfully as she moved across the foggy yard, realizing that she felt no cold. 'Twas Griffith's heart that warmed her, and she welcomed the thought.

She entered the stables and found Carrie. The horse was sleeping but awoke when Kallen called to her. Kallen conveyed her new happiness through word pictures to the mare, who nickered softly in a show of support. Then Carrie sent Kallen an image of

Satan flirting with her, which caused Kallen to laugh.

"Mayhap we are both to be courted, Carrie."

The mare nuzzled her hand. Kallen caught a picture of the four of them strolling along a country lane. Both couples looked happy.

"You're a silly girl, Carrie." She rubbed the horse's velvet nose, hoping the mare's wish for the both of them would come true.

Kallen floated from the stables, the apple core still in her hands.

"What brings you out so early, my lady?"

The voice frightened her, coming from the fog. She turned and saw Sir Rodger standing nearby. What upset her more was that no aura surrounded him. None at all. That never happened before, and especially since his aura had changed on her, Kallen didn't know what to expect.

"I could not sleep, Sir Rodger," she explained to the knight. "Mayhap 'twas all the festivities. I am not used to such celebrating."

He strode forth and stood in front of her. Still, no aura appeared. "Trying out tradition, my lady?"

She followed his glance and saw it rested on the apple core in her hand. "No," she said quickly. "I thought to reward Carrie. She was so gentle and easy to ride on my first attempt. I cannot wait to ride her again today. I did not think 'twould hurt to bribe her with a treat."

The knight laughed. "You speak of her as if she were human."

Kallen sensed the blush crawling up her neck. "I do think some animals are nicer than humans. I suppose that notion seems foolish to you."

He took a step closer to her. Her heart pounded

wildly. Her fear increased with his nearness, yet she had no reason to shy away from this man of Mangeron, knowing he was sworn to protect her.

"I rather think my horse far smarter than some of the men I've fought against," he confided.

Kallen smiled weakly. The need to escape remained. "I shall bid you good day."

She took a step away from him, but Sir Rodger took hold of her arm. She was unused to being touched by any man except for Griffith. The contact caused a strong dread to rise within her.

"'Tis very foggy, my lady. Allow me to escort you back to the keep. My liege lord would not want anything to happen to you."

Her heart raced wildly. "All right," she said softly.

Kallen's mouth had gone dry. She forced her feet to move. This man had given her no reason to fear him. Far from it, he'd been quite the gentleman. But she did not relax the entire way back to the keep.

14

Griffith's eyes were gritty from lack of sleep. All night he'd lain awake, thoughts of Kallen flooding his mind. He still sensed her touch. Tasted her sweetness. Felt her melting into his body.

Why had he told her he would ask Crispin for permission to court her? It could never be. Not after what Crispin revealed to him before Griffith left on this mission.

Kallen would hate him for it. She might hate Crispin once she learned of his plans for her.

If only he'd been loyal to Carina's memory...

If he had, Griffith wouldn't be in such a quandary. Yet at this moment, despite his weariness, life flowed through his body. An excitement. Anticipation of what the new day would bring.

Griffith was tired of being dead inside. Tired of the risks he took, simply because he cared not for this world anymore.

Kallen brought a renewed spirit to him, an interest in what was around the next corner. He grew up, always knowing it would be Carina for him. He never pictured his life without her. When she died, part of him died, too.

Now Kallen entered his life. Griffith finally realized that he could be true to the memories of his beloved wife and still rejoin the living. He was young. Sooner or later, he would inherit his father's title. He could build a new life, with a new wife by his side.

And perhaps children. Almost more than Carina's death, he regretted life had been snuffed from their babe. He loved children and never admitted aloud to anyone he still longed for them. He could have a chance at happiness, a family, with a woman he cared for.

He wouldn't yet believe 'twas love he felt for Kallen. He was taken by her beauty, charmed by her innocence, intoxicated by her kisses. But he wouldn't put a name to his feelings.

Not yet. Especially when he knew what Crispin had in store for her.

Griffith decided in that moment that Kallen was worth fighting for. Crispin was as much a brother to him as if they shared the same blood. He would make Crispin understand that he needed Kallen by his side.

Griffith needed to live again in this world. Kallen had made him realize that. Their fates were joined. Now he must figure out a way they could be together.

"Thank you again, my lord, my lady, for extending your hospitality to our party." Griffith bowed his head in acknowledgment.

"We were delighted to entertain you, Sir Griffith. And especially grateful to introduce Lady Kallen to the old traditions surrounding All Hallow's Eve." Percival inclined his head in return. "Give our best wishes to Lord and Lady de Mangeron."

"I shall." Griffith mounted Satan and scanned the group on horseback. All were accounted for. "I bid you a good day."

He turned his horse, and the others followed him through the gate. He signaled Rodger to ride ahead.

As they trotted along, he fell back to the middle so as to be next to Kallen. He looked her in the face for the first time since their private moments together last night and caught a shy smile from her.

"'Tis a cool but fortunately sunny day, my lady. We should make good time."

"I think the rest from our journey did everyone good," she replied. "I agree that we will be able to ride far today."

Griffith nodded. "Let me know how you fare. I realize 'tis only your second day alone on horseback. If you need to call a halt to rest, you need but ask."

"I shall."

They spent a pleasant morning discussing many things. Despite the group of men that surrounded them, it seemed Griffith rode alone with Kallen. Her observations delighted him, and he laughed aloud several times as she told stories about life in the convent.

They stopped in the early afternoon for a brief respite. Lady Percival had provided fresh bread and cheese and flasks of wine for their party, which prevented them from stopping to shoot game for their food. If they could do the same for the evening meal, they could ride much later than usual.

As they continued on their way, Kallen began to sing. She was quite dreadful, but the men cheerfully joined in with her song. Griffith could not remember the last time he sang. It had to be before Carina's death. He sang along with them, much to Kallen's delight.

"You have a rich baritone, my lord. You should sing more often."

Griffith thought how he'd once composed poetry and set the words to music for his wife. That part of him seemingly died with Carina, but as he sang, he realized how much he enjoyed it.

Just another gift you've returned to me, Kallen.

They stopped for the night after many hours on the road. Griffith was ready. His lack of sleep bothered him. He set up the shifts for guard duty, allowing himself to sleep for the first few hours.

He fell asleep listening to Kallen's throaty laugh as she wove another tale for the men gathered about the campfire.

Screams woke him from a dead sleep. Griffith leaped to his feet quickly, his hand unsheathing his sword. His eyes swept over the camp as men joined him, ready to meet whatever challenge confronted them.

"Who's on duty?" he called gruffly.

"Simmons and Cuthbert," Rodger quickly replied.

A scream tore through the dark night again, followed by a rustling. Griffith pointed to the two men closest to Kallen. Her face was a ghostly white.

"Stay with her. Let not a hair on her head be harmed."

He advanced quickly, the others following him, to the perimeter of the camp. Cuthbert lay on the ground, clutching his leg, writhing in pain.

Griffith bent, the smell of blood assailing his senses.

"Boar," croaked Cuthbert. "Came from nowhere."

Griffith motioned, and two men bent to take

Cuthbert back to the camp. He continued until he found Simmons, less than twenty feet away.

Simmons wheezed as he spoke. "Ran as... fast as could. Saw wild boar gored Cuthbert. Got me. Sorry."

Griffith lay a hand on the soldier's shoulder. "No apologies. We must move you and check your wounds." He stood and pointed to two men.

"Return him to camp. Carefully. The rest of us will find this boar."

A sudden thrashing caught their attention, as the very boar emerged from the woods. It headed straight in Kallen's direction. Griffith charged the animal, his sword raised. He came into the path it ran and plunged his sword into the creature's eye. The boar's screech echoed eerily through the woods.

Then all was quiet.

The smell of fresh blood assaulted Griffith's senses immediately. He yanked the embedded sword from the animal as the others caught up to him, in awe of his actions. Men slapped him on the back, congratulating him for such swift thinking and bravery.

Griffith trembled under the barrage of compliments. He'd acted so quickly because the boar threatened Kallen's life. In an instant he'd pictured her gored as Cuthbert, her perfect skin marred with blood, her life ebbing away. The thought made him insane. He'd charged the boar, wanting to protect her at all costs.

He squatted on the ground and rested his head against a knee.

Suddenly, the scent of lavender invaded his senses.

"Are you all right, my lord?" Kallen called breathlessly. She threw an arm about his shoulders as she knelt beside him. His tremors stopped.

He was safe—because she was.

Griffith raised his eyes to meet hers. He longed to take her in his arms, reaffirm they lived, kiss her senseless. Instead, he nodded.

"I am fine, my lady. The boar is not."

The knights surrounding them chuckled. Griffith's heart slowed from its racing pace.

"We must look after our injured," he told her.

"Let me help. Travelers often stopped at the convent for aid. I have cared for fevers and wounds of all types."

He stood and helped her to her feet. "I need hot water and wine," she said. "Marigolds if they can be found. Clean cloth for fresh bandages. Now."

The men moved quickly at her orders. Griffith marveled as he saw a new side to Kallen de Mangeron.

They found themselves alone for a moment. Kallen reached out a hand. Griffith took it, its warmth bringing him comfort. He brought it to his mouth and kissed her open palm. A blistering heat erupted inside him. He saw the shock on her face.

"I never knew such strong emotions existed," she said in wonder.

And despite the fact he'd loved Carina with all his heart, his wife never stirred such feelings within him. Griffith stared intensely at Kallen.

"Nor I, sweetheart. Never have I been so moved by a woman as I am by you."

She flashed a brilliant smile. It slowly died as she grew more serious. "Let us see to your men."

They returned to the campfire. Water boiled as instructed. Simmons and Cuthbert were placed upon clean blankets next to one another. Kallen asked for a knife and cut away their clothes so she could examine each man's wounds.

"So much blood," she whispered. Aloud, she spoke comforting words to both men, moving from one to the other. She cleaned their wounds with first the heated water and then some of the wine.

"Listen to me," she addressed both of the wounded men, her hands clasping theirs. "The punctures must be cauterized. It will hurt—mayhap as much as when the boar gored you. But this must be done to prevent infection. May I have your permission?"

Simmons merely nodded and closed his eyes, moaning softly. Cuthbert smiled up at Kallen.

"'Tis a might prettier sight you are than that boar, my lady. Do as you must."

Kallen told Griffith, "Please place the blade of your dagger in the fire. As much of the blade as you can. If the hilt gets hot, I can wrap a cloth about it for protection."

Griffith did as she instructed while Kallen designated men to hold the injured down. She gestured for Griffith to bring her the knife. He bunched a cloth about its hilt and took it to her.

"I wish I had new eggs to rub on them. The whites are a soothing balm."

"Just do the best you can," he reassured her. "You could save their lives."

Kallen took a deep breath and wrapped her hands around the dagger's hold. She brought it to Cuthbert's thigh and pressed it into the wound. He struggled a minute before fainting from the pain. Kallen then poured more wine over it and wrapped the leg in fresh linen.

She moved to Simmons, whose wound seemed more serious to Griffith, and repeated her actions against the soldier's side. Then she took their hands in hers again and chanted, "In the name of the Father, Son, and Holy Mary. The wound was red, the cut deep, the flesh be sore, but there will be no more blood or pain till the Blessed Virgin bears a child again."

All watched her work in silence, knowing but for God's grace they might be one of the injured men lying there.

Kallen stood and looked about her. "Did you find any marigolds?" she asked Rodger.

"Yes, my lady." He indicated a bunch gathered on the ground.

"Drop these in the water and then remove the water from the fire. When it cools, I'll try to have them drink."

"What will that do?" asked Griffith, puzzled by the process.

"They will soon have a fever. The marigolds will help reduce it."

Griffith arranged for two men to continue to stand guard the rest of the night. He himself helped Kallen try to get the men to drink the doctored water as the hours passed.

Dawn broke and with it, Cuthbert's fever. Simmons was delirious by this time.

"We cannot travel for several days," Kallen informed Griffith. "They will have no chance to survive if we do. They must not be moved."

Griffith shook his head. "We must press on. I cannot tolerate delay."

He thought at how their numbers were reduced from ten knights to eight. He would need to leave

another one or possibly two men with the injured. That would leave their number at six, with himself making seven, to see Kallen safely back to Mangeron.

"Then we leave them. I know of no surrounding castles nearby. Two of our number will remain behind to care for them."

Kallen nodded. He guessed she knew well enough not to argue with his decision.

"Choose the two who will stay. I must give them instructions. They must know how to change the bandages and what to look for in case infection sets in."

Griffith signaled and two soldiers hurried toward him. "You are to stay and care for these injured men. Lady Kallen will give you specific orders on what to do. I shall send help from the first castle we pass. Mayhap they can spare a litter for when the men can be moved."

Both soldiers reported to Kallen. Griffith had the others prepare for their immediate departure. They packed up quickly, leaving some food and the burning campfire for those remaining behind.

Kallen finished speaking with the men and turned to Griffith. "I am ready."

"I know you are tired, my lady, after so little sleep, but we must continue on. Your uncle expects it."

"I understand."

She moved toward Carrie. Griffith caught her elbow.

"I must ask you to ride with me. We are fewer in number," he explained, "and the threat of any danger is thus greater. I know you've enjoyed riding your own mount, but you will be easier to protect if you are with me. Would you agree to this?"

Kallen's gray eyes showed a bit of sparkle, the first he'd seen in hours.

"'Twould suit me well." Her face remained solemn, but her eyes now danced in anticipation.

She followed him to Satan and stroked the horse's mane. "I'll expect you to behave," she told the horse. She looked directly at Griffith and said softly, "That means both of you."

Griffith hid a smile as he mounted and lifted her up into the saddle. He gave her a minute to settle herself before they rode out.

His arms encircled around Kallen now, relief swept through him. He knew, though, he must be on guard for whatever might occur on the remainder of their journey.

15

K allen awoke with a start. Her hands flew out to steady herself from a swaying motion.

"'Tis on horseback you are, my lady," a reassuring voice murmured in her ear.

She took a deep breath as she relaxed back into Griffith, whose arms enfolded her. She nodded to let him know she was all right.

"You fell asleep," he told her. "Almost three hours now. I should be grateful you do not snore. 'Twould put Satan in a mood most foul."

Kallen laughed. "I did not know that sleep was possible atop a horse. All these bumps in the road should make it impossible."

"I fear you were overtired after ministering all night to Cuthbert and Simmons."

She glanced up at Griffith. "Then you should be slumbering as well, my lord. You tended the wounded alongside me."

He smiled down at her. "A soldier has less need of rest than a convent-bred lady. We are trained to get by on as little as possible."

"You are telling me that men are made of stronger stuff than women, my lord?" she said indignantly.

Griffith laughed. "Nay, lady, I am one man who realizes that the core of many a woman is as the steel of a sword. Females might possess less physical strength than males, but their hearts and minds are sturdy beyond measure."

"You sound as if you have experienced this strength."

Griffith nodded. "My mother is one such woman. She appears fragile, but she rules our castle as a king. Especially since my father's illness."

Kallen caught the wistfulness in his voice. "I did not know your father to be ill. I am surprised you would leave him to fetch me back to Mangeron."

He cracked several knuckles before speaking. "A horse kicked Father in the head nigh on three years ago. 'Twas touch and go for weeks. Finally, the healer said he would live, but he has never been the same. He simply lies abed, never speaking, never recognizing a soul. He is sentenced to a living death."

Her heart went out to him, knowing he already suffered from his wife and babe's death.

"Mother stays with him many hours each day. She reads to him. She tells him of the affairs of the castle." Griffith sighed. "But we all know he will never be whole again."

His grip tightened about her waist. "Mother rose to the occasion. She is the true liege lord of Sommerset now. She'd always advised Father on various matters, but she controls all decisions regarding the castle and our people.

"I assist her, of course, though she has little need of my counsel. As of late, I haven't been of much help to her." Griffith bent, his lips resting against her ear. "But I think things will change soon for the better."

A shiver of pleasure ran through Kallen at his

touch. "And what of your sister, Deva? Is she a lady with this steel core?"

He chuckled. "Deva is just as strong-willed as Mother, but she appears even more helpless. I swear by the Virgin that she has Crispin wrapped about her tiniest finger, and the fool has not an inkling of it."

Kallen smiled. "The women in your family sound quite to my liking."

Griffith stared at her a long moment. "And I know you would be to theirs," he said softly.

"Up ahead!"

She faced forward to seeing Sir Rodger riding back to their party. He reined in his horse next to Satan.

"A castle to our right. Shall we stop?" Sir Rodger asked.

"Yes. If I'm not mistaken, 'tis Lord Bethune's estate. The stop should take no more than a quarter-hour of our time." Griffith signaled the guard to halt.

As the horses' hoofbeats ceased, Griffith addressed the group. "We shall go just inside this castle's gates for protection since our numbers are fewer. I will arrange for help to be sent back to the wounded as quickly as possible."

He looked to Rodger. "You shall be in charge while I'm away. Lady Kallen's safety is of utmost importance."

They continued on, approaching the castle's gates within a short spell. Griffith called out to the gate-keeper, who granted them permission to enter. The party rode into the outer bailey and dismounted, stretching their limbs.

"Stay with the guard at all times, my lady," Griffith cautioned her.

Kallen saw the grave expression on his face. She understood how worried he must be, especially with four knights missing from their group. She'd heard the nuns' talk of how dangerous the roads were and knew he'd much on his mind.

"Do not worry, my lord. I shan't stray."

Griffith rode off once he received her reassurance, his aura one of rich purple. Kallen glowed with pride at the leadership and confidence reflected in the bands about him.

"Your trip has been a pleasant one so far, my lady?"

Kallen glanced over at Sir Rodger. "I would say 'tis the best I've ever had. Of course, 'tis the only journey I have made in my life. Ask me again years down the line, Sir Rodger. Mayhap my answer shall differ."

"You look forward to meeting your relatives at Mangeron?"

Kallen turned and faced him. "Yes. I suppose I should be apprehensive, but I fear 'tis excitement inside me at getting to know them."

She chatted with several of the men over the next half-hour until Griffith appeared again.

"I have assurances of aid being sent back to our men. Lord Bethune is familiar with the area in which we left them. If there are no objections, we shall continue."

Griffith reached a hand down to Kallen and pulled her up into the saddle in front of him. As his arms went around her waist, he whispered to her, "Even a few minutes away from you was too long."

Kallen sensed the heat burning on her cheeks and lowered her head, afraid to have any of the men see her blush. Still, she rested a hand on one of Griffith's and gave it a squeeze to indicate her pleasure in his words.

The party continued on, the melancholy from before now lifted, the men relieved by the promise that those left behind would be cared for.

As the light began to wane, Griffith called a halt to the day's journey. Camp was set up, a fire built, water retrieved, and three rabbits caught for their supper. Kallen was glad they still had some of Lady Percival's bread and cheese although she would have enjoyed some of the sweetened nuts and honeyed eggs from the feast even more.

They sat about the fire, the conversation turning toward home since they were but a few days away now. She asked the men about their families and what they did at Mangeron as they ate, and it became a very pleasant hour's respite.

Once the group cleaned up, Griffith set up the guard duty. Kallen lay down on a pallet and found sleep hard to come by. She was still tired from the long night before and found her mind returning to those events. Her nerves became unsettled. What if another wild boar appeared? What if the high-waymen she'd heard tell of frequented this area? What if they saw the fire and made their way here?

She tried to dispel such foolish notions. Men with great fighting skills surrounded her, their one job but to protect her. Griffith had told her these knights would give their lives for her if needed. The thought should comfort her, but instead she worried even more. When sleep came, it was restless.

Kallen awoke, wondering if the shift of guards had disturbed her. She sat up and rubbed her eyes and saw the camp was quiet. Her eyes fell over the men lying peacefully around the campfire, their auras hovering over them even at rest.

She glanced out and saw two of their number

awake, pacing back and forth in the dark, their auras nestled about them against the black of night.

Kallen started to lie down again when a flash of color caught her eye. She sat as still as she could and gazed into the distance. Far beyond the guards, she saw shimmering colors—and they were coming stealthily toward them.

Her heart caught in her throat, and she froze for a moment. She must awaken the others. Their very lives might depend upon it.

Kallen lay down and turned to her side. Griffith was close by, his chest rising and falling as he slept. She gently touched his arm.

Immediately, he sat up, a dagger in his hand. The sheer suddenness of his movement frightened her.

"My lady?" he whispered. "Is something wrong?"

Kallen nodded. She clutched his wrist. "There are men out there, far past the guards."

Griffith frowned. "You saw them? Heard them?"

Kallen's grip tightened on his wrist. "Please, do not doubt me on this." She swallowed. "Trust me. They are there. *I know it.*"

His eyes clouded a moment. Kallen saw him glance over her shoulder and peer into the dark even as he wrestled with questions. Then he turned back to her.

"How many are there?"

Kallen glanced over her shoulder. Though she could not see the actual men in the darkness, their auras stood out brightly to her. Kallen turned back to Griffith. "I see six in that direction, but there could be more." She looked in other directions and gasped, counting quickly. "At least ten more."

Griffith handed her his *baselard*. "You may need this."

Kallen took the dagger that only last night she'd used to cauterize the injured men's wounds.

"Move next to the base of that tree. Keep your back against it. Stay with Rodger. If we are somehow separated, tell him to meet up at Walmouth Woods."

"Walmouth Woods," she echoed.

Without a sound, Griffith came to a crouch and began to awaken the sleeping guard surrounding them. It amazed Kallen how ready each man came to, clutching weapons that lay by his side. She wrapped her cloak about her tightly, her pulse hammering, her mouth dry as she crawled over to the oak tree Griffith had indicated.

"Now!" Griffith hissed in a whisper, and the men ran in several directions, their weapons gripped in their hands. Kallen realized Griffith had taken time to instruct them on even the smallest of detail. She thanked Blessed Mary for his faith in her.

Her lips moved in a silent prayer to the Virgin as the men dispersed. She prayed for all their safety, but most of all, she prayed that Griffith would return to her.

Alive.

16

Kallen gripped the dagger tightly in her hand and watched the attack unfold before her. Despite her inexperience, she knew the assault was well planned. These were no ordinary robbers roaming the countryside in search of victims.

She knew instinctively they came for her.

Sir Rodger moved in front of her, his thrusting sword before him. "Stay there, my lady. I must know where you are if I'm to protect you."

She nodded, fear numbing her as the sound of clanging swords came closer.

"Walmouth Woods," she croaked out.

Sir Rodger turned with a quick glance. "Walmouth, you say?"

"Yes. 'Tis where Griffith said to meet if we somehow became separated."

Rodger turned away from her, his body tense as he stared out in the night.

Kallen saw a mace swinging high overhead and heard the dull thud when it struck its intended victim. Another man charged into a second with a long pike. The groans came closer, as did the scattered curses.

A pair of struggling men stumbled into the fire-light surrounding the camp. Kallen saw bulging muscles and glistening sweat. She smelled fear and blood on both men.

A noise from her right caused her to turn. Griffith, the bands about him now a dark purple, displayed a warlike aggression as he fought with his enemy. Both hands entwined about his sword's long hilt, he struck blow after blow, forcing the man back.

"We're outnumbered," her assigned protector said. "Hasn't stopped Griffith before, but he would have me see you to safety."

Kallen pried her eyes away from Griffith, reluctant to leave with Rodger even though his words made sense.

It was there again. Stronger than before.

Kallen shrank back against the tree's broad base. She couldn't go with this man. Her initial reaction to him days earlier was correct. She didn't understand how he'd cloaked his true nature since then, but his aura now shone black as night. He was the last person she could trust.

"Now, my lady," the knight hissed. "You must come with me."

"I can't leave Griffith," Kallen stammered, no reasonable excuse coming to mind.

"Trust me, Sir Griffith expects me to extract you before 'tis too late."

Every fiber of Kallen's body screamed out its aversion as Sir Rodger grabbed her forearm and yanked her to her feet.

"Hurry. To the horses, or your reluctance may get us killed."

The knight dragged her along as Kallen stumbled in the dark behind him. She longed to thrust the *baselard* into his arm and run, but she had not the courage. Her dull, uneventful life had not prepared her for such an action even while her mind screamed at her 'twould be a sin to attack another in hatred.

They reached the tethered horses, and he quickly untied his own. Kallen slipped the dagger into her pocket, hoping she might dare to use it later. Before she could protest further, Sir Rodger was atop his horse and had brought her up before him. He kicked the horse's side, and they took off at breakneck speed into the night.

"Walmouth Woods," Kallen repeated. "You know this place?"

Rodger's teeth gleamed a brilliant white in the moonlight. "Yes, my lady. I'm familiar with the rendezvous point. Sir Griffith knows that. He would not have instructed otherwise. Stay calm," he commanded. "I will have you where you're supposed to be before you know it."

His words did not comfort her. Nor did the bands of green that began to sprout about him. They could mean many things—jealousy, greed, an affinity with nature, even ambition.

Kallen hoped she would not be around Sir Rodger long enough to discern what they meant.

———

Griffith pushed his bastard sword into the man on the ground before him. The man grasped the blade as if to try and remove it. Slowly, his hands fell away as the life ebbed from him.

Griffith yanked the sword out and turned in a circle, gazing in all directions for more of the enemy. They seemed to be in retreat.

His mind swirled. These were no highwaymen that had attacked for jewels or money. Instead, his gut told him they had come for Kallen. But why? No one knew she was coming to Mangeron beyond Crispin, Deva, and Alita.

Of course, servants eventually learned everything a family knew. If so, was one a spy? Who would profit from holding Kallen hostage before she reached Mangeron?

Griffith had no proof, but he ventured to guess that the Earl of Nowland was behind the attack on the camp. Kallen was, after all, his daughter. Had Quentin somehow learned of her existence? Even so, why would he want her? It wasn't as if she were a legitimate offspring that he could bargain off in the marriage trade. And with Quentin, everything boiled down to money or power.

Thank goodness, Rodger spirited her away during the worst moments. She would be safely to the southwest, not more than a couple of hours ride away, in Walmouth Woods.

Something still troubled him, though. Even as his men began to return and re-group, lingering doubts hung over him.

"Anyone left alive?" he asked those assembled as he jammed his sword into the ground. He quickly counted and saw all five of his men before him, some bleeding, but none worse for the wear.

"One," John called out. "He's over there. Bawling like a babe, he is. Couldn't believe his mates left him. Do you want him, my lord?"

"Yes. Drag him over. I have a few questions for him."

Two men quickly did his bidding. Soon, the injured man lay before Griffith.

"I care not for your name. What I want 'tis your purpose. Why did you attack this particular camp?"

The soldier gave him a surly look. "Rot in Hell." He spat at Griffith's boots.

He bent and grasped the man's hair and jerked him to his feet. "I shall send you there directly if I don't get an answer to my question."

The man struggled a minute before he realized Griffith would not be letting go.

"All right. I'll talk. Don't owe him nothin' anyway. He's bad about paying and cheap when he does."

"The Earl of Nowland."

The man started in surprise. "How'd you know?"

Griffith shrugged and released his grip. "Just tell me why."

"All I knows is 'tis the girl he wants. He didn't share with us why. He said he needed her brought back in one piece, and we weren't to lay a hand on her otherwise."

Griffith contained the anger that threatened to bubble over. "Bind his leg wound and tie him to his horse. He'll return with us to Mangeron. I'm sure Lord de Mangeron will have an idea what to do with him."

The prisoner snorted. "You think taking me to Mangeron's more important than retrieving the girl? She's halfway to Nowland's arms by now."

Griffith's eyes narrowed. "Why do you say this? One of my men—"

"Hah! *One of your men*. You are a bit of an arse, my lord."

His heart stopped. An icy sweat broke out across the back of his neck. He stared hard at the man.

"Talk fast... if you want to live."

The man began to tremble. "I saw her. I saw her leave. With Sir Rodger."

Griffith immediately thought back to Kallen's warning. How she hadn't trusted Rodger from the very beginning.

And how he'd dismissed her notions.

Griffith spoke with a calm he no longer felt. "You claim Sir Rodger is a spy for Lord Nowland. A traitor?"

The man shrugged. "Don't know exactly what he is, just that I seen him from time to time with Lord Nowland, their heads together. Up to no good, I'd guess. Sir Rodger's bound to have recognized the earl's men since he's around often enough. He's a smart one. He'd know 'twas the girl we was after."

Griffith grew nauseated. Rodger's betrayal sickened him. Here was a man he'd known for a good many years, a strong, reliable soldier, one he'd fought beside on the battlefield. To know the knight was a spy from Quentin's camp only added to the disloyalty.

But more than that, Griffith was upset that he hadn't shown any faith in Kallen. He didn't know what it was about her, but she was different from others. She'd instantly known Rodger for the Judas he was, just as she'd known her mare's name without being told and had been able to see the number of their attackers in the dark of night.

He must find her before she fell into the earl's hands. He must reassure her that he did believe in her.

Because Griffith now realized he believed in them being together.

"We have no time to deal with him. Tie him to a tree." Griffith turned to leave.

"But I'll bleed to death!" the man cried.

Griffith yanked his sword from the ground and

held the tip to the man's chest. "Would you rather die instantly?"

The man's head bobbed back and forth fiercely. "No, no, I'll take my chances with that tree, my lord."

Griffith sheathed his sword. "Come," he told those gathered around him. "We ride to save Lady Kallen."

And to save my soul.

17

Tension coiled in Kallen's stomach. It threatened to erupt at any moment. The black and green bands burned even more brightly around Rodger as the night sky began to lighten.

Kallen estimated they'd ridden three hours or more, making their way carefully since it was still before dawn. Had Griffith said how far it was to Walmouth Woods? Why was the rendezvous point so far away?

She had not spoken to Sir Rodger the entire time. She didn't know if she trusted her voice. Would he hear the fear and doubt within her words? He must have some sign of her uneasiness from her body. It was stiff and unyielding against him as they rode. Kallen was unused to any man's touch. Except for Griffith's. She longed for the comfort of Griffith's arms about her.

She decided she could wait no longer and asked, "Are we far from Walmouth Woods?"

Rodger hesitated before he replied. "Do not trouble yourself, my lady. You are safe."

His answer did not suit her. "Am I?" She glanced over her shoulder at him.

"For now. Who knows what lies ahead?" he asked cryptically.

It was not the comforting response she desperately wished for and only added to her agitation.

Suddenly, Sir Rodger reined in his horse in the middle of the road and dismounted. "We shall stop here and rest the beast. He's been ridden hard for far too long. I doubt we've been followed."

Sir Rodger reached up to help her down. As his fingers captured her waist, Kallen's panic grew. He set her upon the ground but held on to her a bit too long.

He gave her a sly look and said, "No need for alarm. I can protect you as well as—even better than —Griffith Sommersby." He laughed. "I read in your eyes otherwise. Trust me, Lady. I am capable of more than you'd imagine."

"You're ambitious. Materialistic." The words popped from Kallen without warning. She wished she could push him back. He stood too close. She found it hard to breathe.

The knight eyed her carefully. "You are a good judge of character. What you say of me is true. I want what I cannot have, all the finer things in life. Yet I am a second son whose fool of a brother runs our family estate. *I* should, only I was born minutes too late. He possesses all while I have nothing. *It should be mine.*"

Quietly, she said, "We must accept our lot in life, Sir Rodger. 'Tis God's plan for us, and we should abide by it."

"God's plan!" he roared. "Do not talk of God. I wish I could defy Him and slay my worthless brother. Then I could gain everything due me."

Sir Rodger moved away from Kallen and began to pace frantically as he became caught up in a tirade.

"I am the better rider. Better at swordplay. I dance circles around him in the hunt, yet he has all. I am relegated to serve another when others should serve me."

His tone frightened Kallen as much as the mad look in his eye. He plopped upon a fallen log and hung his head for a long moment, cradling it in his hands. When he raised it, his eyes met hers, a fury blazing within them.

"As it is, I shall go to Hell."

"Why?"

He shook his head. "My soul is not my own. It now belongs to the Earl of Nowland. One gambler knows another well. I had debts accrue, and Nowland kept me from prison. I work for him now. I might as well go to Hell, my pockets lined with his gold."

His words confused Kallen. "I thought you in service to my uncle and Mangeron. Who is this earl?"

Sir Rodger's eyes glittered. "Someone who must want you very badly, Kallen de Mangeron."

Kallen shuddered and took a step back from him. "Explain yourself."

"Those weren't common highwaymen tonight who attacked. That band of men belonged to the earl. I recognized one immediately as soon as he fought near us by the firelight. Why do you think I got you out of there so quickly?"

"But we're to meet Griffith at—"

"*Damn Griffith!* He's a self-righteous pig. He could never understand my dilemma. He'll gain Sommerset when his old man finally dies. He'll never have to work as I will."

He stood, glaring at her. "I take my opportunities

when I see them. And you, my sweet, are a plump one."

Kallen took off running blindly, fear driving her, but her cumbersome skirts got in the way. The knight easily caught up to her and tackled her. She fell face down into the dirt.

He whipped her over, his weight pressing her into the ground, and smiled at her. "I like spirit in a woman."

What she saw in his eyes frightened her more than any words he'd uttered.

He leaned in, his breath warm on her cheek. "I know Nowland has a good reason for wanting you, so I'll see you safely into his hands. That doesn't mean we cannot enjoy a little sport before we return."

Kallen didn't understand his words, but his tone made her go cold inside. She already had trouble breathing with him atop her. When would he get off?

Then her captor quickly began to raise the hem of her skirts. He forced a knee between her thighs. Whispered talk of the nuns came crashing back to Kallen.

"...what all men want... a grave sin outside the bonds of marriage... a fate worse than death..."

Kallen knew he meant to force himself upon her. Take her virginity. 'Twould be painful and humiliating.

And wrong. Against God's laws and man's.

She clawed at his hands, trying to push him away, but he only laughed. She turned her nails on his face, digging deeply into the tender skin. He cried out hoarsely in pain and slapped her hard.

Kallen saw a myriad of stars for a moment, then darkness came rushing up toward her. She fought it, knowing if she succumbed, she would awake a ruined woman.

If she awoke. Despite his promise to deliver her to another, she did not know if he could be believed. She felt her very life threatened, along with her pureness. In an instant, she knew what she must do.

Her eyes still closed, she reached into her pocket and slipped out the dagger, gripping the handle firmly. She knew she would have but one blow. It must count. She sent a prayer to the Virgin for help and forgiveness alike.

And slammed the blade into the side of Rodger's neck.

He lifted his head and stared at her, his eyes wide in surprise. Kallen pushed the *baselard* in further and gave it a twist, surprised at the anger that drove her.

An odd gurgle came from him. He collapsed atop her. His heavy weight, coupled with the warmth of blood pouring from his wound onto her, nauseated her. Kallen pushed against him and he rolled onto the ground. His hands went to his throat as blood bubbled from his mouth. He actually yanked out the knife. The helpless cry that followed was like an animal caught in a steel trap.

His eyes focused on Kallen and pleaded with her as his lips moved, no sound coming from them. Sorrow and guilt overwhelmed her. She knelt beside him and took his hand, watching in horror as his aura faded.

"I'm sorry. I'm so, so sorry," she told him over and over. She prayed aloud, appealing to the Blessed Virgin to take his spirit. "God forgives us our sins, Sir Rodger. He will forgive you of yours if you but ask. Even in your mind. Simply give your burden to Him."

The knight's body convulsed. He went still. Kallen

rose, her surcoat's front doused in blood. Her hands were wet and sticky as well. She leaned down and wiped them on the grass.

She spied the dagger lying there and retrieved it. She might need it yet.

Then panic set in. Her mind screamed at her, demanding she flee, not knowing where to go, realizing she'd actually killed a man.

Kallen ran to the horse, hoping it wouldn't shy away from the smell of blood. The horse moved not a muscle, and she thought it must be a war-horse, trained to the sounds and smells of battle.

She spoke gently to the beast. "We must leave. You must take me to Walmouth Woods. Please."

But the horse did not know this place. No pictures came from his mind to hers.

"'Tis all right. We shall get ourselves on the road and find someone who can direct us there."

Kallen mounted the horse. Her whisper—half prayer, half plea—begged God to let Griffith find her or she him.

Before this Earl of Nowland did.

18

The men quickly gathered up weapons and supplies and mounted their horses, Griffith in the lead. He knew only to ride south. He tried to clear his mind from its frantic racing and think rationally. Where would Rodger take Kallen?

Walmouth Woods would be the last place. Of that he was certain. Yet the woods lay to the south, much as Mangeron did. Quentin's estate was to the southeast, just past Mangeron. The road would be the same for much of the way, veering off only near the end of the line.

Should he gamble and keep all the men with him, expecting Rodger to take Kallen directly to Quentin, or should he split his forces and try more than one approach? Rodger might choose instead to swerve off onto a less-traveled road, go into hiding, and try and ransom Kallen to the villainous earl. He would not put it past the traitor at this point.

Griffith decided it was a calculated risk, but he chose to have the entire guard stay together. They were still at least two days away from both Mangeron and Nowland's estate. Griffith felt confident they would catch up to Rodger before then.

Especially if Kallen delayed him in any way.

If suspicion still lingered in her mind, she might try and slow them down, hoping Griffith would realize Rodger's betrayal and come to her rescue. It hurt that she hadn't an idea where Walmouth Woods lay, though. Rodger could head practically anywhere in all of England and lie to Kallen about the name of the place when they arrived.

He had to believe he would find them. He also wanted Rodger brought alive to Mangeron, so Crispin could deal with the man's betrayal. He would leave that judgment and its subsequent punishment in his friend's hands. Right now if Griffith came across Rodger, he would flay the man, stripping each layer of skin away slowly, ensuring an agonizing death.

He knew his men would feel similarly about Rodger, and so he called out as they picked their way carefully until dawn broke, "Rodger is to be taken alive. I insist upon it."

John, riding to his left, questioned his order. "Are you certain, my lord? I bloody well want to tear him apart with me bare hands."

He glanced around him. All the men shared the same determined look.

"Lady Kallen is special," John added. "We want her returned. When we find 'em, you care for her, my lord. Allow us to handle the traitor."

Griffith nodded. He would not argue now.

"God be with us all," John called, and the band of soldiers echoed his sentiment. A hollow feeling rang through Griffith as he focused on the road ahead. He wished he, too, could call upon God for guidance. Part of him wanted to, while the other half rejected any notion of God's existence.

Yet as the cadence of the hooves became a constant throb, a rhythmic thought much like a prayer repeated over and over in his mind.

Keep Kallen safe. Keep Kallen safe.

He didn't think it an offered prayer, but a small part of him hoped someone was listening. And would answer.

It could be hours before they spotted Rodger or any of Quentin's group of soldiers, assuming they headed in the same direction. Rodger had a good half-hour lead, possibly more, with Quentin's soldiers close to that. When they encountered the earl's men, Griffith intended to take no prisoners.

The dawn broke, clearing the faint mist of night. As they now set a brisk pace, Griffith tried to reason why Quentin would want Kallen, much less how he even knew of her existence. Before an answer came, he caught sight of what had to be the remainder of Nowland's soldiers in the distance.

He spurred on Satan like a madman, drawing his arming sword as he rode. Griffith had counted on Quentin's men keeping to a slower pace since they had no reason to suspect that the Mangeron men would know who they were and ride after them in the correct direction. He hadn't expected to catch them this soon but was glad of it.

As his guard closed the gap between the two groups, Quentin's men heard their approach. Shock crossed their faces as they turned their horses and fumbled to draw their weapons before being overtaken. Griffith counted on his men's momentum to plow into the enemy and take as many as possible in that first assault since they were fewer in number.

His sword sliced across the chest of the man first on his left and quickly slit the throat of the next soldier to the man's left. Griffith turned to his right and saw his men making haste with their choice of weapons. Bastons and maces swung, poleaxes ripped, and estocs stabbed into enemies in the breadth of a few seconds. They caught Quentin's larger guard totally unaware. The precious seconds it took them to realize they were under attack cost most of them their lives.

Those surviving banded together and rode full force into Griffith's guard. Men were knocked from their horses, steel clanged against steel, hoarse shouts mingled with bloodcurdling cries. Within minutes, Griffith's angry force literally wiped out the opposing group.

Save for one. Griffith saw him remount in the midst of the confusion and take off down the road. He cut into a grove of trees. Griffith decided the man must be questioned since all others appeared dead.

He turned to John. Before he could speak, the soldier nodded and waved him on.

"I saw him, my lord. Have at him," John shouted, a grin crossing his broad face. "We'll finish the task at hand."

Griffith jumped upon Satan's back and followed. The forest he angled into was thick and slowed him considerably, but he caught sight of the soldier not thirty feet ahead. The rider's horse pulled up lame. He watched the man jump from his mount's back and curse loudly as he held his right hand to his shoulder. As Griffith approached, he saw blood spilling from the wound, staining the man's fingers.

"Ah, by the Holy Christ, just kill me now, Griffith Sommersby!" the man cried as he fell to his knees. "Better ye than that bloody bastard earl."

"You know me?" Griffith asked.

"Aye. The earl said ye'd be in charge of the escort

party. I know ye by reputation to be fair, so run a sword through me and be done with it."

Griffith dismounted, his weapon clutched in his hand. He stepped to the man and touched the tip of the sword to his chest. The man grimaced, his eyes squeezed shut, his mouth set firmly in place.

"Will you talk to me?"

The soldier opened his eyes and studied Griffith. He shrugged. "Why not?"

Griffith backed off a few steps and re-sheathed his sword. "The Earl of Nowland sent you to take Kallen de Mangeron."

The man nodded. "He did. Wants her in the worst way."

"Why?"

"He said she's of his blood, and he must have her by his side. We would recognize her hair of silvery blond, just as his mother and sister and he possess. That things would change once she took up residence at Nowland. Told us where ye'd be and how many in number. He said she would reverse his fortunes. Said not to bother coming back unless we had the girl and not a hair on her head harmed."

The knight took a pained breath and gripped his shoulder. "He's in a bad way, the earl is. There be talk of debts mounting. 'Tweren't always so. When his mother was alive, things was different. Nowland seem to know things back then."

The man shook his head. "'Twas rumored the mother be a witch who could foretell the future. Mayhap 'tis why he wants Lady Kallen now."

The words caused the blood to pound at Griffith's temples. "You accuse Kallen de Mangeron of witchery?"

In a rage, Griffith ran his sword through the man

and yanked it free. The soldier fell backward to the ground. Silence blanketed the woods.

His anger surprised him. He'd killed in haste and passion, wanting to protect her name. He knew Kallen to be an innocent, not a witch. God would never allow one so good and pure to become the spawn of the Devil.

God?

The thought stopped Griffith cold. In their brief time together, Kallen had shown a strong faith in God. Had her talk of the Almighty seeped into his conscience?

Had he been wrong? Did God truly exist? Griffith had blamed Him for Carina's death and that of his son, never giving thought that women died in childbirth every day. Throughout Sommerset's lands, did not most women lose a child or more over the course of their child birthing years? Small crosses littered the graveyard of babes who had not survived. Even his mother suffered the loss of two of her own children soon after birth. Only he and Deva survived from infancy to adulthood.

Was it simply the grand scheme of things in this world? Had he blamed God for the natural order?

And now he had killed a man simply because he couldn't tolerate even a whisper of slander against Kallen.

Griffith admitted to himself nothing but love would be so powerful as to move him in word and deed. If need be, he would go to the ends of the earth to find Kallen. He'd killed for her. He would die for her. He must find her and assure her safety, even if 'twere done with his dying breath.

He returned to his men, more determined than ever.

"The man confirmed 'twas the Earl of Nowland who wished to ransom Lady Kallen," he shared, keeping the heart of their conversation to himself. "Most of you know of the bitter feelings between the earl and the de Mangeron family.

"Come. Only one man lies between us and recovering Lady Kallen."

Griffith wheeled Satan. His men fell in behind him. He resolved they would regain Kallen before this day was out.

They rode only a few leagues before they came to a standstill.

Rodger lay dead in the middle of the road.

But where was Kallen?

19

Kallen held tightly onto the reins as the horse galloped down the road. She wished the morning sun could dispel the dark thoughts that ran through her mind. Over and over again, she relived plunging the dagger into her kidnapper's neck. She could not clear the picture from her mind.

The blood, too, still bothered her. Its tinny smell caused her empty stomach to gurgle uncomfortably. She thought she might be sick and decided to find water to rinse off.

She rode for a quarter-hour in discomfort until she thought she heard running water. She slowed the horse and listened. To her left came a sound that must be a brook. She climbed from Sir Rodger's horse and led him into a grouping of oak trees. The noise grew louder as she approached.

Kallen tied the horse to a low bush and ran to the water. Before she reached it, her stomach lurched, and she was sick. She bent over and closed her eyes, wishing all thoughts of Sir Rodger and her guilt to vanish.

She finally stood and walked on shaky legs to the water. She plunged her hands into the clear stream and rinsed her face and mouth before she scrubbed at her throat and bodice with the cold water. She managed to cleanse the blood from her skin, but her surcoat was ruined. A large stain remained, a reminder of her transgression.

Kallen wrapped her cloak about her. It was dark in color and had been trapped under her when Rodger lay atop her, so it escaped being drenched. She would keep it close around her to hide what blood she could not wash from her clothes.

She sat, exhausted, wondering how she would find Griffith. Her frustration turned to tears that cascaded down her cheeks. She cried at her loss of innocence. For Sir Rodger's death. For being lost and alone.

Less than a sennight ago, she lived a quiet life in a holy convent. Her greatest sins revolved around speaking out of turn or complaining if others shirked their duty. Now a man lay dead, and her penance would be great. She had broken one of the most important of God's laws. She might never gain entrance into Heaven.

She brushed the tears from her cheeks, determined to carry on. No obstacle would be too great to keep her from Griffith or from meeting her family. She must put aside such childlike behavior and take action.

Kallen headed back to where she'd left the horse when she heard riders approaching on the nearby road. She froze. Would they pass or stop to water their horses? Did she have time to reach her own mount? Should she hide?

The decision was made for her as she glimpsed sight of them entering the copse. She lifted her skirts and ran to a fat tree trunk, squatting behind it as two men entered the area.

"Sweet Jesu but I need a drink."

A man hurried to the stream and dipped his hands into the water. Kallen heard a loud slurping.

"Better ale, if ye ask me," a second echoed before he also bent and drank.

Kallen studied them from her hiding place. They were rough looking, dressed very meanly, with unshaven faces and an element of danger about them.

"'Twas a good haul." One stood and wiped the back of his hand across his dripping chin. "Better 'n raiding hawkers along the roadside to London."

The second man ran his fingers through greasy hair. "Nay, them hawkers only have pig bones, corpse's teeth, and stray pieces of wood. How many o' them have true relics?"

The first grinned. "Not like us, bloody likely. These be the originals. I'd bet my soul on it. They have to be, as tight as that old arse held onto them." He snickered. "Before we parted him from his treasures."

"Do ye think they're authentic enough to toss into the fire? We could test if they truly be real. 'Tis the Church that says real relics'll survive fire."

The other man laughed. "I'm not that much of a fool, Rufus. They should make the bishop happy. He'll pay if'n he's happy. Let him be the one to test them by fire."

The one called Rufus emptied his purse and held up two necklaces and what Kallen thought might be a ring.

"The best relics are always protected in small reliquaries like these. And when the bishop has 'em, it'll guarantee his church the biggest number o' pilgrims."

"And all the profits that go with 'em," the other cackled.

Kallen was appalled at their irreverence. The convent she'd been raised in had both a relic of St. Paul's finger bone and one of St. Peter's teeth. It was her small link to the Christ. But these men spoke as if relics were for sale everywhere and not all of them authentic.

Did fakes abound in the outside world? Her faith was already badly shaken by her actions with Sir Rodger. She refused it to be jostled further. 'Twas bad enough Griffith questioned God's very existence though she might have, as well, had she suffered a loss as deeply as his.

"By God's teeth, Rufus, over there. Do ye see it, the horse?"

They'd noticed Rodger's horse. Kallen's heart pounded furiously. Should she stay where she was? Try to move as they walked toward the horse? She saw no place in which to cross the stream, and she had no idea how deeply it ran. She feared wandering farther into the forest and getting lost.

Her only course was to go horizontally with the road. While the horse distracted the men's attention, she would move farther out of sight and then make her way back toward the thoroughfare. They need never see her.

Kallen crept from her hiding place, the voices too far away now for her to catch what was said. She kept low to the ground, praying she would not be seen.

"What's that?"

Fear rippled through her. They'd spotted her. She took off running, pushing through the dark wood, her hands shoving away the low greenery as she made her way.

"'Tis a woman! Catch her!"

A loud thrashing followed closely behind her. Kallen knew the men would soon be upon her. Instinctively, she reached into her pocket and grasped the *baselard*. If these men debased sacred relics of the Church, they would place little value on her life. She had nothing to give them to entreat them to leave her alone.

She would have to fight.

A calm descended upon her, even as she ran. God was with her. If He chose to call her home soon, so be it. She would go knowing she had a family who'd wanted her and having known the kiss of a good man. She was ready to meet her Maker.

But only after she made her stand.

Kallen reached the road. She glanced frantically to her left and right. No one was in sight. She had nowhere to run. Nowhere left in which to hide. She turned back and faced the woods.

Immediately, the one called Rufus and his companion rushed out. They halted in their tracks when they spied her.

"Ah, a lady," Rufus said. A wolfish grin appeared on his homely face. He brushed strands of unkempt hair back from his forehead. "Me and Billy ain't never had no real lady before." He smacked his lips as if readying to eat a delicacy.

As before, when Sir Rodger's eyes gleamed in such a fashion and his tone made her go cold inside, Kallen knew these two would be up to no good. She knew not exactly what, but evil abounded in what Rufus planned.

"Stand back!" Kallen cried. She raised the dagger before her. "I've killed once. I'll do it again."

The two men looked at each other and burst out

into laughter. Her courage began to falter, replaced by a dread of indescribable magnitude.

"She's killed a man," Rufus said in a singsong voice. He took a step toward her. "And I'll wager she aims to kill me."

Kallen's hand shook in front of her. She gripped the hilt until her knuckles went white. As Rufus drew even closer, she slashed the dagger through the air.

"Ah, she's a quick 'un, Billy Boy. I may need yer help."

Billy slowly ventured toward Kallen. She locked her knees, which threatened to buckle under her. Rufus took another step in her direction, and Kallen lashed out again.

"Damnation, she sliced me!" he cried.

Kallen saw the murderous look in his eye. She waved the dagger again, but he grabbed her wrist and twisted it. She cried out in pain and dropped the knife. Billy swept it up.

Rufus pushed her to her knees, his hand still locked around her wrist. Kallen tore at it with her free hand, but the criminal only cackled.

"She's got dash, this 'un," Rufus proclaimed. "Dippin' me tarse in her will be quite a treat."

He then backhanded Kallen so hard, she went limp. The world went dark for a moment before a thousand stars danced before her eyes. She felt her body crumbling to the ground. Small stones in the road dug into her back, through her cloak and surcoat. The pain brought her back around.

Kallen saw Rufus now hovered over her. He'd pinned her arms to the ground, so she began to buck violently, trying to keep him off her.

"Like a wild woman, she is." Rufus lowered his weight onto her. His girth was so great that she couldn't budge him. His unwashed body so close to her made her gag with dry heaves.

"God, make him stop!" Her thoughts became her words.

The men laughed. "Now, me lady, God's just granted me an answered prayer. Be a sweet girl for now, and then I'll see He grants yours, too."

Rufus then plunged his tongue into her mouth. Repulsion filled her. He was *kissing* her, but this was nothing like Griffith's touch. What she had done with Griffith seemed heavenly. This seemed obscene. His hand roughly squeezed her breast. Pain shot through Kallen. He began to push up her skirts. Strong fingers tried to force her legs apart. Kallen held them together until her thighs ached.

She could take no more. She would rather die than be subjected to such degradation. She turned her head, trying to catch her breath. As Rufus pushed her face back toward him, Kallen latched onto his ear.

And bit down as hard as she could.

Rufus's scream erupted as he scrambled off her. She thought it loud enough to be heard all the way to London. Kallen jumped up and took off running down the road.

"I'll rip your nether lips out, whore!" screamed Rufus.

Kallen ran, her cloak streaming behind her. She sensed at least one of the men gaining on her. Her lungs began to burn as if they'd caught fire, and still she ran.

Then she heard horses in the distance.

Sweet Jesu, let it be Griffith. Oh, Lord, please be Griffith.

20

Satan's ears folded back. The horse tensed as if in pain. Griffith knew the animal sensed something out of the ordinary. He signaled a halt, and the guard came to a stop. An unearthly howl died down from somewhere ahead.

Quickly, Griffith spurred Satan, his men directly behind him. He rounded a bend in the road and his heart almost stopped. Kallen ran toward him, her hair and cloak billowing behind her. What Griffith figured to be a highwayman chased after her, a knife in his hand, blood pouring down the side of his neck. Another man followed at a distance. When the second man saw the approaching horsemen, he ducked into the woods.

Griffith pressed Satan harder. He had to reach Kallen before the brigand did. He feared for her life.

Her gaze met his as Satan approached at a gallop. Griffith thrust out a hand and waved Kallen aside.

She somehow understood and veered off the road just as his horse reached her. Now Griffith and Satan came between Kallen and the highwayman. He reined in the horse as the thief ran smack into Satan's flank.

Obscenities poured from the man's mouth. He

lifted his dagger, read to plunge it into Griffith or his mount. With his hand still in mid-air, John rode by, sword in hand, and sliced off the man's arm just below his elbow. The thief's eyes watched in astonishment as his limb fell to the ground.

Griffith cared not a whit for the bleeding stranger. Instead, he wheeled Satan and rode the short distance to Kallen. He leapt from his horse and pulled her into his arms, consequences be damned.

He held her close for a long moment. Her body quivered violently. Griffith stroked the hair that fell down her back, murmuring soothing words. Finally, she calmed.

"Are you all right?" he asked gently, rubbing his hands along her arms as his eyes searched her face. Her cheek was scraped and her face dirty with dust. He hoped that was the only damage she'd suffered while out of his care.

Tears welled in her eyes. She nodded. "A little worse for the wear but all in one piece."

She shuddered and then heaving sobs came. Griffith wrapped his arms about her again.

Kallen tried to speak in spurts. "I... I... killed him... Sir Rodger. I... He wanted... he tried to force... he wanted... I killed him." She broke down again.

Suddenly, John spoke. "There, there, my lady. Weep no more. Traitors need killing. I am just sorry you had to do it yourself."

She raised her head from Griffith's shoulder and smiled weakly at John.

"I suggest you need some time alone, my lord," the soldier added. "We will make camp. Lady Kallen needs no more of the road this day."

Kallen sniffed. "There's a clearing down the road a ways, on the left. Next to a lovely brook. I left Sir

Rodger's horse tied there." A look of panic crossed her face. "I don't want to kill the horse, too! Please find him, John. 'Tis watering he needs."

Griffith turned to John. "Have the men make camp. Take Satan with you. We'll be down there in a little while."

John nodded. "Very good, my lord." He strode off, barking orders left and right.

Kallen watched the men ride down the lane before she turned her attention back to Griffith. "Thank you. You saved my life."

He brought her hands to his lips and tenderly kissed them. "'Tis I who am grateful to see your beautiful face again." He wrapped an arm about her waist for support. "Come. Let us sit under this tree. You can tell me what happened."

He guided her to the tree and sat upon the ground, bringing her into his lap. Kallen rested her head against his chest. They sat for some minutes in silence.

It was a glorious day. Cool and sunny. No wind. And the woman he loved in his arms. As Griffith held her, he knew all was right in his world.

Kallen eventually raised her head. "We must talk. I must explain. I killed Sir Rodger. He frightened me badly, Griffith. He said awful things about you. His loyalty lay elsewhere, not with Mangeron and my uncle."

Griffith stroked her cheek. "He met with the fate he deserved."

"But I *killed* a man! 'Tis a mortal sin, against God's sacred law. I—"

"You did what had to be done, my love. God would not have you burn forever in Hell for protecting yourself from such a wicked sinner."

He paused, not knowing how to frame his question. "Did he... did he hurt you?"

She shivered. "Not exactly." She averted her gaze from his.

Griffith tilted up her chin with a finger. "Where was he when this occurred?"

A lovely blush stained her cheeks. "We were... in the middle of the road." She dropped her eyes again.

"We found Rodger's body, Kallen. The wound was in the side of his neck. Rodger was a tall man. You could not have struck such a blow under ordinary circumstances."

She nodded, her lip quivering. "'Twasn't normal at all. He... was atop me. Trying to push my skirts up."

Griffith brushed aside the rush of anger that swept through him and willed his body to relax. Kallen would feel any tension within him. He did not want her to think he judged her poorly because of Rodger's despicable behavior toward her.

"Then he was not only a traitor to Crispin but to you, as well. Have no shame, Kallen. God will not punish you, for you did nothing wrong. Believe me."

She pressed her head against his chest again. Griffith gave her time to absorb what he'd said.

"Who's Nowland?" she blurted out. "Why would he want me?"

Griffith hesitated a moment. He decided it was best to tell her everything, no matter how painful it would be for her to hear.

"I doubted you before. Never again, my love. We'll keep no secrets in this matter."

Only one thing would he keep from her. Griffith knew he must change Crispin's mind when they arrived at Mangeron. Once he did, Kallen need never know.

"Quentin, Earl of Nowland, is your father. He forced himself on your mother when she was but a young girl, much as Rodger tried to do the same to you."

Griffith saw the look of horror on her face.

"I... I am a child of rape?" Tears welled in her eyes. "I remember Savina skimmed over the truth as she told me of my family. My surprise and delight in discovering I had relatives who wanted me overshadowed the rest of her story." She sighed. "Only now do I understand what happened to Bevia since it almost happened to me."

He took her chin in his hand. "Listen to me, Kallen. I know this upsets you, but you should feel no guilt, no shame, simply because of the circumstances of your birth. You are not your father. You have nothing of him in you. I have never met one with as much goodness in her as you."

She nodded, her eyes closing for a long moment. "Tell me the rest. Hold nothing back."

Griffith drew a deep breath. "Your grandfather abandoned your mother to the care of the convent when it was found she was with child. Your family at Mangeron never knew of your existence. Renton, your grandfather, was a hard man, Kallen. But remember, you go to family now, to your grandmother and uncle and my Deva. They all want you very, very much."

Kallen frowned. "But why me? This earl never knew of my existence in all these years. How did he learn of me now? What good would I be to him?"

He ran his fingers through her silken locks. "Nowland has spies everywhere, Kallen. I'm sure he learned through them of your imminent arrival at Mangeron."

She grew impatient and pushed aside his hand.

"This doesn't explain why he would want me now after all these years. What can I offer him? I am but a simple girl, and his bastard, at that. Of what value am I to a landed earl?"

Griffith explained, "Your hair is a most unusual color, Kallen. It runs in the earl's family, though. What I tell you now is pure speculation, but it may be the twisted reason he seeks you."

He raked a hand through his own hair and closed his eyes a moment, trying to find the right words. "'Tis rumored Nowland's sister killed herself. 'Tis also reputed his mother had some kind of power to see into the future.

"Nowland is said to be near financial ruin. He's a half-brother to our king, a bastard of the first Edward. 'Tis no secret Nowland would love to rule in his brother's place. There's been talk of uprising before, especially because this Edward isn't as strong a ruler as his father before him. I think the earl wants you because he thinks you possess sorcery that would help him accomplish his aim."

Griffith stared at Kallen. Part of him regretted telling her such half-truths, especially since they were mostly spun from lies.

But were they? As he looked deeply into Kallen's eyes, he saw her reaction.

It was true. She did possess some kind of power.

Kallen began to breathe rapidly, panic setting in. Remembered words flooded her mind. She was different. She was odd. Something was wrong with her.

Bevia never understood. She was too simple. Savina called it a gift, though as Kallen grew older it seemed more a curse to her.

She saw the questions in Griffith's eyes. She hated to lose him, but he had been totally honest with her about her father. Her grandfather. Why this wicked earl wanted her.

She must be truthful in return.

"I am different from others," she said quietly.

Griffith's quick intake of breath stung her. Immediately, he apologized. "I assure you, I don't judge you, Kallen. If anything, I want to protect you."

He took her hands in his. "I pledged to do so. Not just for the debt I owe Crispin, but for me—and you."

Kallen took strength in his words, in the warmth of his hands cradling hers. It gave her the courage to go on.

"I see auras. I'm not sure quite how to explain it to you. But around every person I meet, I see a band of color surrounding his or her body. Sometimes two colors. Each color can mean many things."

"What do you mean?"

Kallen saw curiosity and not condemnation. She smiled. "For example, it helps me read into the character of others. I cannot see the future, but the insight into personalities could be quite helpful to someone with political aspirations. It could be used for gain."

"Tell me about these colors."

She sighed. "There are a variety of colors and different shades of them. Blue can mean many things. That a person is sad and wistful and lives in the past. Or that he's peaceful and calm. It could mean someone who is a good listener or one who is patient or honest. The longer I am around a person and the better I get to know this individual, the more I can grasp about him or her and the aura that surrounds them."

Griffith nodded as he listened. It was as if he understood her. It encouraged her to continue.

"Red can indicate anger or rage. Yellow shows

good health and happiness. Silver might show grace or goodness."

She paused. "Savina always called this second sight my gift from God, but I have learned to hide it from all others."

He frowned. "So was it an aura you saw about Rodger that caused you to warn me about him?"

"Yes. What I saw told me he wasn't to be trusted, but you came to his defense so strongly. Then his aura changed totally. I'd never experienced that before. 'Twas something so unusual. 'Tis as if Rodger were two men, one good and kind, one filled with hate and regret."

Kallen shuddered. "'Twas only as the attack occurred and Rodger wanted me to flee with him that his original aura reappeared. I did my best to try and remain, but he insisted I was to go with him."

Griffith grimaced. "'Twas my orders to you both, and I shall regret the words until my dying day."

He placed a hand against her cheek. "I'm sorry I did not trust you when you first spoke, Kallen."

"I was but a stranger to you, Griffith. You knew Rodger to be a good and loyal man for years. I would not expect you to believe me—even if I had told you then about seeing auras."

"I will never doubt you again, Kallen. I promise you that."

With those words, Griffith's lips met hers.

21

Quentin rode through the gates of Mangeron and into the bustling outer bailey. A servant approached him and offered to care for his horse, but Quentin waved the boy away. He had business in the Mangeron stables. It wouldn't do for another to take his mount.

He rode at a leisurely pace, his eyes watchful. Mangeron always thrived. Under Crispin's guidance, the estate flourished more than in previous generations. Quentin searched for any new changes the new earl might have made since Quentin's last visit to the castle had been for Renton's funeral mass. He wondered if the son would surpass his father's touch.

His gaze caught a pretty girl, who blushed profusely when he winked at her. She ducked her head and hurried away, the basket she carried on her hip only drawing attention to her curves. He tamped down the sexual energy that began churning inside. He must stay focused.

The Mangeron stables appeared ahead, and he trotted his horse to its entrance. As he dismounted, Maitland came rushing over to him, a worried look on his face.

"Greetings, my lord. May I take your horse?"

Quentin grunted. "I am particular where 'tis stabled. I shall accompany you and see the steed well placed."

He wanted privacy for their talk, and the darkened stables would help keep prying eyes from their meeting.

The stable hand frowned and shook his head. "Not now," he hissed. "We cannot talk. Simply hand over your horse."

The boy's attitude irked him. He had paid the lad for the information he'd given. Maitland was now in his pocket and always would be. He'd box his ears but good once they stepped inside.

The servant grasped the horse's reins. "They are—"

"Why, good day, Lord Nowland. What brings you to Mangeron?"

He peered over the stable hand's shoulder and saw Crispin de Mangeron emerging from the mews, his arm linked through his wife's. Quentin could make out a faint band of yellow surrounding the woman. He released the reins to Maitland, who scurried off with the horse.

Sweat broke out along his hairline and under his armpits. It never failed any time he was nervous. Whether at cards or in the presence of the king, anxiety always flustered him in the worst way.

Quentin planted a smile upon his thin lips. "I thought I would come and see how the lovely Lady de Mangeron is faring." He studied the noblewoman a moment. "Your confinement draws to an end, I suppose?" He couldn't help but add, "I thought women secreted themselves away at such a time."

Lady de Mangeron answered him. "I doubt I'd describe myself as lovely, my lord. More like a fattened goose. Crispin swears to me I still have feet, but I haven't seen them in a fortnight."

He felt a trickle of sweat roll down his back as she glared at him. "'Tis surprising you are out and about, my lady."

Crispin gave his wife's hand a loving pat. "Deva misses riding. We venture down to the stables every few days so she can visit the horses."

"I know 'tis odd, but I find the smell of hay and horse most refreshing."

Her words had a patronizing air to them, and Quentin realized that Crispin must have revealed to his wife the role Quentin had played in their upcoming visitor's life. Usually, the woman displayed the deference due to one of his position, but today her tone rang differently.

"She also is mad for apple tarts," Crispin interjected. "Eats three or more a day. I do believe we'll name the child Apolonia, for she'll mostly be made up of apples."

"Now, my lord husband, the babe could be a boy as easily as a girl," she chided him, her voice softening as she spoke to her husband. "But as long as we speak of tarts, might you and Lord Nowland excuse me?" She openly glared at Quentin now. "I tire so easily these days. I wish to lie down."

Quentin frowned. "Of course, my lady. Rest is important to one in your condition." He bowed formally. "Then I shall leave you gentlemen to your talk."

Crispin kissed his wife's cheek, and his wife left them alone in the yard.

As soon as she was out of hearing, Crispin turned

to Quentin, his pretense of affability gone. "What say you, Nowland? Why did you really come to Mangeron? 'Tis not as if we are close friends, merely neighbors by circumstance. State your business and leave."

He scowled in return. The pup did not even feign the respect his office was due. He was half-brother to the king, after all.

"Though I suffered poor relations with your father, I had hoped to remedy that. I see you are as narrow-minded as that bastard was." He looked around him. "Your stable boy has taken my horse. I'll fetch it and be off your property."

Crispin stepped in front of him. "I'll see to it," he said curtly and went to retrieve the horse himself.

"Damn the man," Quentin said to himself.

He'd only needed a minute with Maitland to see if there had been any word from the escort party. He figured it was expected at Mangeron in the next day or two. He'd also wanted to pump the spy for any more information he or his sweetheart might have learned. He supposed he'd simply have to return home and wait until Kallen de Mangeron was brought to Nowland instead.

Crispin returned with Quentin's horse and tossed him the reins.

"Do not expect a welcome again, my lord," the Mangeron lord warned him. "We have no friendship nor love lost between us, despite the fact I fostered with you. Keep to your lands, and I shall do the same."

Quentin mounted his horse, biting his tongue and reminding himself to bide his time. 'Twas Crispin de Mangeron who would suffer more in the long run. His precious niece and her escort party would never arrive. He could search to the ends of the kingdom and never know she lay but a few leagues away from Mangeron.

If his soldiers managed to kill every last member of her guard, that is. He'd ordered there to be no survivors, for he didn't want a war with his neighbor. He would play the innocent when Crispin came hunting for his niece, as Quentin expected would happen. How could he have someone in his custody whose existence he didn't know of?

He smiled and said, "Good day," through gritted teeth, spurring his horse and riding out the gates. Crispin de Mangeron would be the first person he took down after he toppled that idiot Edward from his throne.

And Kallen de Mangeron would lead the way.

———

Griffith escorted Kallen down the road at a leisurely pace. As they strolled, the sky darkened. A wind from the north picked up, more true to the November day than the earlier sunshine.

He placed an arm about her for warmth and then thought better of it. He could hear the men and knew the campsite was close.

"Kallen?"

She turned and looked up at him, the dirt still smudging her beautiful face.

"We need to talk a moment."

"We've been talking for quite a while, Griffith."

He brushed a strand of hair from her face. "We are almost to the camp. I must make you understand something. I am your protector, head of this guard. 'Tis not quite acceptable that I've formed such a... close relationship with you. I have not your uncle's permission. Do you understand what I say?"

Her gray eyes darkened and then clouded over a moment. "Yes, I see. We are not to act so familiar in front of the men. Is that what you ask?"

Griffith nodded and gave her forehead a quick kiss. "I think the men will understand why I embraced you when we found you. Most will know I was relieved and wanted to reassure you. A few might guess otherwise, but I do not want to feed those suspicions. We still can remain friendly. We are friends and should act naturally with each other."

She cocked her head to one side. "I suppose I shall have to be content with merely dreaming of your kiss, my lord."

A sweet ache filled Griffith. He placed his hands on her shoulders and gave them a gentle squeeze. "Then I shall meet you in those dreams, Kallen. But until then, may this keep us satisfied."

He brought his mouth to hers in a sweet, lingering kiss. Yet each time he wished to draw away from her, he found himself deepening the kiss. Kallen had become everything to him in such a short time. He brought her close, his arms tightening about her, her heart hammering, matching his own pounding one.

A rustling in the woods caused them to break apart.

"Time to return," he whispered to her.

Griffith allowed Kallen to lead him into the camp, where the men greeted her with a rousing cheer. She blushed at the attention. Each man came over personally to tell her how glad he was she had been found safely. She thanked each one in return for their role in rescuing her.

He watched John approach her, the last of the men to do so.

"My lady, we brought your mare and the bag of clothes tied to her. Would you like to go downstream and freshen up a bit? Wash your face or change your surcoat? When you return, we'll have some fine stew for you."

Kallen wrapped her cloak about her and nodded. Griffith had noticed the dried bloodstains down the front of her clothes when they'd found her and was relieved they were not her own.

John retreated to the horses and brought back her things. "Now stay within a shout, my lady," he cautioned her. "We'll come a-running if you need us."

She thanked him and took the bundle, disappearing after a moment.

Griffith stepped over to John. The soldier smiled at him.

"My lady will feel better once she's splashed a little water on her face and gotten into some different clothing." He shook his head. "She's a brave one, that she is."

He heard the admiration in John's voice. He realized Kallen had captured all their hearts with her sweet smiles and rapturous storytelling and now her bravery in the face of danger.

"She is indeed, John. I don't know if even Deva would have held up as well, and she's the most amazing woman I've known. Until now."

John slapped him on the back. "Stew's on, my lord. Come have a taste. You've more than earned it this day."

Griffith followed John to the fire and dished out a

steaming bowl. As he ate, he began to formulate a plan in his mind.

By the time Kallen returned, most of his strategy was set. His gut told him Nowland was still a threat and must be dealt with accordingly. Griffith turned his thoughts toward Mangeron and what lay ahead.

22

Kallen's nerves tingled as she picked up on the men's excitement. Griffith told her they were within minutes of Mangeron. All seemed ready to arrive back home after such a long journey. She was grateful for the uneventful day yesterday and today, having had more than enough adventure.

"Lady Kallen!" called John. "I hope 'tis hungry you are. After being uncomfortable and poorly fed on the road, I can guarantee you that the Mangeron kitchens will be working overtime to prepare the most delicious food you've ever tasted."

She laughed. "'Twould not be hard to do so, John. The convent food was edible. Barely. Believe it or not, the game I've tasted on our trip was tenfold better than any meal I partook of with the nuns."

The men laughed along with her.

Kallen thought back to Cuthbert and Simmons. She hoped the two soldiers had survived their wounds and were being cared for properly. Griffith promised her he would send a messenger to check on their progress once they arrived at Mangeron.

As they came over the rise, all thoughts of the two

men fled. Her first sight of the castle left her speech-less. Far larger than Lord Percival's, the estate stole her breath. Mangeron sat on a hill surrounded by green pastures as far as the eye could see. Tenant cottages dotted the land, while animals grazed content-edly. In her wildest imaginings, she could never have conjured such beauty and grandeur.

Home... she'd finally come home.

Kallen imagined Bevia running through the castle's halls, petting the sheep, tumbling down hills as she played with her brother—all before the loss of her innocence at the Earl of Nowland's hands. She wondered why he chose Bevia to suffer so and why this earl would conceive of such a horrendous act.

As they approached, many greeted them, some with curious stares, but there were smiles, too. The overall auras showed the people's contentment, and it gave Kallen satisfaction that Mangeron was a happy place.

But her bliss was overshadowed by sudden nerves that gripped her. Now that she knew she was a child of rape, she realized Savina had informed her uncle Crispin of this. The entire family might know. Would they view her differently? Could they really want her as much as she wanted their acceptance?

The minute they arrived at the gates, the doors swung open. The gatekeeper called down to their party.

"Been expecting your arrival, that we did, Sir Griffith. Master and mistress be in a frenzy, wanting things all perfect for Lady Kallen."

Griffith flashed her a reassuring smile. "See?" he said softly.

The group rode through the entrance and more greetings deluged them, especially ones from the guards' families. The men began introducing her to wives and children alike. She nodded and smiled, overwhelmed that she had so many faces and names to learn.

As they made their way into the inner bailey and she could see the keep itself, Kallen realized just how impressive Mangeron really was. They had ridden by more than a few castles and had stayed at Lord Percival's on All Hallow's Eve, but nothing prepared her for the magnificence that was Mangeron.

At the top of the stairs, a couple and an older woman awaited them. The younger woman was large with child but waved as they approached, smiling broadly. Golden bands of yellow happiness bathed her form. The man spoke to her and then rushed down the stairs.

Kallen guessed him to be Crispin de Mangeron. She was pleased at his aura. A bright turquoise hovered closest to his body, assuring her of his compassionate yet practical nature. A wider band of purple surrounded the turquoise. This man was confident and led others with poise.

He lifted her from her saddle and hugged her so hard, she found it difficult to breathe.

"'Tis your uncle Crispin who greets you so, Kallen, and glad am I you've finally arrived. 'Twas long in coming, but we shall make up for the time spent away."

Kallen recognized Bevia in him, which comforted her. He had the same generous mouth and dark blue eyes. But where Bevia's usually contained a blank stare, Crispin's were animated.

"And greetings to you, Griff," Crispin added. "I shall expect a full report from you later."

He then took her hand and brought her quickly up

the stairs, where she was greeted with more hugs from Deva.

"Ah, the sister I have longed for. I knew Griffith would someday do some good, for he has brought you to me." She smiled at Kallen as she rubbed her belly. "And you are soon to have a cousin.

"In fact," and she took Kallen's hand and brought it against her belly, "see how the babe kicks in excitement of your arrival!"

Kallen beamed at the small flutters she felt.

A hand gently rested on her shoulder. "I am Alita, my dearest. Your grandmother." She placed her arms about Kallen and held her tenderly for some minutes.

Kallen was moved to tears. She could not have expected a more generous welcome. This new family accepted her readily, without reserve. It thrilled her that she had a place to call home, surrounded by loving blood relatives. Relief ran through her.

Alita released her and said, "I beg your forgiveness, child." Tears began to spill down her lined cheeks.

Kallen brushed them away. "There's nothing to forgive, Grandmother. I am here with you now and so happy."

Alita glowed with soft shades of blue. Kallen guessed her to be a tenderhearted, serene woman.

"Enough of this!" cried Crispin. "We must celebrate Kallen's arrival. Call a halt to all work in the fields. We will feast. Food, dancing, entertainment— all in your honor, Kallen."

She felt the blush crawl up her neck. "I am honored, my lord. I feel much like the Prodigal Son returned home."

"Let me take you to your room," Deva interjected. "We must wash the grime of the road from you." She slipped a hand through Kallen's arm and chattered away as she guided Kallen into the castle.

She glanced over her shoulder and caught a smile from Griffith. Deva's smile was similar and made her know she was truly welcome.

"Hot water will arrive shortly. I ordered it once they sighted your party. And I've placed some wonderful oils here to add to the water. Crispin does spoil me. He's the best of husbands. What scent would you like to try?"

As servants appeared and began filling the bath with steaming buckets of water, the women spoke of Kallen's journey to Mangeron. While Deva washed Kallen's hair for her, she told her young aunt-by-marriage of the two men wounded by the boar and other tales of the road. She kept the attack by the Earl of Nowland's men and Sir Rodger's duplicity to herself, though. She would speak to Crispin later about that. She saw no need to spoil Deva's joy. She would also remain tightlipped about her role in the knight's death. Her conscience suffered enough as it was. Kallen saw no need to alienate her new family by exposing herself as a murderess.

The hot water relaxed her, and she felt truly clean for the first time since she'd left the convent. As Kallen stood and allowed Deva to rinse her a final time, she repeated how helpful all the men had been.

"I should hope so. Griffith better have been particularly nice to you." Deva paused a moment. "He seemed different to me somehow. Almost happy."

Suddenly, Deva gave her a wicked smile. "'Tis because of you, Kallen de Mangeron. Don't deny it. I know my brother, every smile and frown. Tell me all and leave nothing out."

Kallen wrapped a linen sheet about her. "All right,

but you mustn't say a word, not even to your husband. Griffith said he must seek Crispin's permission to court me."

Deva gave a delighted squeal. "Oh, Kallen, I can't tell you what good news you share."

"Just promise me you'll keep it to yourself for now. Only until Griffith has time to speak to Crispin. Then I won't mind if the world knows."

Alita entered at that moment. "The tenants and servants are gathering now. You should dress." She picked up the blue surcoat that Deva had laid out after Kallen's bag was brought up. "What a lovely shade of blue."

Kallen winced. The clothes the two women wore were so beautiful. "I'm afraid 'tis the only suitable gown I've brought, and even then 'twas a gift from Lady Percival. The convent stressed very simple clothes. I've nothing elaborate as either of you are now wearing."

Deva laughed. "Oh, Kallen, I have many clothes we may share. It will be such fun. Just like sisters."

Kallen's insides glowed at that moment. She wondered if her own aura reflected sunny yellow tones now, so great was her happiness. Nothing could spoil such a wonderful day. She would think back on it when she was an old woman and know it was one of the most magical times in her life. No matter what came in the future, this day would be forever imprinted on her soul. The day she found a family. The day she came home.

The women helped her to dress and brushed her hair until it gleamed.

"You are more than ready to meet the people of Mangeron," Alita told her. "All the men will fall in love with you, and the women will want to be your friend."

A knock sounded at the door, and Crispin entered. Gone was the happy, laughing man she'd met earlier. In his place was a solemn soldier who appeared to be on a mission.

"I must speak to Kallen. Alone."

23

Deva protested. "You look much too serious, Crispin. 'Tis a joyous occasion. Save your foul mood for later."

"'Tis something that cannot wait. We'll be down shortly." Crispin's tone was dismissive, and Alita slipped out quickly. Deva flashed her husband a questioning look before she followed her mother-in-law out of the room.

Kallen was on edge. What was wrong? Didn't he like her? She knew she did not resemble Bevia in the least. How could she prove who she was? She believed she was about to lose everything, and she didn't understand why.

"Kallen, please sit." Crispin's tone was soft, but it came out as a curt command.

"No. I shall stand." Kallen moved to the fire. Its warmth on her back bolstered her a bit.

She studied her uncle. His aura shone the same as before, but she could tell of an anger contained just below his surface. He was strong, determined, and very used to his own way.

"I have just come from speaking with Griff. He asked permission to court you."

Kallen's features softened at the mention of Griffith's name. Then it hit her. This was the problem. Mayhap Crispin had been taken aback if Griffith pressed his suit too firmly. This would be easy to clear up.

"Surely 'tis not a problem, Uncle? Griffith is a good, honorable man."

Crispin snorted. "That good, honorable man knew not to ask such a favor of me."

His words puzzled her. "Why?"

"Because you are to be betrothed to another. And he knew it was to happen."

Kallen gasped as if kicked in her gut. "I'm to be married off? Already?" Her anger exploded. "I have hardly entered the walls of Mangeron proper, and yet you seek to fend me off on another? I'd rather have stayed in the convent than be foisted upon some stranger. I thought my blood kin wanted me, but you simply dragged me from the only home I've known to sell me to some stranger."

"I do want you! Of course." Crispin began to pace about the room. "My cousin... his wife was lost in childbirth. He has a small son. I thought you could be a mother to the boy. 'Twould be but an hour's ride away, Kallen, and we'd see you often. I do want to get to know you and make up for my father's transgressions against you."

Crispin frowned as if in pain. "But Harold's lonely. His child needs a mother. He's ignoring the babe. You're the perfect answer. You're family, as he is, and he would be so good to you. Harold is quite wealthy. You'd have everything you could ever want and still come to Mangeron frequently."

It was too much to absorb. But what hurt her most was that Griffith had known of this planned betrothal before he'd even come for her. Why would he have bestowed sweet kisses and made false promises if he had the knowledge that she was promised to another?

"You say Sir Griffith knew of this arrangement?"

Her uncle nodded. "Yes, I told him myself before he left for the convent, though I did not tell him Harold would be the groom. Griff knew I planned to have the contracts drawn up, ready to sign. What I don't understand is why he's gone against me. He knows of my wishes for your happiness."

Crispin came and laid a hand on her shoulder. "I can tell by your face you have some feelings for Griff already. I love him like a brother, and I'm sorry this has occurred. I never would have suspected it. He's mourned the passing of his wife and child for over two years now."

Kallen lifted her chin defiantly. "There's a time to mourn. Griffith still remembers them, but his mourning is over."

She touched a hand to Crispin's arm. "I beg you, do whatever you must, but free me from this marriage. Let me be with Griffith."

Crispin frowned. "I cannot. I gave my word to Harold. The de Mangeron word has always stood for something. Much as I love Griff and would not see him nor you hurt, Kallen, we must honor this obligation."

Hers hand fell. "I have no say in the matter."

"No," he said softly. "I am sorry you were told in this manner. I wanted to wait a few weeks, let you get to know us, then broach the idea with you. Griff's intentions forced my hand. I apologize for the abruptness."

"I know not what to say. You have mapped out my

future so tidily." She turned away from him and stared into the fire.

Crispin placed both his hands on her shoulders. "Come make a new start, Kallen. 'Tis angry you are now, but family must come above all else. Do your duty, and you'll be surprised how happy you will be."

He turned her toward him. "Come. Let us go to the banquet. 'Tis in your honor."

He offered her his hand, and Kallen took it reluctantly. Her heart filled with loathing for what Crispin had done, yet it broke at the same time.

They left the room and she soon found herself entering Mangeron's great hall, full of boisterous people and music and food. Kallen planted a smile on her lips. She would not embarrass Crispin. 'Twas not the time.

A servant announced their arrival, and the resounding cheers echoed throughout the room.

Suddenly, John jumped atop a trestle table. "I can tell you that are gathered that Lady Kallen is a brave one. And she tells great, wonderful stories."

More cheers erupted as Crispin led Kallen to the dais where Deva and Alita were already seated. Griffith was there, too, smoldering as he glared at Crispin. Crispin gave Griffith a curt greeting and then turned to the women.

Alita rose and leaned upon Crispin for support. "'Tis been an exciting day, but a bit too much for me." She kissed first Kallen's cheek then Crispin's. "I will excuse myself. Until tomorrow."

A servant stepped forward and helped Alita down from the dais and led her from the great hall.

"'Tis only the four of us then," Deva said. "And I am more than ready to eat. Please share a trencher with Griffith, Kallen. I'm sure you already know all his bad habits since you've traveled together." She winked at Kallen.

Griffith offered Kallen a pained smile. "If that suits you, my lady." He seated her and then himself.

Kallen sat quietly, her hands folded in her lap as food and drink were served. She had no appetite, but she knew she better make an effort, else Deva would notice.

Griffith took one of her hands and squeezed it. "'Tis not over yet, Kallen. Be strong. Believe in me."

She glared at him. "How can I?" she accused. "You knew—you *knew*—and still painted a lovely picture of us together, knowing it could never be."

Kallen tried to extract her hand, but he held on to it tightly. "How was I to know your kisses were false?" she accused. "You played me for a fool, Griffith Sommersby. I cannot tolerate your presence. Release my hand. I shall share a trencher with you and nothing more. I will be cordial for Deva's sake, but you are dead to me."

As Kallen drew her hand from his, she was distracted by a servant's shout at the door.

"Lord Hammond."

A handsome man made his way to the head table. He had tawny hair and a ready smile. Crispin jumped to his feet and made the introductions.

"Lady Kallen, I would have you make your cousin's acquaintance. 'Tis Lord Harold."

Griffith cursed under his breath. He could have sworn Kallen heard him, but she didn't bat an eyelash. Her attention remained totally focused on the man before her.

Could she already be taken with Harold? Surely Kallen was not a fickle female?

He stared at the new arrival. Harold did cut a fine figure, though he seemed tired. Griffith knew that look. 'Twas one of suffering. At least the man had his son still—if not his wife.

As Harold made easy conversation, Griffith blamed himself for the mess he was in. His knowledge of Kallen's upcoming betrothal had haunted him, but he thought he could reach Crispin first and change his friend's mind before Crispin revealed his plans to Kallen.

Their meeting had not gone well. Crispin remained adamant that the contracts would soon be signed, and there would be no going back on his promise to his cousin. It would keep Kallen close to Mangeron and in the family, though an offshoot of the de Mangerons proper.

Crispin had raged at Griffith, wondering that Griffith had taken an interest in Kallen since he either constantly moped about or took untold risks with his life, depending upon his mood that day. His closest friend accused him of leading on a simple convent girl with his worldly charms, confusing her with affections she'd never been exposed to.

Griffith could not get in a word as Crispin roared at him, telling him he'd trusted Griffith like no other. Then Crispin stormed from the room, claiming he went to straighten things out because he would not allow it to go further. Griffith hadn't even had a chance to reveal Rodger's treachery and the fact that the Earl of Nowland had sent men to kill the de Mangeron escort party and abscond with Kallen.

Now everyone sat here, all smiles. Even Kallen. Griffith couldn't believe she could be happy in her present situation. It was impossible. She loved him. She had to. He refused to see her in another man's arms when they were meant to be together. He'd been miserable far too long. Kallen made him see what life still offered. He would not lose her to Harold de Mangeron.

Griffith sat mutely as Harold seated himself and continued to chat away with Kallen.

"I am so happy to make your acquaintance, my lady."

"I am happy to be here, Lord Hammond. Everyone's been so kind, especially Deva. I look forward to spending time with her and getting to know my grandmother, as well. I cannot wait to explore Mangeron, inside and out."

Griffith's gloom increased at their prater. The dancing monkey, the jugglers, even the bawdy musician could not raise his spirits.

Then Crispin called for the dancing to begin.

Deva stood and nudged Kallen. "You must dance, Kallen, especially since I cannot. Too many apple tarts and swollen ankles bind me to this chair."

Kallen pinkened. "But I do not know how to dance, Deva. I've never had such an opportunity," she protested.

"I am a good teacher, my lady," Harold interjected smoothly. "Allow me to partner with you."

He stood and took Kallen's hand and led her onto the floor since the trestle tables had been cleared and placed along the walls. Griffith seethed as he watched Harold touch Kallen.

Deva turned to him. "She is quite charming," she mused. "Such a lovely girl. I cannot imagine being raised under the auspices of Julesa. Poor Kallen. And poor Bevia."

His sister chattered on, but Griffith tuned her out. His eyes never left Kallen.

"Griffith? Did you hear me?"

He turned and stared at her. "What did you say?"

Deva laughed. "I asked if you would fetch me another tart." She patted his arm. "Never mind. I see your thoughts are elsewhere."

She glanced at her husband. "Crispin? Would you mind retrieving another sweet for me?"

Crispin lifted his wife's hand and pressed a kiss against her knuckles. "Anything for the mother of my child," and left on his errand of mercy.

Griffith continued to watch Kallen. After three dances in a row, she looked flushed.

"Kallen appears to be worn to the bone," Deva noted. "'Tis probably rest she needs after such a long journey."

He leaped to his feet. "I'll see to her."

He strode across the great hall. The next dance was about to start.

"Allow me to keep Lady Kallen occupied," Griffith said to Harold. "You can go dance attendance on our hosts, my lord. Poor Deva is a bit forlorn now. She feels left out."

Harold turned a sympathetic eye in Deva's direction. "I'll see to her right away. Deva is always so kind to me. My lady." He bowed to Kallen and moved away.

Griffith took his place beside Kallen. As they danced, he whispered in her ear, "Kallen de Mangeron, we belong together. You feel it. I know you do."

His words were met with a stony silence.

"What can I say to convince you?" Griffith tightened his grip on her wrist. "I'm sorry, my love. I did know of Crispin's plans to arrange a marriage, though I did not know to whom and when it would occur. But when I met you, I knew everything must change."

He frowned. "I had no idea Crispin would act so quickly and arrange for the contracts and speak to Harold while I was gone. I thought I had much more time. Though I've always been fond of Harold, I would never tarry if I'd known Crispin plotted like the Devil Himself."

Kallen stared blankly at him, increasing Griffith's frustration. "I tried to explain our feelings for one another to Crispin. He wouldn't listen."

Griffith swept Kallen in a circle. "He will listen, I swear, else..." His voice faded away, for he didn't want to make idle threats toward the man he loved as a brother.

Kallen spoke for the first time. "Else what?"

Griffith stared down at her. Kallen's eyes glittered. Her mouth was lush and trembling.

In a loud voice, he said, "I believe you need a bit of air, my lady. Allow me to escort you."

He left the hall, practically dragging Kallen along behind him. He reached the outer doors and pushed through them. The cold night air hit his face, but it did nothing to cool his passion.

Griffith shut the massive door behind them and jerked Kallen against him. He kissed her hard until they both were breathless. Each kiss demanded more as he branded her with heat. Kallen moaned softly and gripped his shoulders. He pushed her against the door, his body pressed next to hers, the sparks between them like none he'd experienced.

He slowed his assault, though the urgency was still present. He kissed her leisurely, lovingly, drinking in her sweetness. His lips trailed from her mouth to her throat, where he licked the throbbing pulse.

"Griffith," she cried weakly.

He searched her face. "You're mine, Kallen de Mangeron, and no other man's. What we share is rare. I will not lose you."

She began to speak, but he laid a fingertip against her lips. "Hush, sweetest. I love you."

She started in his arms, surprise crossing her lovely features.

"I'll say it again and again until you believe me. You're no light-o'-love, dearest. You are my always. I'll be damned if Harold claims you."

He pressed a soft kiss against her forehead. "Believe me, Kallen. I would go to the ends of the earth for you. I swear my life and my love and my protection. I may have misled you, but I was certain Crispin would agree to a match between us once I made my feelings known. I saw no reason to worry you, with everything you'd been through during our journey."

He paused a moment. Afraid to wait for what her next words might reveal, Griffith kissed her soundly again. He finally raised his head, only to see Kallen dazed.

"Study me, Kallen. I never asked you what my aura is. Can you not tell above all others how I feel about you?"

24

Without hesitation, Kallen began to describe his aura. "You are a mix like no other I've seen. Most people signal one color, or rather varying shades of a single color. Every now and then, I find a person with two dominant colors, traits that are of equal weight in their personalities. From the beginning you have been a rainbow of colors. I knew, in your own way, you were different as I was."

Griffith's fingers gently caressed her cheek. "Go on," he said. "Describe the colors."

"You have many. The blues about you have faded in recent days, which means your sadness has faded as well. The shades left show you are trustworthy and honest. There are streaks of brown, which shows you are dependable, while yellow ones reveal you are idealistic but tempered with great intellect. Purple usually dominates the rings surrounding you, and this is one of the strongest of all colors. It states you are confident and aggressive, athletic and a true leader."

Kallen paused. "But now about you I see a red like no other." She blushed. "'Twas present that first time you kissed me on Saint Crispin's Day."

Griffith's fingers brushed along her jaw. "And what is this red?"

"I can only guess 'tis the red of passion. Of desire. I see it burning brightly in the night. I feel your tremendous heat. It wishes to suck me in and—"

He cut off her words with a kiss that made her belly flutter and her knees go weak.

"Not only passion, my lady. 'Tis much more." Griffith cupped her face with his hand. "I want you, yes. But I need you even more. I love you, Kallen. You and no other."

She whispered, "I love you, too."

This time his kiss was tender and full of promise. Oh, sweet heavens, how she wanted this man. She couldn't fool her heart. There could be no other for her than Griffith Sommersby.

"How... we must... can this be explained to Crispin? He's so committed—"

"I shall approach Harold first. We have known each other for many years. He'll see reason. He must."

He kissed her again gently. "We have tarried far too long. I shall go in first since you are glowing pink, and your swollen lips reveal our love play. Stay outside a minute, or all in the great hall will guess what we've been at."

Griffith linked his hands with hers. "I shall find Harold and take him aside when I return. I won't spare another moment thinking of being apart."

He whispered in her ear again of his love before he departed. Kallen felt on fire despite the November night's cold air. She wrapped her arms about her, a smile growing.

"He loves me," she said to the night. "Griffith truly loves me."

She took a deep breath and let it out slowly. She

turned to go but saw a shadow of color ascending at a brisk pace from the bottom of the stairs. The aura she saw confused her.

"Oh, good eve, my lady, and welcome to Mangeron. 'Tis Maitland from the stables. I hope I didn't startle you. I must see Lord de Mangeron. The mare you rode is feeling poorly. Nothing I do satisfies her."

"Carrie ails? What's wrong with her?"

The groom shrugged. "I haven't a clue. Usually, I'm good with the horses, but this mare moans for no reason. The earl is an expert when it comes to horse-flesh. He'll want to see the filly himself. I must fetch him." He gave a short bow to excuse himself.

"Then go. He's in the great hall. I think I shall go down and see Carrie myself."

"She'll like that, that she would. Stables be that way. You can't miss them." Maitland nodded and entered the door.

Kallen started off at a brisk pace toward the stables. The noise from the great hall began to fade. She hoped she headed in the right direction. The night was very dark, and she wished she had a torch to better light the way.

She reached the stables, grateful for Maitland pointing her the correct way. All was quiet except for the occasional snort. Kallen called out as she entered.

"Carrie? Carrie? What stall are you in?" She caught a glimpse in her mind of the mare munching happily on hay. Her horse was neither ill nor distressed.

Suddenly, a chill enveloped Kallen that had nothing to do with the night. Something was terribly wrong.

Suddenly, a blinding pain exploded in her head.

Stars swirled in an array of colors before all faded to black.

———

A wave of nausea struck Kallen, disorienting her. What happened?

She became aware of the night sounds about her. An owl hooted. The cold breeze. The stillness of the forest. She lay on her side, cool dew against her face.

Voices!

She couldn't sit up yet, but she could listen. She opened her eyes a slit. Her vision blurred. Her head throbbed, but she made out two auras glowing nearby. She recognized the voice of one. Maitland? Had that been the groom's name?

But who belonged to the deeper voice she heard?

"I don't owe Lord Nowland anything else."

"Do as you're told, boy. We all do. How do you think Lord de Mangeron would react knowing you kidnapped his niece on her first day back?"

The Earl's people.

"If 'tis ransom he seeks, he'll get it, whether 'tis gold or stock. Lord de Mangeron will pay. Just leave me out of this. 'Twas hard enough sneaking her out the sally port. I could be at the feast now, dancing with my Celia."

A harsh laugh. "You'll dance to the earl's tune or hang. Now leave. Speak of this to no one."

Kallen knew no ransom was intended. It disheartened her one of Crispin's servants succumbed to the earl's bribes, especially one so tender in years. Maitland had appeared younger that she.

Escape. She must try. But it was hard to think clearly when her head ached so. Kallen pushed herself to a sitting position. Before she had a chance to try and stand, a man grabbed her hands and began to wind rope around her wrists. She gasped and started to struggle.

"Ah, you're awake, my lady." He rubbed her head, and she flinched. "'Tis a big knot you have. One which will be sore for a few days. You must feel very bad."

He moved away a moment and returned. Kallen's vision began to clear as she focused on him.

"Here. Take a sip of ale." He held her chin gently and gave her a drink. The brew was cold and tasted good, and she drank deeply.

"Have another. It will help you." The man patted her shoulder. "Relax now. I won't hurt you. Just sleep. 'Tis cold now, but you'll be warm soon enough."

His voice soothed her. Kallen began to feel drowsy. Too late she realized the drink must be drugged.

Griffith located Harold immediately and went to join him. He managed to run off the two men conversing with the earl with a calculated look.

Harold laughed as the men scrambled to the other side of the room. "You're looking well, Griffith."

He examined Harold carefully. "You could be better."

Harold shrugged. "I've learned when in public to be affable and charming, especially when visiting an important place such as Mangeron. At least I combed my hair before I came to visit tonight, my friend. 'Tis hard to take an interest in my appearance when I have no interest in anything else."

Griffith gripped Harold's shoulder. "You have a son, man. What better interest could there be?"

Harold struggled to speak. "Without my wife..." His voice trailed off, and a sob choked Harold. He turned his back on Griffith and the room.

Griffith lay his hand on Harold's shoulder again. "Harold, listen to me. She lives—through your child. Your son may be your wife made over. Enjoy what you have, not what you've lost."

He took a deep breath as Harold's gaze met his. "You know of my pain these past years, Harold. I lost not only Carina but the son she carried all those months. The son that would one day rule Sommersby."

Griffith wiped a falling tear from his cheek. "You have an opportunity that was taken from me. You still have your boy. You can tickle his toes and teach him to sit a horse. You can be there to watch his first steps and hear his first words. One day you will teach him to hunt and shoot. You can sing him to sleep as you rock him in your arms and watch every breath as he lies there peacefully, content to know his father cradles him."

He swallowed hard. "Do not let sadness overwhelm you, Harold. 'Twould be a crime to let your son's childhood pass by and not share in it, only to awaken one day and find him a grown man and a stranger to you. Please, my friend. Waste not what God has seen fit to bless you with."

An odd look came over Harold's face. "Your words make sense, Griffith." He stood taller. "No one has ever put it that way. 'Tis good advice I will take to heart."

"I have yet more to say." Griffith looked steadily into Harold's eyes. "I know of the wedding contracts drawn up by you and Crispin. Of his promise to give Kallen to you."

The surprise showed on Harold's face. "But how?" He expelled a long breath. "I suppose you would, as close as you and Crispin are. You always were. Yet even Deva does not know of them yet."

Harold smiled. "Kallen seems a sweet girl, very pleasant. She will surely nurture my son and still be close to Mangeron. 'Tis an arrangement that should please us all. I know we will suit. I came tonight not only to meet my future wife but sign the betrothal contracts."

His Kallen sweet and pleasant? Oh, she was so much more. Griffith thought of the hot kisses they'd shared, her body responding to his. He couldn't— wouldn't—allow her to marry Harold.

"You are a good man, Harold, but I must tell you that I have feelings for Kallen."

The nobleman studied him a long moment.

Griffith filled the silence between them. "I did not mean for this to happen. I have not even looked at an-other woman since Carina passed. Yet," he paused, a smile coming to his face, "there is something about Kallen that draws me from my blackest mood. Some-thing that makes me want to live again."

Harold sighed. "You love this woman?"

Griffith nodded. "That I do, my friend."

Harold slapped him on the back. "Well, good for you, Griffith. I know you have suffered. If Lady Kallen has brought the happiness I've seen in your step, so be it."

Harold leaned against the wall, crossing his arms. "Mother has run the household since... since my wife passed. She can continue to do so. I have no imme-diate need for a wife yet." He placed a hand on Griffith's shoulder. "I shall do as you said and get to know my son first. Besides, by the determined look on your face, you'd as soon kidnap Lady Kallen before a wedding could take place."

Both men laughed. The immense burden weighing Griffith down vanished.

"I shall tell Crispin tonight of my wishes to cancel the marriage contracts. Since they've yet to be signed, it should not be a problem." Harold grinned at him. "You have found a wife for your own. You may be asked to locate one for me in the near future, though."

He clasped his hand around Harold's. "I owe you, friend. I will never forget your generosity in stepping aside."

Harold smiled. "'Tis good to have one of your character in my debt, Griffith Sommersby." He excused himself, and Griffith saw he headed in Crispin's direction.

Griffith turned and searched the room for Kallen. He couldn't wait to tell her of Harold's decision.

25

Kallen was so tired. Her eyelids fluttered open and shut several times. She finally found the strength to force them to stay open.

Only a single candle burned in the otherwise darkened chamber. A man sat in a chair next to the bed, his face hidden in the shadows. Kallen could not see his aura. That meant only one thing.

"Awake, Kallen? What a pretty name."

He leaned closer, his leering face coming into the light. She saw the thick band of black encompassing his head, revealing the evil that ran down to his very soul.

She moved to push him away and realized her hands were tied together in front of her.

"Now, now. Let us sit and have a pleasant chat, Daughter. "I am Quentin, Earl of Nowland, but somehow I believe you must have figured out that bit of information."

Kallen eyed her enemy with suspicion. "Why do you want me? I cannot see the future."

Nowland smiled. "Why would you ask that? I didn't say you could. No, I need you for the auras, my dear."

Her heart sank. How could he know of them? "What mean you? I don't understand."

The earl stroked the black beard peppered with gray, which looked so at odds with his silvery blond hair. "Oh, but you are a clever girl. You have the looks and smarts of a Nowland." He crossed his arms and gave her a smug smile. "No, you have the power. I sense it in you. You, Kallen de Mangeron, are the answer to my every prayer."

He stood. "Edward rules now, weakling that he is, but soon I shall take his place. You'll see to that. You will tell me who will support me and who would betray me. You can shed light on where a man's loyalties lie."

Nowland bent and brushed a lock of hair from her face. "You shall be my own little princess. You may have whatever you wish—unless 'tis Edward's head you want. I shall keep that as my own souvenir of the man who thought he was king."

Disgust rose in Kallen. "Even if I could do what you ask, I would never help you." She struggled against the ties around her wrists.

"You will, my dear. Mother thought the same thing. Eventually, she aided me for years. I learned quite a bit from her. I know more how to help you harness your power." He began to pace. "My sister escaped. She lies in unconsecrated ground now for her efforts." He stopped at the end of the bed. "You never will. You're mine, Kallen. For all time."

She blurted out, "Griffith will stop you. My uncle will, too."

Nowland's smile was benign. "Oh, they'll search for you, I'm sure. They'll never find you, though."

"Griffith stopped the men you sent before while

we returned to Mangeron. Even Sir Rodger. None returned to you. You can send as many as you want, and he'll defeat them all."

His wicked grin showed yellowing teeth. "I need send none now, for I have my prize. 'Tis interesting, though, these impassioned feelings you reveal for Griffith Sommersby."

The nobleman thought a moment. "This may be just the way to control you. To take prisoner this knight who's so obviously captured your heart. Yes, 'tis exactly what I shall do." He nodded as he began to pace again, his hands clasped together behind his back. "Surely the mere threat of hurting Sommersby would have you do my bidding."

Nowland moved to her side and leaned low. He twirled a lock of her hair. Kallen cringed, drawing back into the pillows away from him. He twisted the lock tighter and yanked it. Tears came to her eyes.

He sat on the bed next to her, one hand still twisted in her hair, the other stroking her cheek. "I can see it now. You, being stubborn and uncooperative. Typical Nowland. Starving you wouldn't work. But a trip to my darkened dungeon, with its foul smells and sweating walls, and one look at your beloved stretched across the rack? A twist of one, maybe two turns. You'll do whatever I ask of you then." He released her hair and stood. "Thank you, my dear. You have given me the leverage I need." He rubbed his hands in glee as a child would.

Kallen was horrified. An image of Griffith suffering almost did her in. "You'll never take him."

Quentin chuckled. "I took you, didn't I? 'Tis always when you least expect it. Mayhap I will let the good knight worry a day or two. Then I'll send word by messenger of a secret meeting. Come alone or his beloved Kallen dies. He'll do it if he feels as you do. And while his heart is trapped, I'll trap his body and soul."

Kallen jumped from the bed and ran to the door. She tried to twist the knob, but the restraints prevented her from escaping. She started beating her bound fists against the massive door.

Behind her, Nowland cackled as an old woman. "What fun!" He clapped his hands in delight. "I never knew having a daughter could bring me so much joy."

He turned her from the door, his fingers tightening about her elbow. "You must be parched, my dear." He dragged her toward the bed and tossed her upon it. She watched as he poured water from a pitcher into a silver cup.

She gritted her teeth. "I'll not fall for that trick again." She twisted her head back and forth and began to scream.

The earl sighed. "Screams do no good, child. Nowland is my own little kingdom. I said we were not to be disturbed, so we won't be."

Kallen ceased moving and stared at him.

His eyes pierced hers and held them. "I could flay you as well as dine with you," he said, his voice low and threatening. "'Twould make no difference to my people. If I ask for no interruptions, then there are none."

Kallen's spirits sagged. He took the opportunity to hold her head. He forced her to drink.

"I need you good and docile for now. Gulp some down, my sweet, malleable child." After he'd made sure she swallowed several times, he stood, cup in hand. "Oh, we shall be friends, Daughter. Such good friends. I have so many plans, so many decisions. You'll be caught up in it all."

"I won't," she managed in a bare whisper.

He eyed her with fondness. "You'll grow to love the power, Kallen. 'Tis my blood running through you."

Nowland bent and kissed her forehead. Kallen's limbs were too heavy to fight him off.

"Sleep, my precious."

Her mind still fought the drug. She was frantic for Griffith. He would be worried about her. Even Crispin, despite their rough start, would be concerned. She was family and she knew, despite everything, he cared for her.

Kallen's struggles ceased, and she slipped into velvet darkness.

———

Griffith encircled the entire great hall twice in search of Kallen. He doubted he could have missed her, despite the large number of people still gathered. Some sang, some danced, and many still drank from the pitchers of wine. Yet Kallen was nowhere in sight.

Surely, she did not linger outside? Griffith left the hall, headed for the outside door.

"Griffith?"

He paused and turned. "Deva. What can I do for you?"

"Have you misplaced Kallen?" A smile twitched at his sister's lips.

"You know something," he accused her.

Deva shrugged. "I guessed. Kallen did not have to utter a word." She laid a hand on his arm. "I know you, my sweet brother. A different man rode through the gates of Mangeron from the one that left a fortnight ago. One look told me 'twas Kallen that wrought the miraculous change in you."

She laughed. "Oh, I shall not tell Crispin. Kallen swore me to secrecy, but I knew I must say something to you." She raised her eyebrows. "Particularly when you disappeared from the hall together for a good while."

Griffith stroked her shining hair. "Ah, little one, I have never been able to hide anything from you."

"Except Kallen. Where is she? The poor girl must be exhausted after such a cumbersome journey."

"That must be it," he exclaimed.

Deva frowned. "What mean you?"

"I came in first while Kallen..." Griffith struggled for the right words.

"Composed herself?" his sister suggested, a mischievous light twinkling in her eyes.

"Yes, 'tis as you say. But that was some minutes ago. I thought she would have returned by now, but 'twas a wearying day. Mayhap she slipped up to her room unnoticed."

"Then I shall check on her and retire myself. First, though, I must find—"

"Your husband?"

They both turned as Crispin strode toward them. He wrapped an arm about his wife's shoulder and stared at Griffith through narrowed eyes.

"Harold wishes to abandon the contracts," Crispin stated flatly. "I saw you speaking to him, Griff."

"Contracts? What contracts?" Deva asked.

"Marriage contracts for Kallen."

"Oh, then, 'tis been settled," Deva said, relief in her voice. "I don't think I could have kept..." Her voice faded. "Wait. You said 'tis Harold who... withdraws?"

She turned and glared at her husband. "Crispin de Mangeron, I demand to know what goes on."

Griffith shrank inwardly. Both Deva and his mother rarely used that tone of voice, but when they did, the world better watch out.

"'Tis nothing, dearest. I—"

"Do not think of me as your dearest at this moment, Crispin de Mangeron. You'll be lucky if I allow you to claim the child I carry as yours. You've been up to no good, Husband. Tell me what mess you have made and be quick about it."

Crispin, a leader both on and off the battlefield, wilted noticeably under his wife's stern glance. "'Tis no mess, Deva. None whatsoever." He glanced to Griffith for help.

Griffith smiled lazily at him. "Your bed, Crispin. Lie in it—or run like hell. Those are your only two choices." He turned to leave.

"Wait, Griff. You have to help me here."

Griffith shrugged. "All right." He paused a moment. "Crispin decided Kallen would make a good wife for Harold and bring him out of his despair. She could care for his babe and still remain close to Mangeron. He spoke of this idea to Harold and promised him Kallen while I fetched her from the convent."

Deva looked from her brother to her husband and back again. "And?"

"When I returned and told him I had fallen in love with Kallen, he refused my suit since he'd already given Harold his binding word."

"Without consulting me? Or Kallen?" Deva said evenly, her tone deadly.

Griffith grinned shamelessly. "That about sums it up. Of course, I explained the situation to Harold, and he graciously stepped aside, informing Crispin he no longer wished the match between himself and Kallen.

"I am now in Harold's debt forever and," Griffith smiled at Crispin, "I believe you'll spend the next thirty years or so making all this up to Deva. And Kallen, of course."

Crispin looked miserable. "I only did what I thought best for the both of them."

Deva slipped an arm through her husband's. "Thank the heavens Harold saw reason. How many times have we discussed things, Crispin? You know such an important decision cannot be made lightly. Men may see things rationally, but women see things with our hearts."

Deva paused. "'Tis why you wanted to speak with Kallen this afternoon alone?"

Crispin nodded.

"Poor girl. Her heart must have been breaking all through the feast due to the actions of her thoughtless uncle." She tugged on her husband's arm. "Come. Kallen has left the hall. I fear she's upstairs crying her eyes out now. You must go and apologize to her. She needs to know all is now right."

Griffith interrupted. "Actually, Kallen knew I was going to speak with Harold."

"Still, she needs an apology. Shall we all go up and tell her the good news?" Deva linked an arm through Griffith's, as well.

They went to Kallen's bedchamber, and Crispin knocked softly. She did not answer, so he pushed open the door.

The room was dark, empty.

"That's odd," Deva said. "I know she's not at the feast."

"Then if she's neither here nor there, where is she?" Crispin asked.

A sick feeling swept over Griffith. His hands balled into fists. Through gritted teeth he said, "The Earl of Nowland has her."

26

Quentin entered his solar, pleased that Barley had already placed food and drink on the table in front of the fire.

"Have a seat, Malcolm," Quentin instructed.

His old friend eyed the ladened table with a gleam. Quentin smiled. He'd asked this ally here tonight for a reason. "Here, let me pour you a cup of wine."

He did so and handed it to Malcolm, who drank as greedily as he did all tasks.

His guest sighed. "A sweet wine, a roaring fire, and an assortment of fruits and cheeses. Everything a man would need but for a woman with lush lips and lusher breasts."

Quentin shook his head in disagreement. "Nay, Malcolm. Essentials? Yes. But a need is something strong, something to burn with desire for." He raised his wine cup. "I need a throne. I need my kingdom before that idiot Edward runs England into the ground."

Malcolm sipped his wine. "You are correct, Quentin. Edward is an imbecile and an embarrassment to his father's blood. I'm sure old Edward is rolling in his grave at the mistakes the second Edward now makes."

Malcolm laughed. "But I'm sure you did not send for me to speak of the king's tomfoolery. Have you finalized plans for your rebellion?"

"They are formulating as we speak, Malcolm."

"Then have you begun to raise an army? Will the old guard, the barons whose opinions matter, support you with soldiers and their coffers? You know I support you."

Malcolm's eyes gleamed brightly. "Of course, I shall expect a nice reward for championing you, especially in these last few lean years, Quentin."

"You shall receive your due. You remained loyal while others fell away." Quentin drank deeply from his cup. "Plans are in motion, my friend. They must be kept secret for now. But it will soon be like the old days. And this time next year, we shall have our pick of palaces to dine at—you, myself, and... my daughter."

Malcolm's eyebrows raised an inch. "Your daughter? Your wife never saw a pregnancy through, Quentin. In all these years of friendship, I've never seen you claim a brat from another woman."

Quentin smiled. "Ah, she's more angel than brat." He stood. "Come. Let us go across the hall. Kallen is asleep."

His visitor rose and followed him into the chamber across the way. A single candle illuminated the room. The men moved to the bed. Kallen's chest rose and fell. Her bound hands remained beneath the coverlet he'd so thoughtfully placed over her earlier.

"Never was an angel more beautiful, Quentin. Why, the girl is stunning." Malcolm's tone was almost reverential. "Where have you kept her hidden all these years?" He turned to stare at her again. "Such pure beauty from one so evil." Malcolm chuckled softly.

"She's been safe in a convent. The good sisters have cared for her well. She only arrived today."

Malcolm licked his lips. "Then 'tis the start of a new royal family." He stared at Kallen as a wolf appraising a prized lamb. "I suppose you will wish her wed soon?"

"Are you interested? First, you want your choice of office, and now you wish to be my son-in-law?"

Malcolm shrugged. "One can never aim too high. A new monarchy. A new dynasty. And unless you marry and have a son, the throne would pass to her."

Quentin bent and brushed a stray lock from Kallen's face. He possessively stroked her cheek with the back of his hand, valuing the new treasure in his midst. "We'll see. All in good time, friend."

They returned to the solar and settled themselves before the fire again. Quentin took a small slice of cheese and bit into it.

"What do you hear of Piers Gaveston? You were not long ago at court. He's the one I'm worried about, for he's the true power behind this shaky throne."

Malcolm nodded. "I do have news of dear Piers. As a matter of fact—"

Suddenly, the door to the room swung open and crashed against the wall. Griffith Sommersby charged in, followed closely by Crispin de Mangeron.

"I demand to know where Kallen is!" demanded Sommersby.

Barley appeared in the doorway on the heels of Quentin's steward. The steward entered and bowed.

"My apologies, my lord. The gatekeeper allowed them in."

"Well, my neighbor is always welcomed at Nowland."

"But they refused to stay in the hall, my lord." The steward glared at the unexpected company. "I took the liberty of sending for a guard of ten. They should arrive any minute to escort these guests off the estate."

Quentin waved a hand. "'Tis quite all right. I'm sure an old visit between friends is all this is. You are excused. Have the guard dispersed. I have no need of them."

The steward looked as if he wished to override his lord's command, but he bowed to his master.

"As you wish, my lord." The steward and Barley left, but Quentin knew Barley would hover outside until summoned, just like a good lap dog.

He had studied Sommersby as the steward spoke. His daughter had picked a magnificent specimen. The boy who'd fostered under him now fulfilled all the promise of his youth. He was tall, broad of shoulder, and a keen intelligence shone in his flashing eyes. He took a step toward Quentin, but Crispin de Mangeron caught his arm.

"'Tis a pleasant evening, gentlemen," Quentin said. "You know Malcolm, of course. Or do you?"

Griffith threw off Crispin's hand. He strode the few steps that closed the gap between them and placed his hands on the armrests of Quentin's chair. Bending low, their noses practically touched.

"I want no introductions, absolutely nothing from you, Nowland, other than Kallen."

Quentin cocked his head. "Who is this Kallen? Is she the new village whore?"

Griffith grabbed his throat, but Crispin quickly jerked Sommersby away.

"Griff, even you must show proper courtesy. Nowland is of the king's blood."

"Oh, and I should have observed the niceties when he sent a gang of cutthroat soldiers to attack us and take Kallen while we journeyed toward Mangeron? One of his men, Rodger, did make off with her for a few hours. Kallen killed him before we could rescue her."

Sommersby's words shocked but pleased Quentin. Kallen was even more promising than he'd first thought.

"What proof have you this person is here?"

"Proof enough are the dead soldiers we left behind, their bodies littered in the wood. None returned to Nowland, did they, for we killed them all."

Quentin tried his best to appear baffled. "I sent no guard. I am making war on no one, least of all for this Kallen of whom you speak."

He struggled to hide his amusement. Even as a small lad, Griffith Sommersby was not easily rattled. It was interesting to see one with such a cool demeanor turned into a hothead. It did please him to know this knight was as passionate about his Kallen as she was for him.

"No more wasted time, Nowland," Griffith spat out. "Kallen is missing from Mangeron. You have her. I demand a search of the grounds. Every stall in your stables, every room in this castle, each tenant's cottage will I see. She is here somewhere, and I will find her."

Quentin expelled a loud breath. "You grow tiresome, boy. Very well. Conduct your search tomorrow.

'Tis terribly late. I'll not have my staff nor my people upset while they're at their sleep."

He gazed steadily at Griffith. "Return in the morning, and you may look where you wish for whomever this Kallen is."

Quentin turned to Crispin. "I hope you're merely humoring your brother-in-law, my lord, much as you do that wife of yours."

Crispin's eyes narrowed. "Leave Deva out of this. You aren't fit for her name to grace your lips."

Crispin caught Griffith's eye. "Come. Let us return to Mangeron as the earl requests. We shall bring a hundred men to camp outside the gates in the meantime. They shall help us search as dawn breaks on the morrow."

Griffith's mouth set in a hard line. "No. I shall remain here. I'll not leave these grounds unless Kallen accompanies me."

Crispin shook his head. "I would argue with you, but 'tis never done any good in the past." He looked at Quentin. "My lord, may Sir Griffith find shelter at Nowland this eve?"

Quentin rubbed his hands together. "But of course, my lord. He may stay as long as he wishes. I would hope all see me as an accommodating host."

Griffith glared at him, and Quentin did not repress his chuckle.

A knock on the door sounded, and Barley stepped into the room. "Beggin' your pardon, my lord. A messenger from Mangeron just arrived with a message from Lady de Mangeron. He says he must speak to no one but Lord de Mangeron here."

Quentin nodded. "Very well. Show him in."

27

Griffith watched the change come over Crispin as he broke the seal and quickly read the parchment's contents.

Crispin took Griffith's arm. "I must leave at once. Deva's labor has begun. The first babe was lost early. The healer told me this would be like a first babe. The childbirth can go on for hours. I must be by her side."

Griffith remembered Carina's labor. The bevy of women gathered, including his own mother, did not allow him into the bedchamber, much to his later regret. He'd paced for hours, cracking his knuckles until his joints ached. No food, no sleep—he could enjoy nothing while Carina suffered so. And she must have, for the screams became howls that wore on as the day did. Finally, they'd weakened as time passed.

They'd called him in at the end, as it became obvious to all her life ebbed away. The babe had been expelled dead, and Carina herself was minutes later.

Guilt still ate away at him, as if it were his fault. Then Deva lost her own babe just as she began to feel the faint flutters, and Griffith wondered if his family was cursed. He'd sworn never to love again nor get a woman with child.

All that had changed with Kallen. He couldn't imagine life without her. He wanted to see their babe in her arms, nursing at her breast. He wanted them to build a life together at Sommerset.

He must get Kallen back. He knew her father had taken her.

Crispin was almost out the door when Griffith wished him, "Godspeed. Deva will be in my thoughts."

His friend turned and smiled. "If you're lucky, we might name the child after you." He winked and was gone.

"How touching," Nowland proclaimed. "But may I see you to a room, Sir Griffith? Better yet, stay here a while and enjoy some of our fruit and cheese. The wine is especially good this eve."

Griffith wanted no company, least of all the Earl of Nowland's. Even as a boy, he learned what a brutal, immoral man Nowland was. Griffith's own father had been thrilled to have his son foster with the Nowland, since the earl was a king's son, though a bastard one. Lord Sommersby had no idea how regularly Lord Nowland beat his pages and belittled them with cruel words.

Griffith often thought part of why he became such a good soldier was to prove Quentin's taunts wrong.

"Thank you, but no, a room with privacy would suit me best. I have a wish for solitude."

His host stood. "Then I'll have my servant show you one close by. Barley," he called, and the servant immediately poked his head inside the solar. "Place Sir Griffith across the hall—"

"Not across the hall!" the servant cried.

"—and one door to the left."

"But what about—"

"I have the situation in hand, Barley, but I thank you for your concern."

The servant escorted Griffith to a bedchamber. Barley's nervous behavior troubled Griffith. The man's eyes also shifted about, and he wouldn't look Griffith in the face. What was he hiding? Could Kallen be nearby? He'd let the place settle into sleep and then begin his search.

A knock startled him. The Earl of Nowland pushed the door open, carrying a small tray. "Wine. Despite your hostile attitude, I have chosen to be gracious."

The fact his host brought the wine himself only roused more suspicions.

"Thank you for your kindness," he said evenly, and the nobleman retreated from the room.

Griffith lifted the cup and sniffed it. No unusual scent marked the brew. He couldn't help but think how the earl's sister had been rumored to be a witch. Had she passed some knowledge of potions on to her brother?

He left the wine untouched, biding his time before he began his hunt.

Blowing out the candle, he sat in the dark. Kallen's visage shone brightly in his mind. He remembered her throaty laugh. Her atrocious singing. The wonderful stories she told around the campfire. He loved her genuine concern for others, despite her poor treatment at the hands of the good Christian sisters, the supposed chosen of God.

Only Savina had given Kallen love. Griffith remembered how he'd dispatched a messenger back to the abbess to let her know of their safe arrival at Mangeron. Only hours later, Kallen was gone.

Griffith's insides twisted. He'd lost one love. He couldn't bear to lose another. His impatience to start got the better of him, and he decided to wait no longer. Kallen was valuable to Quentin, so he figured the earl would keep her close by. Barley had been extremely nervous when Quentin mentioned the room across from the solar. Griffith decided his search would begin there.

The corridor was deserted as he stepped from his bedchamber and closed the door behind him. Yet no guard was posted at any door, nor was the room next to him even locked. He doubted Kallen would be there, but he was determined to search everywhere. Griffith turned the handle quietly and slipped into the room.

A lone candle burned low, allowing him to see someone in the bed across the room. Griffith crept over and spied Kallen's silvery blond hair spread like silk across the pillows. His heart raced. She looked so peaceful. At least no harm had come to her.

He cupped her face and kissed her. "Wake up, Kallen," he whispered. She did not respond to his touch, much less his voice.

Griffith stroked her cheek. "I've come for you, love. Wake up." Still nothing, so he shook her.

Kallen was dead to the world. He saw a cup next to the bed and retrieved it. He could detect no smell, but he knew she had been drugged. He had to get her away from here.

But how?

She stirred, and Griffith slipped his arms around her and drew her to him.

"Kallen?" He stroked her hair, and she smiled. He decided to speak to her sternly. "Kallen. Wake up. Now."

She attempted to open her eyes and did for a moment.

"Griffith?" She smiled again and fell fast asleep. He lowered her to the pillows.

It was then he noticed her hands bound with leather ties. He swore softly and reached for his dagger. He cut through the ties and removed them. Even in the dim light, he could see her wrists rubbed raw from her struggles against the bonds. Anger flared within him at the perfect skin marred by the burns.

Suddenly, he was struck from behind. Pain exploded in his head. Griffith fought to remain conscious. He still had the dagger in his hand and turned, lashing out at his attacker. Someone grunted in pain, and then he struck Griffith's jaw hard. Griffith went down, his last thoughts of Kallen.

A voice insisted she awaken, but sleep felt so good. Kallen snuggled back down, dreaming of Griffith. He wore a hauberk of hunter green. His aura of purple glowed brightly about him. He stood beside a priest, waiting for her. Kallen knew she must reach him.

"Kallen," said a stern voice. "I want you to see your Griffith."

Griffith? Here?

Slowly, she opened her eyes. Lord Nowland hovered over her. The nightmare came back to her.

She shook her head. "No, you lie."

"Didn't I say when least expected? I knew you'd want him here with you. I am a man of my word, dearest daughter."

He yanked her from the bed, dragging her along

the deserted corridor and down steps and more steps. The cold stones burned her bare feet.

Then it began to be familiar, as Quentin had described to her earlier. The cold. The damp. The foul smells. A rat ran over her foot, and Kallen screamed.

"Don't be squeamish," he snapped and jerked her along roughly. They passed unoccupied cells and then came to a locked door. A guard rushed over to open it, and they entered something out of a nightmare.

Iron devices stood everywhere, ominous and foreboding. Kallen had no idea what any of these apparatuses did, but she caught the smell of fear and blood lingering in the air. She realized these unknown objects were used for torture. Her stomach swirled violently.

Nowland brought her before three guards, and she caught sight of Griffith. He'd been stripped to his waist. Bruises showed about his face and trunk. One eye was completely swollen shut.

"Kallen?" His voice was full of anguish and love. She saw he was tied to some kind of wheel. She threw off the last of the drug's effects and tore away from the earl. She ran to Griffith and fell on her knees next to him.

His hair was damp with sweat, and she could see his muscles straining because of his fixed position.

"See, 'tis as I promised you, Kallen. I keep promises to you, and you shall to me. We are quite a duo already."

She turned and flung herself at him, scratching his face, slapping at him, incapable of words. The guards jerked her away as Griffith hoarsely cried out at them to let her go.

Nowland sneered. "You're in no position to make demands, Sommersby. Behave yourself."

Griffith struggled to break free as the earl nodded to the guard next to him. The soldier turned the wheel a click, and a low groan escaped from Griffith's lips.

Oh, Sweet Jesu, what had she done? Kallen struggled to break away from the guards holding her.

"You, too, my pet. Behave. They'll release you only if you remain perfectly still. Do not go to him, or he'll suffer another turn of the crank."

Kallen went limp. The guards released her. Her eyes cut to Griffith as tears rolled down her cheeks.

She fell to her knees. "I'll do anything, I'll help you in any way, only stop this madness, I beg you."

Lord Nowland stared at her. "Loose him for now."

Kallen let out a muffled sob. Griffith groaned again. She couldn't look at him, knowing she was the cause of all his pain.

"Return him to his cell," the earl ordered.

Kallen watched the guards unbind Griffith. He fought back, but they struck him down and dragged him through the door. She remained rooted to her spot.

"You follow my directions well. That pleases me, Daughter."

"Free him," Kallen said quietly.

Quentin laughed. "I'm no fool. He stays. You'll do as I bid."

"Free him," she repeated. "I give my word, as a de Mangeron, that I will continue to do whatever you ask. For as long as you ask."

He studied her, an amused look upon his twitching lips. "For the rest of your life? That could be a long time, my sweet."

"I can live only if I know he does. If you continue to torture him and try to break him, I will kill myself."

She narrowed her eyes. "As your sister did." Kallen stared at the man whose blood ran through her. "I mean what I say. I would find the way. Do not doubt me, Father." She spit out the last word with contempt.

He nodded slowly. "I do believe you. You have the Nowland stubbornness and the de Mangeron sense of honor. What a lethal combination." He chuckled. "Bevia and I may have created a monster."

He circled her. "You would prostitute yourself to me."

She held her head high. "My love for Griffith is so great, I would sacrifice my life for his."

He stopped. Kallen knew he'd come to a decision. "Very well. I will see him released." He took her arm, but she shook it off.

"I ask but one favor. Let me tell him goodbye."

He nodded.

Kallen left the chamber of horrors and walked slowly until she came to his cell. She stopped and wrapped her fingers about the bars for support. He had been thrown upon a cot, which took up most of the narrow space. His one good eye saw her, though, and he struggled to his feet. She knew the agony he suffered from his aura.

Griffith staggered the few feet, falling twice, finally dragging himself to the bars. He pushed himself upright and clutched his fingers around hers. "Are you all right, my love?"

Kallen forced a brave smile. "I should ask that of you."

He leaned forward and pressed a kiss on her lips. Her heart ached. *I must make him forget me.* She couldn't risk his life any further.

She did not respond to his kiss. He pulled away. "What is wrong?" he asked hoarsely.

"Go home to Sommerset, Griffith. I have chosen to remain here. With my father."

He tightened his grip on her fingers. "Are you mad?"

Kallen struggled to keep from crying. "No," she whispered. "All my life, I have been powerless. I suffered abuse you can only dream of, especially at the hands of the nun, Savina. She was the cruelest one of all. My father has made me see what my destiny is. I can control my own future now with his help."

"*You* are my destiny." She heard the anguish in his voice—along with the first signs of doubt. "We belong together, Kallen. You know that."

Kallen knew she must lose him to save him. "No, Griffith, I need more than you can offer me. With my father, I can live as royalty and help him rule all of England. He's promised to teach me more about my gifts. He understands the auras like no other."

She met his gaze, seeing the desperation there.

"I love you, Kallen. You don't know what you're saying. He's pure evil. Just study his aura. Surely you see what a monster he truly is."

Kallen paused. She glanced over her shoulder at the earl, who'd come to stand behind her, his hand possessively resting on her shoulder. "He is what I am. I am of his blood. I cannot change that. Even if I could, I would not. It is my father who pleases me now. I wish you to be gone."

Griffith's hands fell from hers. She turned and walked away, her heart breaking in two. Griffith called out after her.

"Come back, Kallen. I don't believe you. Come back!"

She placed one foot in front of the other. Lord Nowland's hand remained steady on her shoulder as he led her away.

Keep moving, she told herself. Out of Griffith's life.

And into the darkness.

28

G riffith stumbled back and sat on the filthy cot. Kallen had rejected him.

For Nowland?

The world had gone mad. Numbness set in, gripping greater than any cold he'd ever experienced.

This was not the Kallen he knew. She may have walked away from him just now, but she was lying. When she'd first entered the earl's torture chamber, he hadn't imagined the feelings written so plainly on her face. She'd run to him, begging Nowland to stop.

She couldn't have changed so drastically in the space of mere minutes.

Then it hit him. In the blur of words she'd hurled at him, she had repudiated Savina. Savina, the only one who had ever shown Kallen an ounce of love. He understood the hidden message in her words and realized Quentin forced her. Kallen dismissed Griffith to save him.

Her life—for his.

He tried to take a deep breath, but his sore ribs ached. He caught himself and continued taking slow, shallow ones. Every muscle in his body burned from the strain of being placed upon that wheel. He knew the evil Nowland had only scratched the surface, toying with him as a cat might tease a captured mouse. Griffith couldn't imagine the pain of a man broken upon the wheel.

He heard muffled voices and caught the flickering shadows upon the wall moving his way.

His enemy had returned. Would the torture begin again, this time in earnest? Had the sacrifice Kallen made been all for naught?

The earl came and stood before Griffith's cell door, an apologetic smile dancing upon his thin lips.

"I am sorry if you did not enjoy my hospitality, Sommersby, though I must agree that you found what you sought. I'm afraid your little bird has flown your nest, though." The nobleman's gaze was malevolent. "She has made her choice. Me."

"Kallen would never choose you of her own free will," Griffith spat out.

Nowland smirked. "Oh, but she did, dear boy. Besides, I have decided to acknowledge Kallen as my true offspring. By law, I am her father. I have total control over her. Not her uncle. Not the de Mangeron family. Certainly, not you. None of you hold any rights whatsoever as far as she is concerned."

Nowland leaned against the bars, his voice barely above a whisper. "And my brother Edward, our king? He would never condone any attack to try and spirit my daughter away from me, would he?"

The earl leaned away, fussily smoothing his tunic. "Kallen is trapped behind these walls forever. *My* plaything... for as long as I wish."

A sinking feeling overwhelmed Griffith. This monster spoke the absolute truth. Women possessed no rights in English society. Crispin would no longer have any authority to intervene in the situation. Only a father or a husband would possess the power to decide Kallen's future.

Nowland cleared his throat. "I'm afraid you must return to Mangeron without your prize, but take heart. You will soon be an uncle yourself. Mayhap that will take your mind off this little interlude."

The noble bastard flashed a signal, and a guard stepped forward to unlock the cell door. The earl gestured for him to step out as the guard moved away.

"You're releasing me?" Griffith still suspected foul play.

Nowland expelled a long breath. "Unfortunately, yes. Although I would love to spend hours with you in my special room, Kallen wishes you leave. She may not want you any longer since I can offer her so much more, but she won't see you harmed." He chuckled. "I can keep my word as well as any de Mangeron. My daughter is precious to me, so I will acquiesce to her wishes."

The nobleman tapped his foot impatiently. "Come now. You're free to go. You shall be escorted to the stables for your horse, and you will leave my estate, never to return." He narrowed his eyes and studied Griffith a moment. "Unless you miss being here. You can be a part of it all again if you choose."

Griffith remained silent, squelching the torrent of curses he wished to hurl at this man.

"No? Well, I realize you're needed at home. I know that father of yours is so ill. I was very sorry to hear of his accident."

Griffith glared silently in return.

"You must excuse me then. My best to your sister and her husband." The earl quickly exited the dungeon, his false words of goodwill echoing in Griffith's head.

A guard threw his clothes at him. He hastily dressed, ignoring the pain, and the guard escorted him from the keep. Griffith saw no sign of Kallen. He reasoned it was the middle of the night, but his spirits sank nonetheless.

As he gingerly mounted Satan and galloped through the gates, every bounce caused a new ache. He hurried, though, eager to leave the property.

But a part of him remained behind. With Kallen.

─────────

Kallen returned to her room, totally devoid of emotion. She remained dry-eyed, numb to all that had just occurred. She had pushed Griffith away as hard as she could. Now, she could only pray Nowland would keep his word to her and free him.

And if so, what would Griffith do? Would he believe she'd cut all ties with him? Kallen lost herself in prayer, silently chanting the same phrases over and over, begging God to be merciful and protect Griffith. He must be kept far away from her father's evil.

A rap on her door startled her. She had no idea how much time had passed.

The earl entered with an air of confidence. "Your nobleman is gone, headed back to Mangeron. I hope you're pleased."

She deliberately let no emotion show on her face.

"You have no thoughts about returning there yourself, I hope?"

Kallen held her head high. "No. Why would you ask? I have thrown in my lot with you."

"You have been sheltered your entire life. I want you to understand that the law makes you mine. I acknowledge you as my offspring. That means as your father, I control your every action."

He gripped her arms tightly, his fingers digging into the soft flesh. She knew bruises would appear later, but she kept a bland expression on her face.

"We have a destiny, Kallen. Are you ready to follow me? To learn?"

She nodded, her eyes never leaving his face.

"Good." He patted her cheek. "I so wish you could have met your grandmother. She would have enjoyed knowing you existed."

"And talking of the auras? She saw them?"

Quentin released her. "Yes. She helped me so much. She was afraid of what she saw. It frightened her ever since she was a child. But I helped her to see 'twas a special talent." He began to pace about the room. "She loved me so, much as she did my father. He provided her with all that she needed. I doubt you realize it, but Edward was the greatest king England has seen."

His gaze was steady on her now. "I plan to follow in his footsteps. I may be a bastard son, but 'tis royal blood that runs through my veins. Yours, as well. We will topple this weakling half-brother of mine from his throne, Kallen. I shall rule in his stead, with you by my side."

Kallen wondered how much he would reveal to her. Already he admitted to treason, and she hoped she could eventually use this against him.

"How do you plan to accomplish this? I would think the younger Edward most powerful, with armies of men at his disposal. Surely he realizes you are a threat to him, Father? I'm surprised he hasn't tried to have you killed."

She decided to address him that way, hoping it

would placate him and lull him into thinking she had feelings for him.

He chuckled. "Edward is too stupid and too wrapped up in Piers Gaveston to realize his kingdom crumbles all about him. Besides, I have a few men who recognize England weakens because of such a spineless monarch."

"Who are these men that would risk being accused of treason?"

"We meet here tomorrow night. I sent word to them once I knew when you would arrive at Mangeron." He came close and took a lock of her hair between his fingers, rubbing it back and forth. "You shall attend this meeting, my pet. You will judge who's worthy to stand with me.

"Today, though, you shall meet a few of my underlings and get acquainted with your new home." He clasped his hands together. "I want you to enjoy a certain freedom, Kallen. I want Nowland to become home to you. I can trust you, can't I?"

Kallen placed her hands over his, willing herself not to shrink away in revulsion. She must gain his trust before she could sabotage his plans. Her efforts might cost her her life, but only emptiness and unhappiness stared back at her in a world without Griffith.

In a firm voice she replied, "Yes. I have made my choice, Father. I would be a part of all you plan."

29

Griffith waved to the gatekeeper as he entered Mangeron. He roused a sleeping stable boy to rub down Satan and hurried to the keep. Dawn would break within the hour. That meant Deva had been in labor close to nine hours or so, based upon the messenger's words of last night.

He struggled up the steps, disregarding his protesting muscles, and made his way to the solar. Griffith paused in the corridor outside. He would not invade so private a time but wait here until news came.

He'd only brooded about Kallen's situation for a few minutes when the door opened. A pretty servant with a bundle of bloody sheets in her arms stepped into the hallway. Griffith's heart froze in fear. His hands balled into fists.

"Oh, hello, my lord," the girl said saucily. "My, but haven't you been in a bit of a scrape."

Griffith relaxed a bit. The servant wouldn't be so cheery if Deva's life were in danger.

"Might I ask how things are proceeding with my sister?" he asked hesitantly.

At that moment, Deva's scream broke the quiet, unnerving him.

"Oh, my lady is sailing through. The healer said she's a natural, with wide hips and plenty of heart. The head was crowning just a moment ago. You'll be an uncle in a few minutes, my lord."

The girl turned and took her bundle, leaving him alone in the hall. He could hear muffled voices and then another long cry from Deva. Griffith put his hand upon the handle but chose not to turn it. Instead, he stepped back and leaned against the wall.

Laughter sounded within the solar, and a lusty wail from a babe rose above it. Griffith slid down the wall and plopped upon the floor. Relief flooded him as the door opened and shut several times, servants rushing in and out.

Crispin finally emerged, looking spent. Griffith rose and offered him a hand.

Crispin took it and eyed Griffith warily. "What happened at Nowland?" he asked.

He shook his head, not wanting to worry Crispin. "I'm a little worse for the wear, 'tis all. What news is there of Deva?"

A broad smile instantly appeared on his friend's face. "'Tis a healthy boy," Crispin announced. "He's all red and wrinkly and absolutely the most beautiful sight in my life, next to my precious wife."

"And Deva?" Griffith held his breath.

Crispin shook his head. "Said she hated me close to ten times in the last hour of labor. Said I'd never get even a kiss again unless I promised to be the one to go through the birthing pains next time around."

He grinned. "But that was before she saw the babe. When I left just now, he suckled at her breast

while she glowed. She told me I was the most wonderful man on earth to have given her such a son."

"Thank the Christ," Griffith whispered.

"Would you like to see them?" Crispin asked.

He hesitated. "If I could."

"Of course. She asked about you. She'll be delighted you're back." Crispin grew serious. "I assume
Kallen's not with you although you look like you
fought your way out of Nowland."

"Kallen is at Nowland."

"You saw her?"

Griffith nodded. "'Tis for later. I must see Deva
now."

Crispin led him into the solar. Griffith caught
sight of his sister and the child at once, propped up in
the center of the bed. Deva wore an expression of
contentment he'd never seen grace her face before. It
was the first time he saw his own mother in her.

He sat gently next to her on the bed so as not to
disturb the sleeping child. She took his hand,
frowning at him.

"I see you found trouble," she stated.

"Nothing I could not handle," he reassured her.
"No worries about me now, little sister. Tell me about
my glorious nephew."

Deva smiled. "'Tis a miracle, Griffith, that something so perfect should come out of me."

He ran a finger along the babe's smooth cheek.
"Perfect," he agreed.

Deva looked at her husband. "I suppose you told
Griffith that I guaranteed he would beat you black
and blue for me." She eyed her brother. "Though it
appears as if someone else has beaten you instead."

"'Tis nothing," Griffith said, hoping to ease her

mind. "Why did you need me to beat upon Crispin? I always try to accommodate your wishes."

She sighed. "'Twas probably around midnight when the pains started to become unbearable. I threatened Crispin with you. You always used to fight my battles, you know."

Crispin chuckled. "Told me she'd have you beat me to a bloody pulp, I recall." He smoothed his wife's hair. "She wasn't especially happy with me then."

"Well, I've forgiven Crispin, so you've no need to slay this particular dragon, Griffith."

"Not that you could have," Crispin teased.

The babe sneezed, and the gathered women began fussing over him.

"We shall take our leave now, my sweet," Crispin told Deva. He kissed her brow. "I shall be sure Griff's bruising is tended to."

The healer shooed them from the room, and the men retreated to an adjoining room, which Crispin used as a study to go over the estate's accounts. They both sat.

"Tell me all," Crispin said. "You say you saw Kallen. Please tell me Nowland hadn't abused her as he did you."

Griffith winced as he shifted in the chair. "She was drugged. I didn't have time to learn how he spirited her away from Mangeron, but you have to realize 'twas a spy from within who managed it, Crispin."

His friend nodded. "I know Nowland has spies throughout the kingdom, even here at Mangeron. Believe me, now that Deva has safely delivered, I shall conduct a thorough investigation into everyone. Whoever helped in removing Kallen from my safe-keeping will not go unpunished. But continue."

"Nowland took me by surprise while I tried to

rouse Kallen from her unnatural sleep. When I came to, I was in his dungeon, strapped to the wheel."

Crispin leaped to his feet. "My God, Griff, are you all right? How did you escape?"

Griffith motioned him to sit. "'Twas very uncomfortable but not as bad as it could have been. I believe it was more a test of Kallen."

"A test?"

"Yes. The earl brought her there to witness the proceedings. You know of our feelings for each other, Crispin, and somehow Nowland learned of them, as well. He used her love for me as a bargaining tool. Either she bent to his will, or he would break me on the wheel. It took only one turn for her to promise him what he wished."

Crispin shuddered. "'Twould be difficult for a hardened soldier to see such a sight, much less an innocent such as Kallen."

"The bastard got what he wanted. She agreed to do whatever he asked to keep me from suffering. She even convinced him to release me in exchange for doing his bidding."

Crispin threw his hands up. "What could he want with her? It makes no sense."

Griffith pushed his hands through his hair. "It does, my friend. He has a diabolical use for her."

He stood and paced the tiny room as he gathered his thoughts, cracking each knuckle twice over. Finally, he spoke.

"I want you to listen without interruption, Crispin."

His friend nodded, a frown upon his face.

"You remember how successful Nowland was when his mother was alive? His gambling's always been out of control, but after a time he won more often than he lost. Politically, he was favored, too. There was a reason for that."

Griffith took a deep breath. "The earl's mother helped him in an unusual way. She could see an aura of color about people."

"An aura? What do you mean?"

"A band of faint color. The colors reveal a man's personality. Show where his loyalties lie."

He saw the meaning of his words dawn on Crispin's face. "And Kallen has this same... talent?"

"Yes. 'Tis something she kept to herself since she's never known a soul who possessed this unusual gift."

Crispin gave him a long look. "But she shared this knowledge with you?"

Griffith nodded. "From the day we met, Kallen advised me not to trust Rodger. She wouldn't explain why, and I'd known Rodger for most of my life."

He stared into Crispin's eyes. "I ignored her warning, and it almost cost Kallen her life. Rodger turned out to be a spy for the earl. When Nowland's men attacked our party, Rodger spirited her away."

Griffith slammed his fist on to the desktop. "She knew, Crispin. *She knew.* Just by glancing at him, a total stranger, she had an idea of the kind of man he was. Do you know the guilt I suffered? I was supposed to protect her. Instead, I disregarded her words and allowed my enemy to kidnap her. I almost lost the woman I love because of it."

"And 'tis why Nowland wants her."

"Yes. He must have guessed she would have this power. I've heard rumors since the younger Edward succeeded his father that Nowland would like nothing better than to seize the throne from his half-brother. With Kallen, he might have a good chance of doing so."

Crispin stood. "Then we plan an attack upon Nowland immediately. I will—"

"We can't."

"Griff, you jest. Of course, we can. We cannot let Kallen spend another night under that monster's roof."

"We have no choice." Griffith collapsed into a chair.

Crispin shook his head. "'Tis not like you at all, Griff. I thought you said you loved Kallen. Then you must fight for her, man. You must—"

"The earl told me he now acknowledges Kallen as his daughter. *He is her father.* Legally, he is in charge of her fate. Don't you see? If we try to wage war on the king's half-brother, Edward would have us crushed. 'Twould be treason, Crispin. Your head and mine. Don't tell me you'd make Deva a widow and your newborn son an orphan. The de Mangerons would lose all their estates. Your family would become outcasts."

A wooden expression fell upon Crispin's face. "Then... we've lost her. He'll control her always."

The two men sat silently for some minutes before Crispin spoke.

"What if we warn Edward that there's a plot in the works to dethrone him? Then 'twould be Nowland and his supporters to suffer the king's wrath. Not us."

"Don't you think Kallen would be the first person her father would implicate?" Griffith responded. "Knowing his twisted mind, he would convince Edward that Kallen had bewitched him, and he only did her bidding. She would burn at the stake, Crispin."

His friend looked lost. "So, we do nothing? Simply allow Nowland to use her and hope he topples Edward? 'Twould be the only way Kallen could stay alive."

"Not if I can get to her soon."

"But Griff, even if you could smuggle her out from under Quentin's nose, you have no say over her."

Griffith grinned. "Not unless I'm her husband."

30

K allen studied the men gathering in the secluded room near the great hall. She sat in a chair off to the side, in the shadows. Her father greeted each man that came in by name. He expected her to remember each nobleman by name.

And by his aura.

He hadn't given her details of his planned coup, but she knew he would eventually. He liked to boast, and he would want to brag about each move he made. The information she shared with him would be crucial in his scheme to oust his half-brother from the throne.

That was her dilemma. Should she be truthful with him in whom he could trust and which men should be excluded? Or should she deliberately stack his group with the very men who might seek to betray him to the crown? She hadn't decided what to do yet. She leaned toward the truth. She thought he might test her some in the beginning. Because of that, total honesty would be necessary to convince him of her loyalty toward him. Only later would she have the knowledge it would take to destroy him.

He slipped over to her. "Many of these men have

done business with me over the years. They were used to my mother's presence and should not object to yours."

He took her hand in his. She noticed the dampness of his palm. Interesting that he was so nervous.

"Your hand is cold, my dear," he said as she stood.

"'Tis cold in here, Father, and I am far from the fire."

He frowned. "Does that affect your ability in any way?"

"No. I shall be fine where you have placed me."

Barley entered the room and hurried toward them.

"My lord, there's a new arrival." The look on the servant's face betrayed his worry.

Her father tightened his grip on her hand. "'Tis an uninvited visitor, Barley?" he asked quietly.

"'Tis... 'tis Sir Griffith," the servant sputtered.

Griffith? Here?

Her father remained outwardly cool. "Did he say why he is here?" he asked as his eyes scanned his assembled guests, who enjoyed a fine wine as they spoke to one another.

"He says he's reconsidered your offer."

The nobleman smiled in amusement. "Show him in."

As Barley scurried from the room, she withdrew her hand from her father's. "What offer? What have you done?" she hissed.

He shrugged nonchalantly. "As I had him escorted off the estate, I merely told him he was forbidden to return—unless he ever changed his mind and wanted to join my forces."

"And you believe he's changed? 'Tis but a trick of Griffith's to draw near to me." Kallen crossed her arms. "I don't want him here. I think he would betray us to the king. Get rid of him. I want nothing more to do with him."

She hoped her firm stance would force him to evaluate Griffith's presence at Nowland. Kallen quelled her rising panic. She did not want Griffith tangled in this rebel plot.

Her father cocked his head to one side. "So you say. I'll hear him out first. You will not speak to him or acknowledge his presence in any way. But if I think he might be valuable to me, he'll stay." He took her hand and linked it through his elbow. "Besides, if I doubt him, I'll simply return him to my chamber below stairs."

Kallen's heart beat rapidly as Barley brought in Griffith. Her heart ached at the bruises and swelling that marred his handsome face, all suffered in her behalf. Yet Griffith stood as tall as any man in the room. His aura shimmered with a confidence unlike any she'd ever seen present.

But wait. What was this? Kallen saw a thin band of color closely hugging his body. It was so close to him and so overwhelmed by the others that she had almost missed it. The hue was a shade she'd never seen surround a person before, a rich magenta. Kallen could not say what it meant.

Then she realized it could only mean Griffith was up to something. She wished she knew what he planned.

He came straight to them and bowed. "My lady. My lord." He fixed his attention upon her father. "I see I arrive at the right time. 'Tis a meeting I would most like to participate in," he said smoothly.

The earl chuckled. "Your timing is impeccable. Why are you here? Seek you Kallen of Nowland?"

Griffith focused on the nobleman alone. "Nay. I gave thought to what you said. I know England will be driven into the ground if Edward continues upon the present course. I'm not willing to lose my estates to an invading French force taking advantage of the poor leadership we now suffer. I seek to join you in whatever plans you make. I bring a goodly sum to support your cause and my leadership and men against the king's soldiers."

He stared hard at the older man. "You know my capabilities as a soldier, my lord, for you yourself trained me."

"Aye, indeed. But there's no love lost between us, is there, Sommersby?"

Griffith shrugged. "We have had many differences, but now we work toward a common cause. I know of Kallen's talents, and she can only help speed the way."

She swallowed. He spoke of her so impersonally, as if they'd never shared anything special together. His words, seeking to brush her aside, only confirmed to her that Griffith had some plan up his sleeve.

"Where does your brother-in-law stand?"

"We have parted ways over the matter, my lord. I am no longer a welcomed presence at Mangeron. Unless you give me a task and place to be, I shall return to Sommerset immediately following tonight's meeting."

"You still might have some convincing to do, but I shall welcome you at my table. For now." Quentin indicated the gathering behind Griffith. He turned and went to join the others without a backward glance.

"What does his aura say?" her father hissed.

"That he is indeed a leader among men. Confident. Intelligent. If he is telling the truth, he would be an asset to your campaign."

"If."

Kallen stroked his sleeve. "I can only share what I see and feel, Father. I'm not a mind reader. Hopefully, you can help me learn more about my abilities. Then," she said, "I may know whether or not Sir Griffith is honest in his intentions."

He stared out across the room. "Do you see anyone you like?"

Kallen indicated several men, stating both their names and the qualities she thought they possessed. Her father nodded in agreement with her words. She realized she'd passed his first test.

"Come, let me introduce you. I shall call for you in a moment." He stepped forward from the shadows. "Greetings to all," he called out.

"Greetings," echoed throughout the room in return.

"We gather tonight to plant the seeds that shall grow to fruition very soon. Every man in this room shall have a role in this endeavor, and every man shall be rewarded accordingly once I reign as monarch over all of England."

"Hear, hear!"

Goblets were raised, and several toasts were made. Quentin allowed this to go on for a short time before he cut off the well wishes.

"Before we take a seat, I would like to introduce those gathered to my daughter, Lady Kallen."

Kallen stepped forward on shaky legs and prayed that she would not falter. She held her head high and tried to project an air of confidence and indifference as she took Quentin's hand.

"Lady Kallen is very dear to me. She would like to

speak to each of you individually tonight to thank you for your participation." He beamed at her, and she returned a ghost of a smile in his direction.

———

Griffith's stomach turned as he watched the treacherous Nowland parade Kallen before the assembled group. He heard the murmurs of approval around him, as well. The nobleman on his left turned and said, "What a beauty. I would not mind dipping my wick into that flower."

He seethed at the man's words but merely nodded. "She is quite lovely," he murmured.

Nowland dismissed her, and Kallen returned to a seat away from the group. Griffith guessed she was there to watch each man as he spoke and report to her father what she discovered as they interacted together.

He remained quiet for much of the proceedings. His greatest shock was at how well-formed Nowland's plot was. He'd always known the man to be intelligent, but the depth of the plan surprised him. Quentin must have spent the last several years devising this rebellion. And with Kallen's help, he could see Edward toppled within the year.

"Sir Griffith," Quentin called out.

So much for his anonymity. He only knew a handful of those gathered, mostly by name and reputation. He'd hoped to keep it that way.

"Yes, my lord?"

"What say you of the king's guard in London?" the earl asked. "Though not a regular at court, you must have an opinion."

Griffith launched into an explanation of how they

might possibly foil the troops that protected the city of London. He knew he danced along a fine line. He'd anticipated that the earl would want some contribution from him, and he hoped he spoke with reasonable intelligence. At the same time, he did not want to journey into treasonous behavior. The entire time he spoke, he felt Kallen's eyes upon him, and he had to fight to concentrate on his words.

"Yes, that could be done," agreed Lord Westerbrook. "But what if...?" The nobleman added several ideas to those Griffith had espoused, elaborating as only a court regular could.

Others murmured their assent as Westerbrook spoke, and after a few minutes, Nowland returned to different matters. After several hours, he ended the session.

"Much was accomplished here tonight, my friends. We shall start the wheels in motion and meet here again in two fortnights. All should be in place at that time."

The earl pushed away from the table and stood, and those gathered did likewise.

"'Tis late, but there's food and drink in the great hall. My servants will vacate it tonight, and you shall all bed down there in the comfort of new rushes." He smiled, his hands held wide. "Please, let us adjourn there now."

The noblemen's chairs scraped loudly as they pushed from the table and began to file from the room in small clusters. Griffith passed Kallen but did not glance in her direction. He followed the mass of men down the corridor into the great hall, where the trestle tables were laid out. Though the hour grew late, the tables were burdened with enough food for a feast.

The wine flowed freely in the next hour. He noticed that Nowland called each man forward and let him speak with Kallen for a few moments. Gradually, all six-and-ten men had spoken directly with her.

Except for him.

Griffith drifted over to stand near the fire. Nowland joined him.

"What do you make of my plans, Sommersby? Are they solid?"

"More so than I would have imagined, my lord. You have taken even the smallest details into account. I am impressed by the group you have gathered and their commitment to your cause."

The fire's shadows played against the earl's face, making it hard for Griffith to read him.

"I see you've had all those present meet with Kallen for her approval," he continued.

"You are observant indeed."

"A good knight always knows what goes on about him."

Nowland nodded in agreement. "I shall meet with Kallen tonight for her impressions of each participant, while they are still fresh."

"You have thought of everything." Griffith stared out over the room. "If I am welcome to stay the night with the others, then I shall leave in the morning for home. I have been absent for nigh close to two months and have much to do."

"Then I bid you a good night."

Nowland left Griffith and went to Kallen, escorting her from the hall.

The waiting game had begun. If all went as expected, Kallen would be safely away from the earl's clutches by dawn.

31

Griffith grew impatient. The last guest finally stumbled onto his pallet after Lord Westerbrook had challenged several of the noblemen present to a drinking contest. Silence now filled the great hall. The only sound heard was the crackling of the fire and heavy snores from at least a dozen men.

He deliberately bedded down as far from the fire as possible. He wanted to remain in the shadows so he could more easily slip from the room unseen. He hoped to locate Kallen in the same bedchamber across from the solar. His plan depended upon speed. He had no time to search for her.

He studied the room through slitted eyes. A good half-hour had passed since the last man stirred. Griffith hoped their drunkenness would lead to a deep sleep and allow him to ease from anyone's notice.

Yet something nagged at him, a feeling that all still was not well. That's why his gaze roamed the great hall, watching for whatever was out of place.

There, in the doorway. A shadowy figure appeared. Griffith knew even from this distance the profile was Lord Nowland's. He checked up on his guests.

Their host moved stealthily among the slumbering men. Griffith closed his eyes and steadied his breathing, willing his chest to rise and fall as if in deep sleep. He sensed the earl paused next to him before he finally stepped in another direction.

After a sweep of the entire room, Nowland returned to the doorway. Griffith suspected the nobleman would post Barley or some other guard immediately outside to keep any guests from wandering freely about Nowland.

Griffith counted on that. If he weren't seen exiting the hall, Nowland would assume he was still within it.

He waited another few minutes and decided the time to act had come. Rolling silently to his feet, he remained crouched. He moved close to a tapestry that he'd avoided since the time he served in Nowland's household.

King Alfred's glories were portrayed in the scene. As a young page in the earl's care, Griffith had been fascinated with it. He imagined himself riding as noble a steed as Alfred did, leading men in battle against the Danes amidst glorious cheers. Crispin often led him away from it, hurrying him along to whatever duties the earl had assigned them.

Except for once. Long ago. At eight, he and Crispin were deemed old enough to be assigned to polish sugarloaf helms, cuirasses, and scabbards in the armory. Griffith had other ideas, however. He'd taken to following around Timothy, one of the older squires. Griffith promised Crispin he'd only be gone a few minutes, but he had to see what Timothy bragged about to Joseph, another of Nowland's squires.

Griffith found the two in the stables, whispering like fishwives. He hid behind several bales of hay while Timothy told Joseph of a secret passage he'd spied the earl using late one night. Timothy followed the nobleman and found a network of passages that ran behind the walls throughout the keep. The boys conspired to wait until late that night and explore them.

Then Nowland himself had interrupted the two squires' conversation, lashing out with both tongue and fists. Griffith quivered in terror as the earl beat the boys, Timothy in particular, for revealing his secrets. As the young men begged for mercy, Griffith lit out, running blindly until he reached the armory. He slipped inside, out of breath, finding Crispin hard at work. He dared not tell Crispin what happened for fear of how the earl would respond.

Crispin, despite his youth, calmed his friend and quickly put him to work, even giving Griffith half of what he'd already polished. Minutes later the man they fostered with appeared, roaring at the top of his lungs. Nowland demanded to know if either page had been anywhere near the stables, as he'd caught sight of one there minutes earlier. Crispin spoke for them both and showed Quentin how hard they had been working.

The earl left, disgruntled, and Griffith told Crispin he owed him a debt which he would someday repay. That fact was reinforced the next day even more so when both squires were sent home to their families in disgrace. Rumors abounded as to what mischief they'd been caught at.

Only Griffith knew it had been because of the boys' knowledge of the concealed passageways inside Nowland. He kept the information to himself, never sharing it with Crispin, lest they be found out and returned home, dishonored.

Only on the night they rode to Nowland in search of Kallen did Griffith finally tell Crispin of that long ago day and the fate Crispin had saved Griffith from —and the fact that he had explored the hidden hallways a few times during the years they remained at Nowland. He'd always been a bit of a risk taker, and the secret knowledge ate away at him until he satisfied his curiosity. He came close to being caught only once, and he lost his taste for the game after that.

So now, many years later, he entered the panel hidden behind Alfred's tapestry. He knew exactly how to reach the room Kallen stayed in. He also was aware of the tunnel under Nowland that would help them escape the estate. It was how he'd planned to free Kallen the night he finagled an overnight invitation, only to lose his opportunity.

Griffith realized this would be his best and only chance to reach Kallen. He moved his hand along the wall for guidance until he touched the table he searched for. His fingers were sure in the dark as he lit the candle that he knew would be there, just as a store had been years earlier.

Within two minutes, he arrived at his destination. It suddenly dawned on him that he'd prayed the entire way there for Kallen to be the girl he knew and for her to want to escape from her father's clutches.

Griffith eased the well-oiled panel aside and slipped into the darkened room, his candle dim in the large chamber. He spied Kallen, kneeling in prayer at the foot of the bed, her hands clasped tightly together, her eyes closed. Her lips moved silently.

He did not want to startle her. For all he knew, Quentin would have a guard posted outside her door with so many visitors inside the keep. Any noise might bring in a rush of men. Stealthily as any warrior would move, Griffith crossed the room and set the candle aside. He quickly grabbed hold of Kallen, one arm encircling her waist, drawing her tautly against him. His other hand closed over her mouth, preventing any screams.

She struggled briefly, her head lashing from side to side, and Griffith tried to calm her.

"Kallen, love," he whispered in her ear. "'Tis I, Griffith."

Her rigid body relaxed immediately, and a soft whimper sounded from her throat.

"No noise, sweetheart, else will be the rack for me."

He turned her in his arms. The look on her face would be etched in his mind for all time. This was the woman he loved, and her love for him shone like a beacon. Despite the danger of the situation, desire flickered in him.

Griffith lowered his mouth to hers in a hungry kiss, one so sweet, he wondered if this was as the forbidden fruit Adam and Eve had been tempted to consume. As Kallen's body melted into his, Griffith knew he would risk everything for the woman in his arms.

He lifted his lips from hers and told her, "We must flee this moment. I'll not have another chance to free you."

Kallen's eyes filled with tears. "But he'll only bring me back. He explained to me how he owns me, body and soul. Despite his evilness, despite my loathing for him, we have no choice, Griffith. He is my father, and I am his by law."

She pressed a quick kiss upon his mouth. "I shall bring him down, though. He already begins to trust me, even after so short a time. But you must not succumb to his plot for my sake. Flee while you can. Say you've changed your mind, that you want no part in his schemes."

Griffith brushed a tender kiss upon her brow. "Nay, my sweet. There is a way around the law. You'll not belong to him for much longer."

She stared at him blankly. "How? I cannot claim another as father."

He smiled down at her. "But I shall claim you as my wife. A husband's will takes legal precedence over a father's. What God joins together, no man may put asunder."

Kallen's eyes widened, and then she broke out in the most brilliant smile.

"Now hurry," Griffith whispered. "We have a ways to go, and a priest awaits us." He retrieved the candle before guiding her toward the hidden passageway.

"Stay close behind me. The way is narrow, but I know it well. Take hold of my hand. I promise I shan't let go. Simply trust me."

Kallen said, "I shall merely follow your aura, Griffith. 'Tis burning brightly now. That will allow you free use of your hands."

He maneuvered them cautiously through the concealed path. He didn't want any unusual bump in the night to stir an alarm. Kallen remained as his shadow, never faltering, until he led them to a ladder.

"You go first. I'll be right behind you. When you reach the top, knock twice."

Kallen did as she was told, tapping twice. Suddenly, the trap door opened, and she gulped a breath of the fresh, cold air, so different from that which had been in the musty tunnel. A hand reached for her and lifted her through. Griffith scrambled up after her.

She found herself staring into Crispin's eyes. He smiled broadly and hugged her tightly.

"Forgive me all, Kallen," he apologized. "I hope you will allow us to make a new start."

"Thank you, Uncle." She embraced him again and felt a burden lifted from her.

Griffith closed the trap door and covered it with dead leaves and a large rock. "Is he here?"

"Just in the woods, beyond the copse," Crispin replied. "Here, Kallen, I've brought a cloak of Deva's. She warned me the night air would be chilly. 'Tis just like a woman to think of such creature comforts."

"Then let us hurry," Griffith said. He took her hand, and Kallen felt herself rushed along before she could ask about Deva. She was glad for the soft wool cloak, for the November night air was quite chilly.

They reached the copse, and Kallen saw two men standing there. One was John, her favorite among the guard that had escorted her to Mangeron. The other was a priest. She'd met him at the feast when she'd arrived at Mangeron. Had it only been a few days ago?

"Good evening, Lady Kallen." His voice was low and musical. "I am Father Thomas. I hear you wish to be married?"

"More than anything, Father," she replied earnestly.

"And you love this man, Sir Griffith Sommersby of Sommerset?"

Kallen clasped her hands to her breast. "I do, Father."

"And you love this woman, my lord?"

Griffith wrapped an arm about Kallen's shoulder and brought her close. "She is my reason for being, Father. She has brought love into my life and God back into my heart."

A rush of strong emotion poured through Kallen at Griffith's words.

This was the finest man she'd ever met, one that she knew God sent to her for a purpose.

"Then let us begin. I understand time is of the essence. Lord de Mangeron and Sir John shall act as your witnesses."

And in a darkened wood in the middle of a cold November eve, Kallen pledged her love and her life to Griffith Sommersby.

The priest concluded the brief ceremony by allowing the couple to kiss. Despite their audience, Griffith kissed her at length till Crispin interrupted.

"Come on, Griff. 'Tis cold out here."

Griffith broke their kiss, and Kallen flushed with embarrassment at the eyes that stared at them.

"Don't worry, my lady," John assured her. "'Tis nice to see the two of you embrace as husband and wife."

"Thank you, John. 'Tis nice to have such a husband," she replied.

"John, fetch the horses," Crispin ordered, and the soldier hurried off. He turned to Griffith. "We will return to Mangeron. Shall you make your way to Sommerset? If you leave now and ride hard, you should reach it by dusk."

"We will head there soon enough. Something else must be accomplished first."

Kallen wondered what could possibly be more important than reaching her new home, but Crispin seemed to understand.

"My best to you both," her uncle said. He kissed Kallen on her cheek and shook hands with Griffith. "I hope our next visit will be in more pleasant circumstances."

John led Satan and Carrie into the clearing, and Griffith helped Kallen to mount.

"May Almighty God be with you," Father Thomas said as he made the Sign of the Cross. "God speed you on your way."

"Follow me," Griffith instructed Kallen and gave a wave to the trio of men. They took off at a gallop. Kallen focused all her attention on the road ahead since she'd never ridden at so fast a pace. Carrie assured Kallen she would be safe in her saddle, reassuring Kallen that their escape would be successful.

After a half-hour, Griffith slowed Satan to a steady clip.

"We'll ride at this rate for another two hours," he told her. "Then we have a stop we must make."

She nodded. They rode side by side in silence until Griffith eventually turned off on what seemed to be a little-used road. After another ten minutes, Kallen spotted an abode somewhat larger than a cottage.

Griffith signaled to her to follow him, and he rode around to its side. A small stable awaited them. Griffith dismounted and lifted her from the saddle.

"We are stopping here?" she asked. "I thought you wished to be as far away from Lord Nowland as possible."

He cupped her cheek. "We have a good head start. It will be another hour or more before he arises. Does he come to check on you immediately?"

"He did the first day. Yesterday, I went directly to mass in his chapel and then saw him afterward when I broke my fast."

"With all of his guests, he may look to their needs first. That shall buy us a little more time. I also think he'll first rush to Mangeron and demand to see us. By the time he discovers we are not there, we will be well on our way."

Kallen was baffled. "Then what are we doing here? I would think we would hurry to Sommerset and safety."

Griffith took her hands. "And we shall, love. But before we ride further, we must make this a legal and binding marriage."

"We are not already married?"

He laughed. "Yes, of course we are. But the first thing your father would try to do is annul the union." Griffith paused then looked at her steadily. "We must consummate this relationship, Kallen. Now, before Nowland would tear us apart."

32

Griffith watched the puzzled look gracing Kallen's face. In all her innocence, she did not understand what he asked.

He framed her face between his palms. "Sweetheart, consummate means to make perfect. To put the finishing touches upon something. In this case, 'tis the marriage act itself. When a man loves a woman completely. Do you know what I am saying?"

Kallen nodded, biting her lip. "Yes." She frowned. "I have seen both dogs and cats at their love play. Savina explained it to me."

Her face puckered as if she were about to cry. "If 'tis what we must do, then so be it."

Griffith drew her close, resting his chin atop her head. "Kallen, do you remember how you felt when we kissed? I know the same turbulent emotions ran through you as through me."

He stepped back and brushed a lock of hair from her cheek. "This will truly complete us. We will be as one, man and wife. How God intended us to be."

"All right," she said softly.

Griffith knew the next part would be a delicate matter, especially as skittish as Kallen now looked.

"There is but one problem. The first time we couple, you will experience some pain. 'Tis only natural, and will not occur ever again. I simply want to warn you so you will be prepared."

She frowned. "I thought so. The female dogs I saw whined and whimpered. They did not look very happy."

He hugged her tightly. "I think you are worrying overmuch, Wife. Let me rub down the horses and give them a bit of hay. They need the rest, as hard as we've pushed them this night." He indicated the house. "Why don't you go inside where 'tis warmer? As soon as I'm done here, I'll build us a fire."

"I can do that," she said. She appeared relieved to have a task to accomplish. "Is there any firewood that has been cut?"

"Yes, there is always some left in the grates. This is a hunting lodge long in the de Mangeron family. They shared it with my family over the years, especially since we knew the families would be united in marriage once Deva and Crispin were of age."

He accompanied her to the entrance. "Light the fire in the upstairs bedroom at the top of the stairs. 'Tis the nicest room in the lodge. I'll be up shortly."

Kallen hesitated a moment and then stepped inside. Griffith went to care for the horses and then drew water to wash in. After quizzing her about the earl's routine, he knew they had some time to spare. He hadn't wanted to rush things between them and was glad they had several hours' jump on the earl.

He entered the lodge and heard no noise from upstairs. He hoped Kallen had the fire started since the rooms were chilled. He realized she must have done many manual labors at the convent. Now he wanted nothing better than for her to become a lady of leisure. He found a jug of wine in the cupboard and retrieved two cups, hoping the wine would relax her nervousness.

Griffith climbed the stairs and knocked upon the door before she called out for him to enter. He did so and closed the door to better contain the heat. A cheery fire burned in the grate. Kallen sat perched in a chair next to it, warming her hands, but she jumped to her feet as he entered.

"I hope 'tis to your liking. I could add more wood if you wish."

Griffith heard the worry in her voice. He set down the items in his hands and crossed to her. He placed his hands upon her shoulders.

"I don't want you to be troubled, sweetheart. I know 'tis something you've never done before. I also wish we'd had a roomful of friends and family toasting our vows and a fine feast afterward to celebrate, but that will have to come later."

He kneaded her shoulders and neck, noticing how tense she was.

"I brought some wine. Would you like a glass to warm you?"

She nodded, and he went and poured some for them both. He brought the cup to her and as he placed it in her hand, he raised his own to her.

"To Kallen Sommersby, my wife. My life. May we live long and love well."

Griffith saw tears form in her gray eyes.

She lifted her cup to him. "To my husband, Griffith Sommersby, the best of all men. You are my hero, for you have saved me from impossible situations not once, but twice. I pledge my love and my loyalty to you."

They drank deeply, and Griffith savored the words his bride spoke.

When she finished, he took her cup and placed it along with his on a table. He wrapped his arms about her and held her close, relishing her very nearness. He could feel her heart beating rapidly, revealing how anxious she was. He sought to comfort her.

"Kallen, you know that I love you."

"Yes," she replied, her voice but a whisper.

"And I will always protect you."

"Yes."

"I've asked you before, and I shall again. Trust me, Kallen Sommersby. Trust me."

Kallen stared into Griffith's eyes of darkest blue. He was the most handsome man she'd ever seen, and she had given her heart to him long before this moment.

"I do have faith in you, Griffith. I always have."

"Then let me show you how much I love you."

His mouth came down on hers, his kiss gentle and sweet. The same thrill as before rushed through her, a feeling of excitement and anticipation. Kallen gripped his tunic front with both hands as the kiss deepened. Her heart began to pound faster and faster.

Griffith's tongue mated with her own in a dance that teased, that drew an immense heat between them within seconds. She became lost in his kiss, in his nearness. He was her entire world.

His hands ran up and down her spine, his fingers working their magic on her tense muscles. She began to cling to him now, a fire started within her. Griffith cupped her breasts, his thumbs slowly brushing across her nipples. A deep ache surged through her.

"I know not what I need, but I need more," she said breathlessly. "Help me, Griffith."

Her husband gazed at her lovingly. "We shall help each other, love." He swept her into his arms and carried her to the large bed, drawing the curtain aside.

"Remember. Trust me," he said as he laid her down gently. Griffith eased off her slippers and then removed his own boots before lying next to her.

His hands and mouth continued their exploration of her. Griffith slipped off her surcoat. Kallen was left in her kirtle. He stroked her breasts until they ached then bent his mouth to them. Nudging the kirtle downward, he used his tongue to tease first one nipple and then the other. Griffith pushed the kirtle over her hips and tossed it onto the floor. Then he slipped his hand against her, touching her intimately. Kallen tried to sit up, but he calmed her.

"Let me love you, sweetheart."

His hand cupped her and began to stroke her. Her breathing grew more rapid as a throbbing pulsated in her lower body. Griffith continued to kiss her mouth, her neck, her breasts, all while his hand brought her to a frenzy.

Kallen began to call his name over and over as he pushed a finger within her, then two, stroking her. Suddenly, a sweetness exploded inside her, and she rocked up and down.

"Yes, go with it, Kallen. That's my girl," he encouraged.

Kallen rode a wave of pure pleasure until she was dizzy and weak. Then Griffith doffed his tunic and quickly undressed. She'd never seen a man fully unclothed before, and she knew not all men could look as her husband. His shoulders were broader than she'd realized, and his chest strong with muscle. He hovered over her, his aura burning bright red, full of passion and love.

"You are as ready as I can make you, my sweet. Remember that it will only hurt this once. Every time after this when we make love, there'll be no worries."

Kallen tried to relax, not really knowing what to expect. Then Griffith began to ease into her. She felt him pushing and didn't know where he thought to go. One quick thrust later, she gasped aloud, clinging to him.

He held her close, his body still against hers. "Just get used to me a moment. Then we shall pleasure each other."

Already, the brief pain had subsided. Kallen knew Griffith was where his fingers had been. She began to experience the throbbing sensation again and without thinking, she pushed up toward him, eager to ride the wave of passion again.

"Yes," he whispered as he nuzzled her neck. "'Tis exactly right."

She reared up again and then again. Each time he met her. A wonderful tingling began with each movement.

"Keep it up," he encouraged her, nibbling on her earlobe, his breath warm in her ear.

Kallen began a new kind of dance with her husband, one that seemed a little awkward at first, but then they found a rhythm together. He kissed her deeply, his tongue imitating his body's actions. She found herself turning to liquid as the wave of pleasure rose again.

She clung to him then as the dance became harder and faster. She cried his name again and again as he buried himself within her. Then colors exploded around them, a rainbow of blues, greens, yellows, and oranges swirling in the air. Tears of happiness began to stream down her cheeks.

Then he shuddered and grew still. Griffith looked down at her, desire still flickering in his eyes.

"Are you all right?" he asked as he brushed the tears from her face.

Kallen sighed. "I fear all right is an inadequate term, Husband." She beamed at him. "I feel absolutely wonderful."

Griffith kissed her soundly. "Thank the heavens." He rolled over, taking her with him, until she hovered above him. She leaned in and kissed him.

"'Twas not nearly as painful as I imagined," she informed him. She laid her head upon his chest.

Griffith stroked her back. "I'm glad, love. I would never want to hurt you in any way."

They lay together, her hand upon his heart. Kallen felt when it finally began to slow. A smile curled about her lips. She had made her husband's heart race. He desired her. He loved her. It was the most thrilling feeling in the world.

"Kallen?"

"Mmm?"

"I would stay here with you for all eternity if we did not have a mad earl in hot pursuit."

She flew up. "Oh, my precious Lord Jesu. I had forgotten all about that monster."

Griffith smiled lazily at her. "Yes, 'tis what the love of a good man can do. Put out of his wife's mind all but the two of them."

Kallen dropped a kiss upon his chest. "Then I am blessed to have this great love in my life."

He sat up. "Come, we must dress. As much as I'd rather lock the door and make love to you another ten times, we must be on our way."

She stood, a little shaky on her feet. "I fear you have worn me out, my lord."

"Wait here a moment." He rushed from the room, flinging his tunic over his head as he went. He returned a minute later with a basin of water and a cloth.

"Come, let me cleanse you. As a virgin, you have spilled some of your blood for me."

Though embarrassed, Kallen let him minister to her, knowing he did so out of love. She steadied herself by wrapping an arm about his shoulder while he cared for her. Then he helped her to dress and did so himself.

"We shall return here someday, sweetheart, and I shall take my time, loving every inch of you. In fact, I plan to do that every night of our lives together." He kissed her tenderly, and Kallen knew in that moment just how much this man treasured her.

As he stepped away from her, Griffith's eyes grew large. His brow knitted in concentration as he looked away from her and back again. Then his gaze roamed from her head to her feet and back up again.

"Griffith, what is it?" she asked nervously.

His jaw opened and then closed, and he shook his head in wonder. Finally, he found his voice.

"Kallen, I don't know how to tell you this, but... I see... I see..." His voice trailed off, and a smile slowly spread across his lips.

"I see an aura about you, my love. Silver hovers in a close band to you, and the yellow of the sun glows about it."

Kallen wondered if this were a blessing or a curse.

33

Quentin buzzed about the great hall, observing the favored guests that would become the leaders in his new kingdom. A few attended morning mass, but most gathered here, breaking their fast.

His eyes fell upon Westerbrook, talking with Applegate in a secluded corner of the room. Kallen hadn't thought Applegate trustworthy after their brief conversation last night. Quentin intended for the pair to speak again before Applegate departed back to the north. He could take no chances at this point. Indecision about a man's loyalty could mean his head on Edward's choice of platters.

He scanned the hall but did not see her. He realized she must still be at mass. The convent life had bred the typical Papist rules and restrictions into her. He smiled to himself. It would be up to him to teach her a few wicked ways.

Several men began to stream into the room, heading to the trestle tables laid out for the morning meal. Quentin watched the door until the last person entered. Kallen did not appear. The first beads of sweat broke out upon his forehead.

Immediately, he signaled Barley over as he tried to quell the rising panic.

"Have you seen Lady Kallen this morning?" he hissed in the servant's ear.

"Nay, my lord. Have you need of her?"

Quentin turned his attention to those gathered in the room. He cursed under his breath. Griffith Sommersby was not present either. They must be together. Quentin could not afford for Kallen to be with child. His mother had revealed to him long ago that the auras disappeared when she'd carried her children within her. He wouldn't allow his plans to go by the wayside because of two amorous lovers.

"Find her, Barley. A quiet search is what I need. Locate Lady Kallen or Sir Griffith—both would be preferable—and bring them to the solar. I shall meet you there as soon as the last of the guests takes their leave."

Barley moved away from him, slithering back into the crowd. Quentin's heart began to pound uncomfortably. His palms started to sweat. He refused to fall apart in front of his fellow conspirators. That would be unacceptable. He needed to project confidence at all times.

"Quentin!"

He turned and saw Malcolm and Westerbrook approaching him. In the next few minutes they and many others leaving Nowland distracted him from his worries. He remained calm. He smiled. He even sounded witty to his own ears.

An hour later, Quentin approached the solar, dread spreading throughout his gut. He entered to find an anxious Barley pacing the large room, wringing his hands.

"No sign of them, my lord. 'Tis as if they vanished from the earth."

Quentin returned to the hall and opened the door to Kallen's chamber, searching for some clue. He crossed the room and stopped in front of the bed that had not even been slept in. At least they hadn't rutted like animals here, thank the heavens. But where could they be?

Quentin saw the pair together in his mind, their naked limbs entangled as they made love. A fresh fury poured from him. By the Christ, he would break Sommersby on the wheel. Quentin cursed himself for not realizing the nobleman had never wanted to be a part of his schemes. He had only wanted Kallen.

"Search the entire castle, Barley."

"I have, my lord. They are not present within these walls. Shall I send for a guard to look outside Nowland?"

"Leave me a moment. I must think." He sank onto the bed, rubbing his temples.

How could they leave and no one see them?

Suddenly, Quentin shuddered. "The tunnels," he whispered to himself. 'Twas the only way to escape from the castle sight unseen. Yet the couple could have no knowledge of such thoroughfares.

Unless Kallen was psychic? Did she find this bit of information deep within his mind? He hadn't thought about, much less used the tunnels in years, though Barley kept all the hinges in good working order. Quentin doubted Kallen would have been able to keep something of that nature from him.

Yet the hidden pathway would have been the only way Sommersby could get from the great hall to her chamber without being seen by the guards he'd posted in the corridors. And Quentin had never let the two of them have any contact last night. He'd made sure, watching Kallen like a hawk. He'd seen no sign from her that the pair had communicated in any way.

That meant that Sommersby was the one with prior knowledge of the escape route. But how? True, he'd grown up here. Still, it was the best kept secret Quentin possessed to this day, and he was a man of many secrets.

And then it dawned on him. The lads he'd expelled so long ago. 'Twas hard to remember even who they were or when it had happened. Had Sommersby been here at that time and overheard the boys' conversation? Had he known about the secret passageways for all these years?

Yes, it seemed just like him. He'd been a bright boy and one that would have possessed the nerve to explore such hidden corridors under his liege's very nose. His mother always told him she recognized from Griffith's aura that he was a natural leader, even as a youngster. Now he realized Sommersby would in all likelihood lead men against him.

In that moment, Quentin wanted Griffith Sommersby dead even more than he wanted Edward dead.

Kallen felt a bond with this man, but who was she? An innocent, inexperienced girl, dizzy with promises of love. What could she know? Her trust was badly misplaced. A few stolen kisses, and she'd lost her head to the handsome knight. Quentin decided he must keep her on a tight rein from now on.

He would summon a guard to ride to Mangeron. Certainly, they'd gone into hiding there. Yet he was a neighbor, a powerful earl. He would easily enter Mangeron's gates without a fight, what with the master busy with the mistress and a new babe. Then he would reclaim what was his, by law.

If he didn't, his dream of ruling England would be in tatters.

"Barley!" he roared.

The servant scurried into the room. "Yes, my lord?"

"I am going to fetch Lady Kallen back from Mangeron. Alert my guard. I shall take no more than twenty men with me."

The servant bowed and hurried from the room. Quentin went back to the solar and poured a generous glass of wine. He downed it in a single swallow. The pleasant warmth spread throughout his chest, filling him with confidence.

He smoothed his hair and took his time attaching his sword, mostly for show, but he wanted Crispin de Mangeron and Griffith Sommersby to know he meant business. Quentin strolled leisurely down to the inner bailey. His horse was already saddled, and his men awaited him with an expectant air.

"We ride to Mangeron," he said and then mounted his horse.

The party rode from the gates of Nowland in rows of two, Quentin at its head. He worked on breathing in and out, slowly, confidently. He would refuse another attack of nerves getting the best of him. He would keep his head. He would recover his daughter.

He *would* be king.

A quarter-hour later they arrived at Mangeron's gates. The gatekeeper called out a deferential greeting and allowed them inside. They rode through outer and inner baileys and arrived at the keep. No one stood to greet him.

Quentin frowned as he dismounted. He climbed

the steps, motioning his men to remain seated upon their horses.

At the top the door opened, and Crispin de Mangeron stepped out.

"I am surprised to see you here, my lord. We did not part upon the best of terms. I suppose you have come to congratulate us on the babe? 'Tis a healthy boy."

Quentin did not trust this nobleman. He sensed something afoot.

"You know why I am here. I will search the grounds if I must."

De Mangeron shook his head, his eyes narrowing. "I'll not have my place torn apart nor Deva disturbed."

Quentin grinned malevolently. "Then I shall be sure my men take special care. But we shall search Mangeron, my lord. With your permission, of course."

Crispin began to speak but must have thought better of it. He bowed his head in submission. Quentin was glad the pup understood he dealt with royalty. He would hunt for Kallen whether given permission or not.

Crispin lifted his head. "Be my guest. I shall return to my wife and son." He turned and stepped back inside the keep, the heavy door slamming behind him.

Quentin returned to his men and gave orders for the place to be explored. "Do not damage anything nor offend any person, but I want Lady Kallen and Sir Griffith brought to me. Unharmed."

The guard quickly broke off into factions and left on their search. Quentin remounted and began the waiting process. He'd rather have spent the time indoors in front of the fire, but hospitality had not been forthcoming.

Hours later, the men returned in pairs. Each reported no sightings. The head of his guard pulled Quentin aside.

"My lord, we have searched everywhere. Spoken to many servants. No one has seen either the Lady Kallen for many days nor Sir Griffith since he left for Nowland yesterday. They seem sincere."

"So be it." Quentin made his way once again up the steps and entered the keep without knocking. A young servant looked astonished to see him there.

"Take me to the solar. I must speak with Lord de Mangeron."

The boy hurried up the steps, Quentin following at a slower pace. He arrived at the solar's door, which he found open, the servant watching for him with round eyes.

Quentin stepped in to a picture of domesticity. Lady Deva sat in the large bed, a child nursing at her breast. Her husband drew the bed curtain and crossed the room toward him.

"May I offer you wine, my lord? Some cheese?"

"You may offer me my child. We have searched high and low, in every nook and cranny. Where are they? My daughter. And Sommersby."

"Where are Kallen and Griffith? Is that what you wanted? You never asked if they were here. You just barged in and demanded to search the estate."

Pressure rose in Quentin's chest as his heart hammered wildly. He needed to know their whereabouts now. Precious time had already been lost.

He glared at de Mangeron. "Do not play games with me, my lord."

Crispin smiled benignly. "Of course, I shall tell

you where they are. You had but to ask. They are gone to Sommerset."

"What?" Quentin cried. "How dare he take my child! He had no right."

"He had every right," Crispin said with utter calm. "They are husband and wife."

34

How could it be? *Griffith now saw auras?*

She'd never spoken with anyone possessing this gift. Kallen was shocked by his words.

"We came together, Kallen. As close as two people can be. I can't explain how it happened, but it did. I see them." He studied her again. "What do the colors mean? Silver, close to you, and yellow streaming from it?"

She felt herself blushing. "'Tis hard to interpret my own aura, for I have never seen it."

"Then at least tell me what the colors have meant in regard to others. Surely, you've seen them before?"

Kallen rose from the bed and stepped to the lone window. She stared out at the forest.

"Silver is rarely seen," she began. "I have seen it around Savina. It has grown in hue over the years. Two priests that once visited the convent shone with it, as well. The best I can guess is that it stands for a goodness and grace, a selflessness that few possess."

Griffith came and stood behind her. He wrapped his arms about her waist. "I can see that is you," he said softly, his lips caressing her ear. "And the yellow?"

She smiled. "That is easy. It reflects my happiness."

He pulled her even closer and brushed his lips along her nape. "Then mayhap I should work to bring out more yellow about you."

A tingle of pleasure ran through Kallen, and she shivered. He turned her in his arms and pressed a kiss upon her mouth. She opened to him, longing to taste him again. Griffith's tongue ran lightly along the inside edge of her mouth, teasing her.

Boldly, Kallen allowed her own tongue to dance with his. He groaned softly and tightened his grasp on her, his hands slipping to caress her bottom. The kiss grew more heated before Griffith broke away.

"You tempt me, sweetheart, but we must be on our way." He held her at arms' length. "Oh, how you do shimmer with color. I wonder if will last, this sight of mine."

"We must keep this to ourselves, Griffith. There are few that understand something of this nature."

"Of course." He kissed her soundly. "I'm just glad 'tis something I can share with you."

He released her and doused the fire. He wrapped Deva's cloak tightly about her then took her hand and led her out to the stables. Griffith saddled the horses and reached to help her mount.

His hands tightened about her waist. "Are you truly happy?"

Kallen whispered, "More than ever in my life."

He kissed her and placed her in the saddle. "I love you, Kallen Sommersby." He turned and glanced at the horses. "Do animals have no aura?"

She laughed. "From words of love to animals'

auras? No, I have never seen any animal project an aura."

She saw Griffith was now bathed in a golden yellow. Her own aura must reflect the same, and she smiled at the thought.

He returned her smile and took her hand. "Ride with me," he said. "I don't think I can go the remaining hours to Sommerset without touching you." She nodded, and Griffith removed her from the mare.

He tied Carrie to Satan and then set Kallen upon Satan's back. Griffith climbed up and secured her to him.

"This is the way to ride," he murmured in her ear.

Kallen snuggled against him. She understood at once that Satan was happy because his master was happy. She informed the stallion that she, too, was pleased with the situation.

Griffith set a steady pace, and they arrived at Sommersby about an hour past dusk. Kallen wished they could have approached the estate during the day, for it was too dark to see her new home clearly at this hour.

Still, friendly greetings abounded as they rode through the gates and into the bailey. She noticed at once how happy the people of Sommerset seemed at their young lord's return. It caused her to glow with pride.

"Come," Griffith urged her. "Let us go to the solar. I'm sure Mother is with Father. She often spends time with him after the evening meal, telling him about her day."

They passed the steward, who rushed to catch up with them.

"My Lord Griffith?" he called.

"Yes? Is something wrong?"

The plump man nodded. "'Tis your father, my lord. He has taken a turn for the worse. Lady Braea does not expect him to live through the night. I sent word to you at Mangeron just this morning."

Griffith frowned. "We must have missed the messenger along the road." He turned to Kallen and clutched her hand tightly. "Come, love. Let us hurry."

Kallen shook her head. "No, Griffith. I am but a stranger here. You need time alone with your father. I understand."

He took both her hands in his. "Understand that I need you now, my sweet. Please come with me."

They ascended the stairs together. She grew nervous, knowing she would meet Griffith's mother at any moment. She had wanted to make such a good impression upon his parents. Now she arrived with her hair mussed by the wind and the stains of travel upon her, stepping into a trying situation, one that she felt inadequate to help with.

They quietly entered the solar. The darkened room was large, with high ceilings and massive furniture. The only light burned from a large fireplace. A woman sat next to the bed, a band of turquoise burning brightly about her. She turned, and Kallen's eyes met hers.

Brows arched, the woman assessed her in the blink of an eye. Kallen could tell she'd been a great beauty in her own time, and she still was impressive. Her face was unlined, and her cheekbones high. Her jaw was strong. Kallen determined that she would not suffer fools gladly.

Lady Braea watched as Griffith crossed the room and kissed her, and her face lit up in a radiant smile.

"'Tis good to see you, my son." Her eyes flicked back to Kallen again. "And who is this visitor you bring?"

He held out his hand and she took it.

"'Tis Kallen de Mangeron, Mother. My bride." He gazed with love at her and squeezed her hand in reassurance. "A long story for sure, and one we'll share with you shortly."

The noblewoman's lips twitched in amusement. "You always were full of surprises, Griffith." She embraced Kallen. "I welcome you to Sommerset, child. I am Braea."

Griffith's mother glanced to the bed, and Kallen's eyes followed. A man lay there, emaciated and pale, his breathing shallow. He had a look of Griffith about him, but what concerned Kallen most was his aura.

Braea turned back to Kallen. "You seem exhausted, dear. 'Tis a long ride from Mangeron."

"You don't know the half of it, Mother," Griffith interjected. "Could you see to Kallen's comfort? A hot bath and some food and wine would be appreciated." Her husband smiled at her. "I'll be along shortly, love. I want to spend a few minutes with Father."

Braea took Kallen's arm and escorted her into the dimly lit corridor. "I'll see to the hot water and food for you both. Why don't you stay here, Kallen? Griffith needs your strength."

Kallen frowned at her new mother-in-law. "Griffith asked to be alone, my lady. I would honor his wishes in such a time of sorrow."

Braea laughed softly. "I am strong. My daughter Deva is, too. Griffith couldn't possibly be attracted to any other kind of woman. He needs your strength now. Return to him." With a gentle squeeze of Kallen's hand, Braea left her.

Kallen paused at the door before entering. She had admired Deva from the moment they'd met and now added Braea to that list. She entered the room again and crossed to where Griffith knelt beside the bed, his hands wrapped around his father's.

He looked up and smiled. "I see Mother is already ordering you about."

Kallen placed a hand on his shoulder. "She probably could see how much I wanted to be with you."

He placed a hand atop hers. "She is a remarkable woman. You'll grow to love her. Her aura was turquoise, was it not? I could see it clearly."

"Yes. She must be a very practical woman, very organized, and yet compassionate."

Griffith nodded. "That describes her well." He turned his attention back to the bed. "And Father? What do you see about him?"

She stared at the bed. It so reminded her of Bevia when her mother lingered between life and death.

"I see a murkiness about him, muted tones of green. They are shot through with red and orange flecks." Kallen bit her lip. "I'm sorry, Griffith. This signals his end is near."

"I see the same thing." He sighed. "He's been ill for some time. A horse kicked him in the head, and he's lain abed for several years, never able to communicate with us. But this is different."

"Yes."

He hesitated a moment. "What will death bring, Kallen?"

"As he dies, his aura will start to weaken. It will fade from view until almost the very end. Then just before death, it will expand. Bevia's was a beautiful pale blue shot with silver sparks. It hovered over her for only a moment, and then it dissolved until nothing surrounded her."

Her eyes returned to the bed. The aura encircling Griffith's father already became faint.

Then his eyes opened. He blinked several times, focusing on those gathered around him.

"Griffith?" he said weakly.

"Yes, Father, I am here."

The dying nobleman frowned slightly. "Who is this?" he rasped.

"This is my bride, Kallen de Mangeron. Both Deva and I have married from the same family."

"Give me your hand, child."

Kallen slipped her hands around the old man's. His eyes closed. A contented look appeared on his face.

"Care for him," he said, his voice but a whisper. "Love him. 'Tis a good man he is."

"Yes, my lord," she replied. "I already love him beyond measure."

"Tell Braea... she was... my... life." His eyes closed. The aura about him faded until there was no color present, then a brilliant gold shone, quickly melting away.

35

Quentin was speechless as he stared at Crispin de Mangeron, a smug look upon his face.

"How dare you!" he finally sputtered.

Crispin crossed his arms over his chest. "You never asked, my lord. You demanded to search Mangeron, and I acquiesced to your request." He flicked a speck from his tunic. "Your rights regarding my niece are terminated. I suggest you take your guard and return home before further humiliation comes your way."

"I'll have it annulled," declared Quentin. "She had not my permission to wed."

Crispin eyed him slyly. "Knowing Griff as well as I do, I'd say the union is consummated by now. Mayhap already a babe grows within Kallen. No, 'tis much too late for an annulment."

Quentin stormed off, his mind whirling. He had been so close to realizing the dreams of a lifetime. He refused to give up on them. He made an instant decision, to ride to Sommerset. First, he and his soldiers would return to Nowland, though. He would need every available man armed and ready to ride.

"Griffith Sommersby might have the rights by law now," he said aloud to himself. "But he shall have none from the grave."

He rushed back to his guard. He would be willing to give up his fantasy of exquisite torture of Sommersby, slowly bringing the man to within inches of death before he gave him hope that he might live after all. Time was of the essence now. Quentin must immediately eliminate the threat of Griffith Sommersby and return Kallen to his fold.

He wondered if she were already with child. If a boy, 'twould give her rights to Sommersby through the babe. Quentin visited the estate many years before. 'Twas beautiful beyond words, and he would love to have it within his grasp.

Still, if Edward fell, Quentin would have many properties from which to choose. He mustn't become wed to the idea of one plot of land as inheritance. He must set his new plans in motion. They would ride the rest of the day and reach Sommerset late at night, if he were not mistaken.

There he would contact his spy present within the castle.

———

Griffith took a deep breath, glad that Kallen recognized his need to be alone with his father for a few minutes. She'd gone in search of his mother, in order to break the news to her. He thought back to incidents from his childhood. He wished the custom of fostering children never existed, for he would have loved to grow up under his father's tutelage and encouragement.

"My son."

Braea entered the room. She came and embraced him. Griffith held her tightly, willing strength from himself into her. Though he loved his father deeply, he knew how close his parents had been. His mother must be devastated at her husband's death.

Braea moved away. "Kallen told me your father spoke at the end."

Griffith nodded. "He was the best of men."

She wiped a tear from her cheek. "Yes, he was. I am fortunate to have loved such a man." She studied him before she spoke. "I am glad he met Kallen before he passed. You have made a good choice in a wife, Griffith. I know these things."

She ran a hand lovingly through his hair, smoothing it as if he were once again a small boy. "I thought you would never choose to marry again after Carina's passing, but I see now that God wanted you to wait for Kallen."

"She was worth every minute I have suffered alone, Mother."

"I know." Braea smiled at him. "I will vacate the solar for you on the morrow. You are now head of Sommerset, with your wife."

"No," he protested. "I'll not have you thrown out in such a manner."

Braea placed her hands to his face. "No, my child. I know my place. I am fortunate, for I have done more than women usually have the privilege of accomplishing. Your father always treated me as his equal. Few men do so.

"We recognized each other's strength and formed a firm partnership over the years." She smiled. "And love eventually came."

She kissed his cheek. "I see you already have the

love. How did you meet? I knew nothing of this de Mangeron relative."

Griffith led her away from the bed to two chairs before the fire.

"Kallen was raised from birth in a convent where Renton's sister was abbess. She is Bevia's daughter, Mother."

Braea frowned. "But Bevia died years ago. Some accident, I recall."

"No. Renton told the world, even Alita and Crispin, the same lie. Bevia was taken by force and found with child."

"The Earl of Nowland," Braea whispered. "I thought Kallen's hair such an unusual color. 'Tis exactly as his is, and his mother before him."

Griffith nodded. "Yes. Renton abandoned Bevia and let the world think her dead. She gave birth to Kallen, and they remained at the convent."

"And all the while Kallen knew not of her family at Mangeron?"

"No. Only when the abbess and Renton left this life did the new Mother Superior contact Crispin. He did not want to leave Deva so close to the birth, though."

"So, he sent you to fetch her." Braea chuckled. "And you fell madly in love."

Griffith sensed the blush on his cheeks and thought to change the topic. "Deva is well. She delivered a healthy son before I left Mangeron."

Braea hugged him tightly. "Oh, what wonderful news! I shall write to her immediately and plan a visit." She patted his arm. "A grandson and a new bride. What news you bring, Griffith."

He grew solemn. "I'm afraid there's more news, and 'tis bad. The earl is still a threat to Kallen."

"But why? How would he even know of her existence?"

Griffith briefly explained how Nowland had taken Kallen by force from Mangeron and of his plans to overthrow his half-brother and seize the throne.

"This is serious indeed, my son. We must warn the king." Braea thought a moment. "Do you think the earl will seek Kallen here while he plans his rebellion?"

His jaw tightened. "I'm certain of it. 'Tis more than I should share now, but suffice it to say that Lord Nowland desperately wants Kallen returned to his custody."

Braea stood. "Then I shall prepare the defenses."

Griffith objected, but Braea stood firm. "You are tired. You must rest. Go to your wife. If you've chosen as well as I think you have, you will draw strength from one another." She embraced him again and departed.

He realized how tired he was as he went to his bedchamber. He found Kallen already there, her hair damp from her bath, trying on clothes a little too large for her. Griffith realized they must be cast-offs Deva had left behind.

Kallen's face lit up as she saw him. "Look at all these marvelous clothes, Griffith. Your mother is so thoughtful. She knew we arrived without any belongings, and she has provided so generously."

She locked her arms about his neck. "I quite like her," she added. "She is an unusual woman."

Griffith embraced his wife. It amazed him how right she felt in his arms.

"I am sorry about your father. I wish I could have known him." Kallen's palms slid down his chest. "At least you have your memories of him."

"Shh... no more words, my sweet. I need you. Make love with me."

Kallen's reply was to rise up on tiptoe and kiss him. A hunger for her gnawed at him. Griffith didn't know if it ever would be satisfied. He swept her into his arms and carried her to the bed, lifting her surcoat and kirtle from her and tossing them onto the floor.

He buried his face in her neck, the alluring scent of roses from her recent bath rising to greet him. Though tired only moments ago, his body began to hum with energy. He kissed his wife deeply. He didn't know which gave him more pleasure—the fact that she was now his—or the kiss itself.

Kallen responded to Griffith's kiss, her fingers stroking his chest, almost kneading him like a cat. She no longer experienced fear of the unknown. Their previous coupling had been something of wonder and passion. She was eager to try it anew.

She kissed him with every bit of love she held in her heart, holding him tightly, wishing it never would end. And as before, he pleasured her beyond imagination. His touch, his kiss, his closeness, all spoke to the love he had for her.

They finally lay spent in each other's arms, her head resting next to his heart. She sensed it beginning to slow, and his breathing became deep and easy.

Kallen could have burst at that moment, her love for Griffith was so great. She was the luckiest woman in England—nay, in all the world, for she had the heart of a wonderful man.

Worries began to creep in, though, as she knew the Earl of Nowland would come for her. She might lie safely in her new husband's arms for now, but was their love worth the risk? What would Quentin do?

Lay siege to the castle? Have King Edward intervene on his behalf?

Her anxiety kept her awake. Her heart and mind began to race violently the more she worried about what she would bring upon Sommerset and its inhabitants. Kallen began to tremble. Even her teeth began to chatter. She decided to slip from the bed before she disturbed Griffith's rest, but as she sat up, he pulled her back, wrapping her close to him.

"What ails you, love?" he asked quietly, his lazy smile causing her heart to skip a beat. He stroked her hair. The soothing motion caused her breathing to ease, and some of the tension left her body.

Griffith lifted his head from the pillow and stared into her eyes. "I think I would be happy to see your sunny smile, your beautiful aura, for a thousand years or more."

"You can still see my aura?" Kallen asked.

He nodded. "Yes. I see it, as I saw Mother's and Father's. Those close to me burn brightly. Others' bands are dim. I can see but a faint trace of them."

He rested his head next to hers, his finger lightly tracing along her face.

"You are worried about your father coming for you?"

"Yes," she whispered. "I have tried to pray about it. 'Tis one thing I am good at. The nuns saw to that. But I cannot find the right words, Griffith."

"God knows what is in your heart, Kallen."

"But if I ask God to keep him away, I should believe He has the power to do so. Yet the doubts creep in, even as we speak. What if God isn't listening to me anymore, Griffith? What if when I killed Sir Rodger, He decided to abandon me?"

She began to weep. "I no longer understand a God

that would bring you into my life, only to have Lord Nowland, an instrument of evil, tear us apart."

Griffith cupped her face with his hands. "God doesn't always act as we wish, Kallen. He answers prayers in His own way, in His own time."

She gazed at him. "You sound as if you truly believe what you say."

"Ah, but I do. God knew I needed time alone from Him to lick my wounds after Carina's death. I was miserable and thought He'd abandoned me, but He had other plans. He brought you to me, Kallen. I don't think He'll desert either of us.

"Now rest," Griffith told her. "'Tis been a long time since you slept."

She began to relax in his arms, hoping beyond belief that he was right. Just as she started to nod off, though, a light tap sounded at the door. She knew the moment of reckoning had arrived.

36

Griffith slipped from the bed and threw on a robe. He knew his mother would not let them be disturbed unless something very troubling had occurred. His words to Kallen rang shallow in his ears as he opened the door.

Braea stood there, fire flashing in her eyes. She motioned him to step out into the corridor. Griffith did so, shutting the door behind him.

"Lord Nowland is here," she said bluntly. "He waits in the inner bailey. He says he is alone. The watch guards can see no soldiers in any direction."

"That just means they are hidden from our view," he said grimly. "I assume he demands to see Kallen."

"Yes," Braea said.

"Then I shall speak with him. Kallen is in no condition to confront him. She had no sleep last night, and we rode hard most of the day. She is worn to the bone."

"Then dress hastily, Griffith. See him gone from here. I don't want him on Sommerset land."

Griffith turned and found Kallen stood in the doorway. He saw she was dressed in the surcoat she had worn on their journey to Sommerset.

"I know 'tis Lord Nowland. 'Twas inevitable he would come. He will expect to see me."

He gripped her by her elbows. "You're safe here. There's no need for you to see him. Ever."

Kallen's chin lifted. "I will see him."

"I forbid it," Griffith replied. "He has no power over you."

A defiant look came into her eyes. "And you have this power now?"

Braea placed a hand upon his arm. "My son, 'tis not a battle you'll win. Kallen must see him herself in person. He'll not be gone otherwise, I'll wager."

Griffith looked from one woman to the other. "Then we shall both go. We shall stand strong. Together."

He turned to Kallen. "You are right. Forgive me, dearest. I fear that Nowland is a trickster, not to be trusted. I simply wanted to protect you." He took her hands in his.

"You are my life, Kallen. Though 'tis but a short time since we've known one another, I know you are the other half I was missing. You've brought love into my life and faith back into my heart. I cannot lose you."

"I assure you, Griffith, you won't. I shall make him understand we are to be left in peace. If he is wise, he will give up this foolish attempt to unseat the king and try and keep his head."

Griffith quickly dressed and they left the solar, their fingers intertwined as firmly as their resolve.

Torches were lit in the courtyard. The Earl of Nowland sat atop his horse, no guard accompanying him. Griffith knew the wily man must have an army hidden just beyond their sights.

He eyed his enemy warily. An air of confidence

enveloped the earl. Instinctively, the pit of Griffith's stomach tightened. Why would Nowland be so calm? He'd lost every advantage, yet he appeared as if he were truly England's king, so great was his poise.

"Greetings, Daughter," Nowland called as he dismounted. He placed a hand on Kallen's arm and bent to kiss her cheek, but she averted her face.

Griffith's grip tightened on her hand. Kallen glanced at him, and he smiled encouragingly at her.

"What? No welcome for your loving father?"

Her low voice carried in the still of the night. "I am a child of rape. I have no father. You betrayed my mother in the worse sense. Robbed her of her innocence. Her own father ostracized her because of your actions. He let her family believe she was dead, so deep was his shame. I want nothing more to do with you, my lord. Leave us in peace." She took another breath and added, "And for your own sake, put aside your foolish schemes. Be happy with Nowland. 'Tis more than most men have."

He gazed at her intently. "Would you shame your own family, Kallen? The de Mangerons? And now the Sommersbys? Besmirch their good names until they are reviled by all in the kingdom?"

Griffith saw the confusion on Kallen's face. His stomach twisted seeing the earl's evil smile.

"What do you mean?" she asked, her voice faltering.

Nowland sighed. "If you do not return with me this very hour, Kallen, I will ruin both of your new families."

He waved a hand in front of him. "How, you ask?" His eyes narrowed. "I will let the Church know what you hide from the world. That you are a witch, Kallen Sommersby. That you see what others cannot. That you know the future, even twist it for your own benefit."

As he spoke, Kallen went cold inside. For years, she'd prayed for a family above all else. She'd begged God to allow her to leave the confines of the convent. Now the dreams she'd been granted would be cruelly ripped from her grasp.

"No!" Griffith interjected. "You cannot. You know of the goodness that lies within her. Kallen is pure and innocent. These are nothing but lies."

Nowland smiled. "What you see as lies, my lord, others will proclaim as the truth. She will burn at the stake, at the very least. More than likely, they will torture her, seeking a confession to cleanse her soul. Before she burns."

A deep shudder ran through Kallen. She thought back to this man's chamber of horror and Griffith straining against the pain as he was spread on the rack.

Her husband's arm went about her. Still, her shivering continued.

"And Kallen's death is only the beginning, Sir Griffith. By the time I have finished spreading my rumors, the de Mangeron and Sommersby names will be thoroughly ruined. You know of Edward's horror of witches. You'll lose your lands. Your wealth. Your titles. And quite possibly, all the women in your families will also be executed for witchcraft."

Nowland chuckled. "Association with a witch will certainly be taken seriously. The Church and good King Edward will want this threat wiped from England."

Kallen felt faint. As she stared at the evil streaks surrounding the earl, she knew he would deliver on his promises. How could she jeopardize those she had grown to love in so short a time? Images of Alita, Crispin, and Deva with a babe in her arms swarmed her thoughts.

And Griffith—her love, her life—how could she put him and his loved ones in harm's way?

In the end, her father would win, no matter what Kallen decided. She could not—would not—be the cause of so much suffering.

She swallowed and straightened her shoulders. Her voice was calm and belied the fear and frustration racing through her.

"If I go with you now, will you hold your tongue and allow my family peace?"

"No!" Griffith's hoarse cry did not surprise Kallen. She knew he would be hard to convince.

Griffith spun her around and shook her violently. "Are you mad?" She saw the fury in his eyes.

"You are mad to think to keep me," she said quietly. I'll not let you sacrifice both our families and their holdings for me." Kallen stroked his cheek. "He has the power to do what he says. You know 'tis the truth. If you love me, Griffith, you must let me go."

"No," he whispered. "The light will go from my world." He embraced her. His lips brushed her ear. "I cannot."

Kallen looked up at him. "You must. Please. I already have Sir Rodger's death staining my soul. I refuse to allow innocent people to suffer because of me."

She pressed her lips to his, all the longing and love she felt passing from her to him. Then Kallen broke the kiss and turned away.

Nowland smiled benignly. "That's my girl." He offered his hand and Kallen took it, moving away from Griffith's warmth. Her father put his hands on her shoulders. "You have made the right decision, Daughter. Your loved ones will be safe. Come, let us return to Nowland, where you belong."

He placed her atop his horse and mounted behind her. Kallen made the mistake of meeting Griffith's stunned eyes.

"Goodbye, my love," she said softly as the man she was tied to by blood turned his horse and spurred it on. Hot tears quickly followed as they rode through the gates.

Kallen knew enough this time not to look back.

37

Griffith felt as if Quentin might as well have ripped open his gut. 'Twould be less painful and end his suffering more quickly. How could he have let Kallen ride off with that monster?

More importantly, how could he get her back?

Griffith knew he'd led a magical life before Carina died. Everything came easily to him, whether using his skills as a warrior or in his relationships with people. With his wife's death and the loss of his son devastating him, though, he'd wandered through life, empty, with nothing to give.

Until now. Kallen brought back his love of life. For his land, his people.

And her.

Was God some vile puppet master, pulling strings as he watched the emotional turmoil unwind? Or had God granted him gifts enough to meet Nowland's challenge head on? The decision he now made would affect the rest of his life.

He could not give Kallen up as she asked. She had almost withered away within the prison walls of the convent. He would not see her stranded in a prison of no escape.

He would fight for his beloved. In doing so, he would risk everything—his good name, that of his family, even that of the de Mangerons. They could lose their lands, their wealth, their position in society.

Even their very lives.

He must find a way to get Kallen and protect both families. Griffith realized he would have Crispin's unequivocal support and that of his mother and sister, too. He must ride after Kallen and permanently eliminate the threat her father posed.

But should he warn King Edward of Quentin's plot? That would also risk the lives of the men in that room. Some faces present at the secret meeting at Nowland surprised him. Many were the older barons whose loyalty to the first Edward had been unwavering. Dare he implicate any of them?

Or could he simply expose Nowland's role in the rebellion and protect the others?

Turmoil raged within him as he stood in the inner bailey. Griffith needed to organize his thoughts, and he could think of no better place than up on the wall-walk. He quickly made his way to the outer bailey and up the ladder. As he reached the top, dawn broke over Sommerset. He took in the rolling pastures and the calm lake. The beauty of the land took his breath away.

Yet Griffith knew in his heart he would risk this land—and so much more—to be reunited with his wife. Many might scoff at such a reckless venture, all for one woman, but he had no choice.

Kallen completed him. He would be useless without the woman he loved by his side.

His unwavering certainty allowed a calm to descend over him. Now he must think clearly and more rapidly than ever before. Nowland already had the jump on Griffith and Kallen in hand.

How could he extract her from such an impossible situation?

His eyes skimmed the horizon and returned, catching sight of a rider. Others followed half a league behind him. Griffith made out the insignia and realized 'twas Lord Applegate headed his way.

He hurried along to the watchtower. The soldier on duty was alert and identified Applegate's colors to Griffith as he approached.

"Allow them inside the gates."

"Yes, my lord."

Griffith scrambled down as the gates swung open and the party of riders entered. He spotted Lord Applegate in the center of the guard, as assured here as he had been when the conspirators met at Nowland.

"I see you are an early riser, Sir Griffith." Applegate swung from his horse and stared at him. "God's teeth, man, but you look like hell."

He shrugged. "Sleep has not been a priority."

Applegate placed a hand on Griffith's shoulder. "We must talk. 'Tis a matter of urgent importance."

"Let us go into the great—"

"There's no time," Applegate interjected. "I would speak to you alone. Now." He noticed the Sommerset soldiers who had gathered around them.

Griffith nodded and led him away from the crowd.

"Do you stand with Nowland or against him?" Applegate asked when they had privacy.

He had not been prepared for so direct a question, yet his speedy answer came from the heart.

"I am against all the earl stands for. He took my wife Kallen not a half-hour before your arrival, my lord. He threatened to name Kallen a witch and black-mail my family and the de Mangerons unless she departed with him."

Griffith closed his eyes and shook his head. "I acquiesced to Kallen's wishes and let her go with him against my better judgment."

"She's the daughter Nowland paraded about?"

He opened his eyes. "Yes. The earl never knew of her existence. He raped Bevia de Mangeron years ago. Kallen is the result of that encounter. Nowland only recently learned of her existence."

Applegate nodded. "So, he plays a political game with you?"

Griffith's fists clenched in anger. "You could say that. But despite his threats, I must reclaim Kallen. He will destroy her otherwise."

Applegate studied him. "And we will not rest until Nowland is destroyed."

Griffith's quick intake of breath revealed his surprise.

"The barons used the earl as a way to meet. If the rebellion were discovered, Nowland would have suffered the blame. We do seek to unite against Edward, though. In fact, we have drawn up a group of ordinances. We are readying to ride united and force the king to sign them."

Lord Applegate cleared his throat. "And we wish the Earl of Cornwall removed, as well. He has ruled England through Edward far too long. The barons have known all along what must be done ever since Edward ascended the throne three years ago. Nowland merely gave us the way to meet and hatch our own plans in privacy."

"Then you don't intend to overthrow the king?" he asked.

Applegate chuckled. "Edward may be the worse king England has seen, but his half-brother would be far, far worse."

Relief flooded Griffith. "I speak for my entire family as Lord Sommersby, as my father has recently passed. When do we ride?"

Applegate eyed him with approval. "We gather now with our list of ordinances."

"What might those be, my lord?"

"That the king must not leave the realm without the knowledge of the barons. That he must not appoint a keeper of the realm, as we fear Piers Gaveston, as the Earl of Cornwall, may become. That Parliament be required to meet at least once a year and have greater control of his finances. Also, five lords would be assigned to hear complaints against the king's ministers. There are others, but I haven't the time to continue. I have one thing left to ask. Are you with us, Lord Sommersby?"

"Your goals are ones good for England," Griffith answered immediately. "I shall support this endeavor."

Applegate smiled. "I knew you would. Of course, Edward will be no problem, spineless idiot that he is. We will remove Piers Gaveston immediately. I'd prefer to disembowel the man and lop off his head, but most favor that he merely be exiled. He'll also be excommunicated if he sets foot inside England ever again."

Griffith thought a moment. "What about Nowland? Once he learns he was merely a vessel and never in control, how will the barons deal with him?"

Applegate waved a hand in front of him. "His gambling has him in severe debt. If he agrees to quietly live off his land, he'll be left alone. He truly has no political support. He was simply used as a means to an end."

"Will he be told of the ordinances? I ask because of Kallen. She is now my wife, and I will do anything to see her returned safely to me."

"Lord Peters rides to Nowland now. He is to keep Lord Nowland occupied until the barons have forced Edward's hand. It will not take long, for we are led by Henry Plantagenet, Earl of Lincoln, and the king's cousin, Thomas, Earl of Lancaster. We are united in our purpose. Once Edward has agreed to our demands, I'll send word to Lord Peters, and he will reveal Nowland's fate to him."

Applegate gave Griffith a sympathetic glance. "I see how concerned you are about your wife. If you can halt Nowland's progress now and hold him at Sommerset instead while the barons act, I see no harm in altering the plan in such a small way."

A rush of excitement ran through Griffith. "Thank you, my lord. I am in your debt."

"Godspeed to you, Griffith Sommersby." Applegate turned and made his way back to his horse. He gave a wave to Griffith before he and his men departed.

Griffith motioned for the captain of his guard to join him.

"Philip, we must—"

"We are ready to ride, my lord. We have been since shortly after Lady Kallen rode through the gates with the Earl of Nowland." Philip grinned. "We knew we would be called to hunt down that spineless bastard."

Griffith gripped his captain's shoulder. The weariness fled him. He felt battle-ready.

"Then call for Satan and my sword, Philip, and let us be off."

———

A cold ran deep inside Kallen. She felt its icy fingers grip her soul. She realized her sacrifice was great, but she would do it again and again... for love.

She only hoped God would be appeased by her actions and forgive her for murdering Sir Rodger. She said a silent prayer begging God to keep her husband and family safe—and to keep Griffith from following them. She would not have him give up so much for her. 'Twas too much to ask.

She wrapped Deva's cloak more closely about her. Dawn had broken, but a chill still lingered in the early morning air. Quentin's soldiers had camped a few miles from Sommerset. Once they'd arrived, a kind soldier escorted her to a horse of her own, for which she was grateful. She couldn't imagine riding all day next to her father. His black aura had become almost physical in nature. It smothered her when she was near him.

Kallen beheld the soldiers that surrounded her. They looked to be capable men with auras showing their reliability. Yet she picked up from them the same unspoken feelings she had the night her father's conspirators gathered in her presence.

Something was in the air. Kallen didn't know what. Reading auras couldn't reveal the future. She couldn't even tell of a man's loyalty to his master, though her father assumed she could. She let him think so and had studied the gathered men with care. She had no idea whether they would be loyal to the plot hatched that would put the Earl of Nowland on England's throne.

Instead, she knew which of the men who had gathered were intelligent and which were curious. She could tell who was dependable and those who excelled at leadership. A few even showed signs of spirituality.

But whether they would honor a commitment to the planned conspiracy, Kallen couldn't say. Her gut told her something had been afoot, though. An undercurrent ran through the room of gathered noblemen. She sensed it but couldn't put her finger on its nature.

She wondered if these men simply used the Earl of Nowland in some way. She was sure she would soon find out. For now, she must wait. Continuing to fool her birth father and keeping him off-balance was her priority. She determined to do whatever she could to see him and his rebellion fail. She would not be disloyal to her king. Despite all the rumors that swirled about Edward, despite his foibles, he was England's lawful ruler.

And she would do her best to see he stayed on his throne.

The sun rose higher in the sky. Kallen began to tire. The past few days had been emotionally as well as physically draining, culminating in yesterday's long ride to Sommerset. The only good that had come from it was her time with Griffith. It gave her such pleasure to know she was his wife. Thoughts of their couplings caused her cheeks to heat. Kallen rested a hand against her belly, wondering if she carried his babe even now. The thought brought her happiness.

"Christ's wounds!"

The party slowed and then came to a stop. The earl jumped from his horse.

"This stupid beast has thrown a shoe," he grumbled.

"My lord?" A soldier next to Kallen worked his way through the ranks, stroking his neatly trimmed black beard. "I suggest we stop. The noon sun is high in the sky. This rest will allow us a chance to water the horses. I'm sure Lady Kallen could use a brief respite, as well."

Nowland agreed and called for a smithy to shoe his horse. "Be quick about it," he instructed the stout man.

Men began to dismount in small pockets. Their laughter made Kallen think of Crispin's men and the journey to Mangeron she had made with them.

"My lady?"

Kallen looked down and saw the same soldier who'd placated her father offering to help her from her horse. She allowed him to unseat her, enjoying being out of the saddle and able to stretch her legs. As she moved about, the man shadowed her. She realized she must be his responsibility.

She turned. "Sir? I am afraid nature calls. Might you help me find a private place away from the men?"

His eyes searched out his liege lord and came back to rest upon her. "All right. Follow me."

The man led her some distance away, off the road and into the woods.

"Go behind this clump of trees," he instructed. "Stay within the sound of my voice. Keep talking, else I'll think you've run off."

His dark, penetrating eyes stared into hers. "Do not be foolish, my lady."

"I shan't."

Kallen walked to where he had indicated, carrying on a one-sided conversation.

"'Tis beautiful countryside here. I grew up in a nunnery and never left its property. I imagine I have seen more in two weeks than in a score of years."

Kallen stepped into the grove and stopped dead in her tracks.

Griffith stood before her.

———

Griffith had almost twenty soldiers creeping through the woods, ready to attack Nowland's men as they rested. His lead scout had informed them of the respite they took, allowing them to quietly move into position for an attack. Another thirty men approached from the other side under Philip's leadership.

And then he heard her voice. Joy leaped in his heart. Kallen approached, talking about the countryside. She stepped into the clearing. Her eyes widened. A smile appeared on her lips even as she continued to talk.

"Sir? You can still hear me, I hope. I have found a perfect place. I'll only be just a minute."

She reached him and whispered, "Griffith! You must go."

He heard the worry in her voice. He motioned for her to continue speaking, aware that her escort was nearby.

Kallen didn't miss a beat, though. "I'll tell you this. The nunnery was so boring. Prayers could last an eternity. Do you know how many times a nun must pray in a day? I fear I could never be so pious."

Griffith rested his hands on her shoulders as she

spoke. Kallen prattled on as several of his men circled around. He heard a grunt and a thud and knew Kallen's guard had fallen.

She fell into his arms as he embraced her. Warmth flooded him, a sense of rightness in her being with him.

38

Holding Kallen close was a mix of sweet relief. Griffith thought ahead to the task at hand. He'd once entrusted her to Rodger, and that had been disastrous.

Still, he needed to capture Quentin himself. He couldn't very well carry Kallen into battle on his back, which meant he must turn her over into another's hands. The man he most trusted was Philip, who now led the other contingency.

Griffith stepped back and studied her. Her aura burned brightly. He saw the love she had for him. It only made releasing her more difficult.

Kallen glanced over his shoulder and nodded to a man. "That one. He's trustworthy." She gave him a wisp of a smile. "Rely on him, Griffith. Leave me with him. He'll not fail you."

He touched a hand to her cheek. "You read my thoughts, love." He brushed a quick kiss on her lips then signaled Edgar over.

"Stay here with my wife. Her safety is in your hands."

The young soldier blinked in surprise. "I would die protecting her, my lord," he said earnestly.

"Go," Kallen urged him.

Griffith squeezed her hand and broke away to move alongside his attacking men. As they approached the camp, he stepped over the body of the guard who'd watched Kallen. Anger rushed through him, though he knew the soldier only had been doing his duty.

This anger built, coursing more swiftly than anything he'd ever experienced. Griffith knew he must use it—but not let it consume him.

They circled around, bits of conversation from Nowland's men now within their hearing. The troops were in a relaxed posture. Griffith knew Philip would be in place. They must make their move while Nowland's men were so unprepared.

Griffith caught sight of his enemy berating a smithy as he worked hunched over a horse's hoof. A tremendous heat enveloped him, so real was his fury against this one man.

He drew his sword and silently signaled his men. The Sommerset soldiers rushed into the makeshift camp, immediately surrounding the unsuspecting men of Nowland. While Griffith's men outnumbered their enemy, the fighting was fierce. The sound of clanging swords rang through the forest air, along with screams and hoarse grunts.

Griffith kept a steady course toward the Earl of Nowland, running his sword through one man, yanking it back quickly and attacking another. The second man put up a brief challenge, but soon Griffith awarded him a mortal blow.

The soldier fell wordlessly to the ground, blood soaking the grass below him.

Methodically, he killed twice more, making his

way closer to Nowland. He wanted the pleasure of running his sword through the earl's black heart.

But where was he? In the confusion of battle, Griffith suddenly lost his enemy. No, wait. He spied a horseman riding off to the west. With that shock of silvery blond hair, it could only be the earl.

Griffith grabbed the nearest horse and swung into the saddle, sword still in hand. He kicked his heels hard and the beast took off. It had an unusual speed for so powerful a war-horse, and Griffith easily closed the gap between him and his mortal foe.

Nowland kept peering over his shoulder, sheer desperation written across his face. Finally, he pulled alongside his enemy.

"Stop!" he thundered, even as Quentin shook his head.

"You'll not dictate to me, Sommersby."

Griffith's temper snapped. He threw a hard punch that connected with the older man's jaw. The loud crack could be heard over the rumble of horses' hooves.

The earl went tumbling from his mount as his horse ran off. Griffith reined in his mount and returned to where the earl rolled on the ground. One hand cradled his jaw, while his arm was wrapped around his center. Griffith guessed Quentin had broken a rib or two in the fall.

He dismounted and stood over the man with his sword drawn. Griffith knew Lord Applegate said to hold Nowland until the barons had addressed Edward, but how could he let his adversary go afterward? If alive, the monster would always be a threat to Kallen.

Blood bubbled from Nowland's mouth. Griffith looked closer and saw the blood that oozed between the earl's fingers. He glanced quickly about and spied a dagger on the ground. Nowland must have had it out to use in defending himself, only to fall on it as he lost his balance after Griffith's punch.

More blood erupted from between his lips, and he moaned. Griffith recognized the sound of a man dying, one he'd heard too often before on the battlefield. He could find no pity in his heart as he watched Kallen's treacherous father take his last gasps of breath.

The earl's glazed eyes met Griffith's gaze. "I could have been king," he whispered then fell still, his eyes wide as death took him.

Griffith was thankful it hadn't been necessary to make a decision as to Nowland's fate. The evil nobleman sealed it himself and died by his own hand.

He lifted the body and placed it upon the stolen horse, which had circled back around, unsure what to do without a rider commanding its way. He returned the dagger to Nowland's scabbard, careful not to touch the blade. He couldn't trust that Quentin hadn't poisoned the knife.

He grasped the horse's reins and began walking back to his men.

To where Kallen waited for him.

EPILOGUE

Griffith stood just outside the chapel at Sommerset, his fingers entwined with his wife's. Even after all these years, he still experienced a quickening of his heart whenever Kallen entered a room.

He smiled down at her, and she returned his smile. She was still as beautiful as the day he'd first seen her more than twenty years ago. A few laugh lines graced her face, but her aura still burned brightly around her. Griffith saw the love she had for him, as well as the happiness reflected of this day.

He glanced at his sister. Deva stood next to Crispin. She caught Griffith's eye and grinned. Then Griffith admired at the couple standing before the priest. His daughter glowed with lovely shades of yellow sunshine. Griffith could not read her betrothed's aura, but the gaze of the young man gave away what he felt in his heart.

"'Tis nice to know will be a love match," he murmured into Kallen's ear.

His wife leaned into him. "Just as we are and always shall be."

The priest finished speaking and welcomed those

gathered to witness the ceremony to now enter the chapel. As the crowd moved inside, Griffith held Kallen back a moment.

"I love you, my dearest love, my wife and my life." He kissed her deeply. As always, she felt so right in his arms.

"Father," a voice hissed. "Can you at least come watch the rest of the ceremony? You and Mother will have plenty of time for that later."

Griffith glanced over Kallen's shoulder at his son, so like him, and saw the mock exasperation on the boy's face.

"You're right, of course. I always make time for your mother."

He took Kallen's arm. "May I escort you to a wedding, my love?"

"Only if you promise to behave." Kallen's eyes glowed with both mischief and passion as they entered the chapel.

ALSO BY ALEXA ASTON

To Heal an Earl

To Tame a Rogue

To Trust a Duke

To Save a Love

To Win a Widow

THE ST. CLAIRS:

Devoted to the Duke

Midnight with the Marquess

Embracing the Earl

Defending the Duke

Suddenly a St. Clair

THE KING'S COUSINS:

God of the Seas

The Pawn

The Heir

The Bastard

THE KNIGHTS OF HONOR:

Rise of de Wolfe

Word of Honor

Marked by Honor

Code of Honor

Journey to Honor

Heart of Honor

Bold in Honor

Love and Honor

Gift of Honor

Path to Honor

ABOUT THE AUTHOR

A native Texan and former history teacher, award-winning and internationally bestselling author Alexa Aston lives with her husband in a Dallas suburb, where she eats her fair share of dark chocolate and plots out stories while she walks every morning. She enjoys travel, sports, and binge-watching—and never misses an episode of *Survivor*.

Alexa brings her characters to life in steamy historicals, contemporary romances, and romantic suspense novels that resonate with passion, intensity, and heart.

KEEP UP WITH ALEXA
Visit her website
Newsletter Sign-Up

MORE WAYS TO CONNECT WITH ALEXA